Sunrising

Also by Susan Hubert

FICTION

Sabi Star

The Sun is Bright – Book 2 of the Sunrising Series

Sunrising

A Novel

SUSAN HUBERT

Copyright © Susan Hubert 2020

Susan Hubert asserts the moral right to be identified as the author of this work.

ISBN: 978-0-7974-9035-2

Cover design Duncan Watson

For Jeremy

Prologue

A brief synopsis of the history of the territory leading up to the time this novel is set

Mzilikazi, King of the Ndebele (also known as Matabele) people, was arguably the first leader to have a profound influence on the part of Southern Africa in which this book is set.

He was born in the late 18th century, into the Nguni ethnic group, of which the Zulu were the most dominant tribe. The Zulus dominated the part of South Africa which is now known as KwaZulu Natal. After escaping death at the hands of King Zwide of the Ndwadwe, a rival tribe to the Zulus, he became a soldier in King Shaka's army. He showed great promise and initiative, making him both an asset and a threat to Shaka. Believing he was going to be killed, Mzilikazi took at least 500 of his supporters and left Zululand, walking approximately 800 kilometers to what came to be known as the Transvaal, in South Africa. His original group was later boosted by more Nguni refugees from KwaZulu who were fleeing from Shaka's tyranny. Mzilikazi conquered the Transvaal and subjugated everyone he found living there. He lived in the Transvaal for approximately 10 years, until Dutch voortrekkers/wanderers, who had escaped English domination in the Cape, also started settling there and immediately clashed with Mzilikazi's warriors for the control of the area. This caused Mzilikazi to take his people and head northwards, crossing the Limpopo River around 1837 into the territory that is now Zimbabwe. By this time his tribe numbered around 50 000 to 70 000, and they were known as the Ndebele.

The land north of the Limpopo River was sparsely populated by many different, fragmented, fighting, territorial groups. The most dominant tribe was known as the Karanga. They would hide during battles, leading the Ndebele to call them 'shona/tshona' (meaning to hide/disappear). From then on, they have been known as the Shona tribe. Other tribes in the territory were the San Bushmen, the Kalanga and the Rozwi, to name some. Mzilikazi brought formal governance to the area, again subjugating all these scattered tribes and forcing them to live under his rule.

Mzilikazi is credited with preventing the slave trade from spilling south of the Zambezi River.

On their way north from the Transvaal, Mzilikazi had divided his people into two groups for security reasons. One group, comprising mainly of women and children, was placed under the care of Chief Khondwane Ndiweni, who took a much shorter route by way of Thuli and Limpopo confluence, arriving at Matopo Hills in 1837. Meanwhile the King and his group travelled to the west through the Botswana desert, until they reached the Zambezi River in 1839. The two year absence of the king created a lot of anxiety among his followers. They concluded the King had died with the rest of the tribe in the desert. After a lot of arguing and debate, it was agreed that Nkulumane, Mzilikazi's most qualifying prince, should be installed as the next king.

When King Mzilikazi was eventually found and brought to join the rest of his people, he found his son as the new king. This was a treasonous offence. Most chiefs who had participated in the scandal were punished, whilst a few escaped and lived in exile. Nkulumane himself escaped with a sizeable number of his followers and trekked back into Transvaal, where he settled among the Bafokeng tribe of the Tswana, until he died in 1883. The treason trial of chiefs involved in the installation of Nkulumane was conducted on top of the hill which later became known as Ntabazinduna (Hill of the Chiefs) but was never used as an execution field, contrary to common belief.

During this time the few white people in the area consisted mainly of missionaries, hunters and traders. King Mzilikazi developed a special friendship with the missionary Robert Moffat, a friendship that had started many years earlier when he was still in the Transvaal. It is assumed, because of this friendship, he was tolerant of white people.

King Mzilikazi died in 1868 and was buried in the Matobo Hills. Another of his sons, Lobengula, ascended to power by crushing anyone who was a threat to him. Life under King Lobengula was less strict than under King Mzilikazi, but he still led an efficient and disciplined army that continued to subjugate the rest of the population.

Initially King Lobengula set up his royal homestead north of the Matobo Hills. He was wary of whites, but he did make concessions. For instance, he allowed Sir John Swinburne the right to search for gold in the extreme south of his kingdom, in 1870. But when the Jesuits built a mission close to his homestead, in 1880, he moved approximately twenty kilometres northwards to the area where State House (formerly known as Government House) now stands. He named the place KoBulawayo (meaning 'A place where he is being killed'). Except for the missionaries, who lived at their missions, he insisted all other whites in the area live close to his homestead. This became known as "White Man's Land". He wanted them there so he could keep an eye on them. He got to know and befriend several white people this way. A special friend of his was John Moffat, Robert Moffat's son.

The next person to have great influence on this part of Africa was Cecil John Rhodes. He came to South Africa from England in 1870 as a sickly 17 year old. He spent a year working for his brother on a fruit farm in Natal, but decided this was a waste of time. He moved to Kimberly, where he worked in the diamond fields. 19 years later he had made a fortune and, through the company he set up, De Beers, he controlled the value of diamonds throughout the world.

Rhodes became involved in politics and was made the Prime Minister of the Cape Colony, which was under British rule. The

Transvaal, where vast deposits of gold had been found, was under Afrikaner rule and, with no hope of taking this over, Rhodes started looking northwards. He formed the British South Africa Company (BSAC) and, in 1888, sent a team comprising of Rudd, Thompson, and Maguire, amongst others, to meet King Lobengula and persuade him to grant the BSAC the right to trade, hunt and prospect for precious minerals in the Ndebele territory. The negotiations were long and laboured, as the king could not read or write. After discussing the terms and writing them down, they had to be read back to be discussed further. The king finally signed the concession in October 1888, and it was rushed to England for Queen Victoria to sign. King Lobengula's friend John Moffat, who had advised him in other dealings with white people, convinced him that the BSAC would protect his kingdom from the Portuguese, Germans and Afrikaners who were all showing interest in it. In exchange the BSAC agreed to pay him a monthly rental of 100 pounds, plus 1000 Martini-Henry rifles, 100 000 rounds of ammunition and a gunboat.

The king soon became wary of the agreement he had signed. It seemed that some of the conditions they had discussed were not being upheld. The King wanted to consult the 'white queen' Rudd and his party said they had been representing. He also wanted confirmation that she actually did exist. So he sent two of his emissaries, Babiyane and Mtshede, to England to meet Queen Victoria. However, their long trip via Cape Town was delayed, partly by Rhodes' manipulations, and then, when they arrived in London, they were invited to attend many functions and meetings. Several months passed before they met the queen, and, when they did, they were told that it was too late to change the agreement and that the concession Lobengula had signed was unbreakable.

Armed with the Rudd Concession, Rhodes approached the British government to apply for a Charter to move into Lobengula's kingdom to look for precious minerals. The Royal Charter was signed on June 18th 1889 and was initially valid for 25 years. It stated that only the British could settle or gain concessions in Matabeleland and Mashonaland.

It was agreed the traditional leaders would retain significant powers over their people. It is estimated their number was around 300 000 at this time, spread over a vast area.

Rhodes, using his own money, organised a column of white pioneers to move into the territory. This column comprised approximately 290 colonists, 78 wagons, 250 cattle and 130 spare horses. One of its leaders was Frederick Courteney Selous, who had hunted in the area for decades and knew it well. The column was protected by 200 volunteers who would become the first recruits of the British South Africa Police (BSAP). They crossed the Thuli (now Tuli) River, a tributary of the Limpopo River, via the Thuli Circle and travelled north east until they arrived at a place called Mount Hampden (near what became Fort Salisbury, now Harare), about 400 km north east of Bulawayo. They hoisted the British Union flag on the 13th September 1890. They initially started prospecting for gold but, when it became apparent there were no gold fields like the ones in the Transvaal, they were encouraged to go farming instead.

In 1891, boundaries were set in Africa, distinguishing one country from another. Lobengula's kingdom gradually started to be called Southern Rhodesia, after Rhodes, by the settlers living there.

(Rhodes went on to seek other treaties with local leaders elsewhere in Africa, but these have no relevance to this book.)

King Lobengula, still living in KoBulawayo, continued to assert himself as the ruler of his people, and in July 1893 the First Matabele War broke out. It started with a skirmish between the Ndebele and Shona tribes somewhere near Fort Victoria, now Masvingo. The British High Commissioner authorised the present military to respond. Major Forbes left Salisbury with an army of approximately 700 men with the aim of crushing any further unrest. They had 5 Maxim guns which they used with great efficiency against anyone who threatened them. It soon became apparent that Lobengula's soldiers, armed mainly with assegais and knobkerries, were no match against these Maxim guns. After heavy defeats near Bembesi/Gadade (near Bulawayo), on the 1st November 1893, King Lobengula ordered his homestead and the whole area around KoBulawayo to be burnt, and he and his bodyguards fled northwards. Everything was still smoldering when Forbes and his men arrived in KoBulawayo. They had been joined by the Administrator General of the BSAC, Leander Jameson, and they raised their flag in a tree at "White Man's Land" on the 3rd November.

On the 13th November, Forbes left Bulawayo with a column of men to try and capture the king. Jameson sent a letter to King Lobengula saying:

'I send this message in order, if possible, to prevent the necessity of any further killing or burning of your kraals. To stop this useless slaughter, you must come at once to see me in Bulawayo, when I will guarantee that your life will be saved and you will be treated kindly. I will allow sufficient time for this message to get to you and return to me, and two days more to allow you to reach me in your wagon. If you do not arrive I shall at once send out troops to follow you, as I am determined to put the country in a condition where whites and blacks can live in peace and friendliness.'

In response, King Lobengula sent back two bags of gold dust. Unfortunately, his soldiers inadvertently gave these bags to the wrong men – two privates by the names of Daniels and Wilson, who promptly stole the gold and hid it. Some time passed before anyone knew of the king's gesture and, by then, any chance for peace had been destroyed.

The column sent to find the king failed in its endeavour. 37 men, led by Major Allan Wilson, left the main group and, disobeying orders, crossed the Shangani River in their enthusiasm to capture the king. With no Maxim gun, they could not prevent themselves from being surrounded by the Ndebele about 8 kilometres from the river. 34 of them were killed, with 3 scouts, Burnham, Gooding and Ingram, managing to escape. This was to be the first major victory for the Ndebele army against the whites. King Lobengula could not be found and the column eventually made their way back to Bulawayo. It is believed the king died of smallpox a few weeks later.

The British House of Commons initially charged the BSAC for deliberately provoking the Ndebele, but they were later exonerated by Lord Ripon, the Colonial Secretary.

On the strength of the Maxim gun, the whites imposed their rule on the Ndebele.

However, in 1896, the Second Matabele War broke out. This has been renamed the First Chimurenga, in a move meant to distance alleged Shona collaboration with Whites in the First Matabele War. It is believed the Second Matabele War was started when the Ndebele spiritual leader, Mlimo, told the Ndebele people that the white settlers were responsible for the drought, locust plague and outbreak of the rinderpest disease which had killed so many of their cattle. It was a good time for them to start a war, because Jameson had taken most of his troops to the Transvaal to try and overthrow the Afrikaners there. White settlers living in remote areas of Rhodesia were easily overrun, as the Ndebele attacked and burnt hundreds of homes and mines. 141 white people were killed in Matabeleland and 103 were killed in Mashonaland. The Ndebele also besieged towns. In Bulawayo the settlers formed a laager in the centre of the town to protect themselves. Fearing the Maxim guns, the 10 000 Ndebele warriors who surrounded the town did not attack this laager, but remained a threatening presence within sight of the people in the laager, waiting for their provisions to run out. The conditions in this laager became very harsh, although the settlers only had to stay there at night. However, the Ndebele warriors made the mistake of not cutting telegraph wires, so the settlers could call for reinforcements. When these arrived from Mafeking and Salisbury, the siege of Bulawayo was broken, but the war continued.

50 000 warriors retreated into the Matobo Hills where fierce fighting continued, as well as in other parts of the country when the Shonas joined the war a year later. The whites concluded the only way they could bring the war to an end was to assassinate Mlilo. Burnham and another scout, named Armstrong, were told by a Shona informant where Mlilo's cave was in the Matobo Hills. This cave was deep in Ndebele territory, so it was with great fortitude that they managed to creep in and shoot him. They were lauded as great heroes by the settlers, and even as far away as England, until it became apparent that the man they killed was not Mlilo, and the unrest continued. After many more battles and deaths on both sides, Rhodes eventually went unarmed to the Matobo Hills and spoke to Ndebele chiefs led by Prince Nyamande, Faku, Mpontshwana, Mlugulu, Siginyamatshe and other senior indunas. He persuaded them to lay down their arms so their people could get on with planting their crops.

The war was effectively over, although the fighting continued for another year in Mashonaland.

After this there was relative peace, although everyone in the country had been deeply scarred by the war.

The powers of the local chiefs were gradually eroded, as the settlers encouraged their own officials to take over administrative roles. This gave them the freedom to develop the country in earnest.

The railway line reached Bulawayo from South Africa via Mafeking (Bechuanaland) in the west, in October 1897, and reached Fort Salisbury from Beira in the east in February 1898. Bulawayo and Salisbury were linked by a railway line in October 1902.

When you have acquired the taste of dust,
And the scent of our first rain,
You're hooked for life on Africa,
And you'll never be right again,
Until you can watch the setting moon
And hear the jackal's bark,
And know they are around you,
Waiting in the dark.

When you long to see the elephants,
Or hear the coucal's song,
When the moonrise sets your blood on fire,
Then you've been away too long.
It is time to cut the traces loose,
And let your heart go free,
Beyond that far horizon,
Where your spirit yearns to be.

Africa is waiting – come!
Since you have touched the open sky,
And learned to love the rustling grass,
And the wild fish eagle's cry,
You'll always hunger for the bush,
For the lion's rasping roar,
To camp at last beneath the stars,
And be at peace once more.
Author Unknown

Chapter 1

Bulawayo 1905

ANTHONY woke to the sound of whimpering. Despite sleeping in separate rooms, he could still hear Isabella through the thin corrugated iron wall. He knew from experience that her whimpering would turn to crying, and her crying would turn to wailing, if he did not go through and calm her. He pulled his mosquito net back, swung his legs over the side of the bed and felt for his slippers. Sighing, he lit a candle.

'Isabella, Isabella, it's alright.' He put a hand on her shoulder and shook her gently. She opened her eyes and stared at him, tossing her head. He sat on the side of the bed, holding the candle so the light shone in her face. When he saw that she was awake he put the candlestick on the bedside table and felt her face with the back of his hand. Her forehead was hot and clammy and her long hair, which he knew she would have plaited neatly earlier, was now matted and untidy. He took his handkerchief from his dressing gown pocket, walked to the nightstand and dipped it into the bowl of water. He wrung it out before coming back to the bed to wipe her face.

'Were you having your bad dream again?' he asked.

She nodded. 'I was dreaming. I, I had just arrived here on the train, and there was, there was a baby. It was crying and....'

He put his fingers over her mouth. 'Hush lass. Here, have some water. It will make you feel better.' She lifted herself to take the glass. She sipped the water, then slumped back against the damp pillows.

1

'I will stay with you until you fall asleep,' he suggested, but she shook her head.

'No, please don't. I would prefer to be on my own.'

A momentary flash of pain crossed his face, but he said nothing. He knew this was how she now felt.

'Well I will leave you to get some rest then. Shall I blow out the candle?'

'No, you can leave it lit, thank you.'

Anthony rose from the bed, pulled the mosquito net back into place, lit a second candle from the first and left the room, closing the door behind him. He trod lightly down the passage to the room he used as a study, trying to prevent his footsteps creaking on the wooden floor. He winced as the door squeaked when he pushed it open. He lit two more candles, placed them either side of his desk and sat down wearily, the leather chair groaning at this unexpected encroachment. It was well after midnight and Isabella's crying had woken him from a deep sleep, but he was awake now and he knew further sleep would elude him for many hours. The night seemed grave like still, breathless and silent, until he heard the intermittent short, short, long, trilling of a nightjar and the whining of mosquitoes flying around the room. One landed on his wrist and he slapped it dead. He checked to make sure his ankles and feet were covered by his pyjama pants and slippers.

Isabella and I cannot go on like this, he decided. With this he opened the top drawer of his desk and found a piece of writing paper. He took the pen from the holder in front of him and dipped it into the ink as he thought what he should write in his letter.

*

Philip and Muriel Weir were sitting at their dining room table, finishing their breakfast, when they heard a horse entering their yard.

'What the heck?' Philip said, laying down his napkin and going to the window to see who had arrived. 'Ah, it is Anthony Craig. Now why has he come here so early?' He and Muriel walked onto their veranda to greet Anthony, who was just getting off his horse. He looked tired and drained as he lifted his hat to them.

'Philip, Muriel. Good morning. Sorry to call round at such an inconvenient time, but I wanted to see you on my way to work.'

'Not at all,' said Muriel. 'Why don't you come in and join us for a cup of tea?'

'No, I cannot, thank you. I have come, because Isabella had another bad turn last night and I am worried about leaving her alone all day. Would you be so kind as to drop in and see her this morning Muriel?'

'Of course I can do that. I have nothing urgent that needs doing today. I will make time for her. But what about Mabel, is she not company for Isabella?'

'No, she keeps to her room all the time. She appears to have recovered physically from that malaria she had three months ago, but mentally, she is still very weak.'

'Such a shame,' Muriel said, thinking how Isabella's maid had seemed such a godsend when she first arrived from England, but had since become more of a hindrance than a help. 'Maybe I should try and cajole her into some activity too.'

'I doubt very much she would be interested,' Anthony said.

Muriel felt sorry for Anthony, having to deal with two fragile women, on top of everything else that had come his way in recent months. 'Are you sure you won't come in for a cup of tea? We have a fresh pot in the dining room.'

'I need to get home early this afternoon, so no thank you. I must be on my way now.' He climbed back onto his horse, and was about to urge it along, when he hesitated; 'I wrote a letter to Sir James Brooke last night, you will be interested to hear. I told him I would take up his offer after all. I finally realised I have to do something to change our lives.'

'By goodness yes. Best thing you could have done,' Philip said.

*

Isabella slumped into an armchair in her sitting room and stared at the painting above the dresser. She had painted it back in 1900, or was it 1901, shortly after she had married. She pulled herself out of the chair and went to check the date: 1901, of course! She would have been too busy sorting out their home for the remainder of 1900 to do anything else then. This painting was of the mud huts near the Matsheumhlope River where Anthony had lived when they first met, back in 1898. He, and two other bachelors, had lived in these huts whilst they established themselves in Bulawayo and built more permanent accommodation. For the Craigs, this was the house they lived in now, built entirely from corrugated iron, except for the wooden floors. It was a compact little house comprising of combined sitting room and dining room, veranda, three small bedrooms and an adjacent rondavel. This they used for Mabel's bedroom. The kitchen was beyond this rondavel and the latrine the other side of the yard.

If only I could bring myself to paint now, Isabella thought as she flopped back into the chair, but then she shook her head. No, no, I am still too distracted these days, she told herself.

She continued staring at the painting until Muriel found her like this when she arrived an hour later.

'Isabella, my dear. Goodness, you are still not dressed? And I have come round to ask you to join me on a little jaunt to Mrs Holdengarde. You remember her, don't you? She lives about two miles from here.'

'I do, but no, I am not up to visiting anyone this morning. Go without me.'

Muriel hesitated, but just for a moment. 'Now, now Isabella. It will be so much more fun to have your company. Come dear, I will not take no for an answer. Let us have a nice cup of tea before setting off. I will go to the kitchen and ask Mananga to put the kettle on the fire while you change into your daywear.'

She could tell Isabella needed to be chivvied along; otherwise she would just sit and mope all day.

Muriel considered for a moment to suggest they invite Mabel to join them, but then resolved against this. She could see that Isabella was poorly and did not need further distractions right now.

They rode in Muriel's cart to the Holdengarde's property; it being too far and too hot to walk. The Weirs and the Craigs lived on the western side of a suburb of Bulawayo known as Hillside, while the Holdengardes lived on the eastern side, down the hill and near the stream. This stream had been dammed a few years before, to make water storage reservoirs for the town. There were two dams, named the Bulawayo Waterworks Reserve. In happier days, Anthony and Isabella had gone there often for picnics, as many of the residents of Bulawayo did.

The Holdengardes had a plot big enough to keep a small herd of dairy cows. These were grazing in a field in front of their house when Muriel and Isabella arrived. Hillside was developed enough now that livestock was no longer threatened by wild animals like lions and hyenas. This had been a big problem when white settlers had first started building there ten or more years before.

Mrs Holdengarde came down the steps from her veranda as the cart drew alongside it. Muriel tied the reins to the hitching post next to the steps, giving the mule enough length to drink from the trough nearby.

'Hello Mrs H. I trust you received my message this morning. My Cookie came back saying he had delivered it safely.'

'I did indeed.'

'You know Isabella Craig, I believe?

Mrs Holdengarde was in her fifties, and, unlike Isabella and Muriel, had lost all trace of elegance she may once have had when she first arrived in the settlement in 1895. But she was warm and welcoming and delighted to have company.

'Oh yes. Indeed I do. Come in my dears. Let us have a cup of tea before I show you my new puppies. Or would you prefer a glass of my homemade lemon juice?'

'The lemon juice sounds delicious, thank you,' Muriel said.

She nudged Isabella as they went up the steps and into the relative cool of Mrs Holdengarde's house.

'Unfortunately, she has spoilt the surprise. Mrs H has some adorable Staffordshire bull terrier puppies. I want to see if she has one available for you.'

'But I do not want a puppy Muriel' Isabella said.

'Just wait till you see them. I think you may change your mind.'

*

Anthony walked out of the post office on Main Street. He worked as the manager of a bank two blocks away in Fife Street, and he had ridden his horse, Gunner, to the post office so that he could get back to the bank quickly. He knew there would be miners coming in later that morning to deposit their gold, and he did not want to keep them waiting. However, after he had posted the letter to Sir James Brooke he decided, while he was still in the post office, to send a cable too. Sir James had homes in England and Cape Town. Although he was staying in Cape Town at present, it occurred to Anthony that it could take more than two weeks for his letter to reach James and for the reply to get back to him. Now that he had finally resolved to take the plunge and accept James's offer, he wanted everything to move as quickly as possible. He did not want to wait for nearly a month before they could start making the necessary arrangements.

Anthony had been working at the bank in Bulawayo for ten years, and he felt nervous about giving up the security of his job there. He did not have the resources that James had, to fall back on, if this venture of theirs fell through. The bank Anthony had opened had become ever busier as more and more people arrived in the settlement to try their hand at mining, mainly for gold.

James Brooke knew the potential of prospecting and gold mining, and it was in this venture he had asked Anthony to partner him.

*

Isabella heard Anthony galloping into their yard when he returned home from work. Oh good, she thought; now I can show him. She picked up the puppy, which had been asleep in her lap, and went onto the veranda. It lolled sleepily in her arms. She bent her head to breathe in his warm, milky, puppy smell, but grasped him when she saw Anthony's Labrador, Trigger, barge round the corner to greet his master.

Anthony looked up from loosening his horse's girth and was surprised to see her, and even more surprised to notice she was holding a puppy. Trigger spotted or smelt the puppy a moment later, and Anthony had to steady him with a hand through his collar. They both looked at Isabella and the puppy, Trigger wagging his tail.

'Muriel took me to see Mrs Holdengarde, and her bitch had a litter of puppies,' she said. 'She did not have a home for this one so she offered him to me. Do you mind if we keep him? I am sure Trigger will soon get used to him and enjoy having him around.'

'What type of dog is he? Looks like a Staffordshire bull terrier to me. Is he?'

'Yes, he is, and so adorable. I have been quite taken with him in the few hours since I brought him back.'

Anthony felt a surge of relief, seeing Isabella interested in something again. She had been moping around for too long, and if this puppy changed anything, it was good enough for him. The puppy wriggled in Isabella's arms, wanting to get free.

'Put him down Isabella, let's introduce Trigger to his new brother,' he said, as he handed his reins to the gardener who had come to fetch the horse. 'Have you come up with a name yet?'

'Archie, do you think this suits him?'

'Aye, I do indeed,' he answered as Archie came bounding down the steps and started jumping up at Trigger. Anthony let go his collar. 'I am sure these boys will soon be best friends.'

He wanted to tell Isabella his other news, but decided it would be best to wait for this introduction to be over.

Chapter 2

ISABELLA Braithewaite had been in love with Africa for as long as she could remember. Her love for Africa was linked to her love for art, and these were interwoven in a most interesting way. Her family had lived in King's Lynn, Norfolk, for several generations. In the early 1850s her grandmother, Mrs Eliza Braithwaite, had acquired a painting by one of King's Lynn's more illustrious citizens, the artist and explorer Thomas Baines. Baines' mother was passionate about establishing her son's career and initially exhibited his paintings in the window of her front room. Mrs Braithwaite was an acquaintance of Mrs Baines and, besides this, had more than a passing interest in art herself. She managed to purchase a painting from one of Mrs Baines' window exhibitions when the artist was just starting to make a name for himself. This painting had become a family treasure; a panoramic African scene set above the Victoria Falls. It hung above the fireplace in the Braithewaite drawing room and, as a child, Isabella would sit for hours in the armchair opposite the painting, wishing she could paint scenes like the ones depicted in it. When she was older, and trying her hand more seriously at painting herself, she found, in the local library, a copy of an album of Baines' prints entitled "The Victoria Falls, Zambezi River" and another publication of folios and lithographs based on his paintings called "Scenery and Events in Southern Africa". She spent hours examining these, as she dreamed of becoming an explorer and painter like Mr Baines. She considered the sketches and paintings she did of English scenes boring, always falling short of her expectations.

'It is not just the subject matter,' she would tell her sister Celia, who encouraged her in her painting; 'It is the light too. The English light is pale and watery, except in the height of summer of course, yet, I believe the light in Africa is bright and glowing all year round. How I long to paint that light.'

*

Isabella Craig, as she now was, was immediately aware of this light as she stepped onto the veranda of her house in Hillside, noticing the radiance that remained from the setting sun. If only it could inspire me like it used to, she thought to herself.

Anthony was sitting in his usual chair, watching the garden. Isabella frowned at the sight of him; rifle in hand, eyes darting about, looking for any sign of movement.

'Oh, Anthony. Do you have to do that tonight? I mean, surely the spring hare population that you keep complaining about is going to be of no concern to us, now that we are leaving?'

A guilty look crossed his face. 'You are right lass, but as you will have deduced, I do enjoy shooting them.'

'Poor little creatures, I cannot understand why. And it causes such reverberations. Look at poor Archie. I am sure he will end up gun shy if you carry on shooting from the veranda like you do. We all get such a fright every time your gun goes off without any warning.'

'Aye, lass.'

'And as for the wretched mules. I am sure one of the reasons they keep breaking loose and running away is because of your shooting. We cannot have this happening tonight, of all nights.'

'All right, all right. I get the picture. I won't shoot at anything tonight.' He leant the gun against the wall behind where he was sitting.

'Thank you,' she said, sinking into the chair next to him.

'Want a drink?' he eventually asked, getting up to refill his glass from the tray of drinks which was set on the veranda every evening.

'Yes please,' she answered, stroking Archie's back as he lay down at her feet. 'Oh my, I am so tired. Packing up this house has been much harder than I first envisaged.'

A month had passed since Anthony had come home and told her that he had accepted Sir James Brooke's offer to partner him in what was to be called The Mining and Exploration Company (MEC). This offer not only meant that Anthony would be changing professions, but that they would also be moving house. They were going to live in the house Sir James had built seven years before, a grand establishment called Sunrising, approximately three miles north of the town centre. It was so much bigger and better than their present home in Hillside, they could not turn down this offer, even though it meant leaving their friends and neighbours in Hillside. However, Anthony had assured Isabella they would arrange house parties and invite friends to stay for weekends at their new home.

They had sold the Hillside house to a Mr Colquain and this was their last night before they moved.

The smoke from the paraffin lamp, set on the drinks table, soothed his frayed nerves as he poured their drinks. The house was almost empty, with just their two veranda chairs, the drinks table, and their bed to be packed before they left in the morning.

'I am sorry I have not been more help,' he said, as he handed her a glass of sherry. He knew that she had spent hours coordinating the planning, wrapping, packing and loading of the carts. During this time he had been busy tying up his own loose ends at the bank, and he was always tired and dusty after the ride back from town in the evening. By the time he had dealt with his horse and tack it was usually almost dark, and he longed to do nothing more than seek out the drinks tray and his gun for his evening sport. Whatever misgivings he may have initially had about changing their lives had diminished as he watched Isabella gradually improve. It was such a relief seeing her doing something constructive again, the first time in months she had involved herself in anything. Both this, and her obvious attachment to Archie were steps in the right direction as far, as he was concerned.

'To Sunrising,' he said, lifting his glass as if in a toast. 'It is certainly an intriguing name for a house, don't you think? A positive sounding name for what I hope will be a positive new start for us.'

'Yes, yes,' Isabella said, but she was distracted by another thought. 'You have not forgotten Mrs Meikle's invitation to what she calls 'a simple little supper' tonight, have you? Of course, knowing her, it will hardly be simple?'

He glanced at the dusk sky. 'No, I have not forgotten, and I will freshen up just as soon as I have finished my drink. The moon is nearly full tonight so we can walk there, as it won't be too dark. Are you happy to do this, rather than dragging out that wretched mule of ours?'

'Absolutely, it is quite close enough to walk, as long as we take the lamp. I would hate to step on a snake lying in a dark patch along the path.'

'Well, let us go and change for dinner,' he said, draining the rest of his whisky.

*

For Mrs Meikle, a 'simple little supper' meant using her second-best linen, silverware and glassware, and inviting just one other couple to join them. Isabella found herself sitting between Mr Meikle and Colonel Napier at the dinner table. It was 'an oldies' get together, as far as she was concerned. She could never call any of them anything other than Mr and Mrs or Colonel and Mrs, and she was always on her best behaviour in their company.

'We are going to miss you two youngsters very much, here in our little neighbourhood,' Mrs Napier said.

'Indeed, we will,' agreed Mrs Meikle. She glanced at Isabella. She had been through a great deal with Isabella and knew she was still in great pain, despite putting on a brave face.

'Thank you, we will miss you too.' Isabella said.

'We will only be six or so miles apart,' Anthony said. 'It is hardly as if we are never going to see each other again.'

'Quite,' agreed Mr Meikle.

'I know dear,' said his wife, 'but it is just so reassuring, all of us being close together. We ladies draw great comfort from each other, living in this country as we do, with no family to speak of. It is all very well for you men, working in your shops and banks, or whatever, but we ladies spend a great deal of time visiting one another.'

'I am trying to work out how long you have been here,' Colonel Napier interrupted, not wanting his wife to get onto the subject of the difficulties of living so far away from family in England. This was one of her pet grievances.

'Five years now,' said Anthony.

'How time flies,' said Mrs Napier. 'It seems like just yesterday when you, Anthony dear, invited us all to that delightful croquet party you had, when you were living in those huts on the banks of the Matsheumhlope River. I do believe that is when you and Isabella first met, am I not right?'

'You are indeed, Mrs Napier. That was in 1898, when Isabella first visited this continent. I took one look at her at my croquet party, standing in a pile of cow dung, and I was smitten.' He winked at Mrs Napier.

'Oh yes, oh yes,' Mrs Napier giggled. 'I remember well what happened. Your manservant. What was his name again?'

'Mananga.'

'Oh yes. He was supposed to pick up all the manure after you had asked everyone to graze their animals near your huts, as a way of cutting the grass.'

'Exactly, and he 'forgot'. Well that is what he told me afterwards.'

'And we spent the afternoon punching our croquet balls out of all that manure with our mallets. Oh yes, it was too funny.'

'Except that my best shoes were quite ruined,' Isabella added. 'At least it was not too long after that, that I returned to England and could replace them.'

'What ever did happen to that lovely brother and sister-in-law that you had come out to visit, Isabella?' Mrs Napier asked. 'I can't quite remember their names.'

'Edward and Alice Braithewaite. They moved to the Cape shortly after I left to go back to England, early in 1899.'

'Well, at least it was not too long before you came back to all of us again. Mr Craig was determined to have you.'

'I was, even if it meant travelling all the way back to England to ask for her hand in marriage. It was the first time I had left Africa in ten years, and as soon as we were married we returned,' said Anthony.

'Well we are very pleased you accepted his offer, Isabella dear. Our little community is that much better for having women like you willing to come and join it,' said Mrs Meikle.

*

'I think I will turn in straight away,' Isabella said, as soon as they got home after their dinner. This had become their usual routine in recent months and they were both reluctant to talk about it. Isabella would go to their bedroom early, and Anthony would retire later, sleeping in the bedroom next door.

'Aye, you do that lass. I will just go onto the veranda for a glass of port and a cigar before retiring. I will try not to disturb you when I come in.'

Neither of them wanted to risk making their problems worse by trying to talk about any of their issues.

Anthony sat back in his veranda chair and lit his cigar. How he hoped this move would change things. Somehow, they had to put what had happened behind them and try to enjoy their life together again. Everyone had told them that time was a great healer, yet up until now, their pain had not diminished.

The floorboards creaked and he was shaken from his thoughts.

'Oh, it's you Mabel. What on earth are you doing up so late?'

She stood at the far end of the veranda in her long cream nightgown, without shoes, her hair hanging loose down her back.

'I saw the glow of the lamp and I wanted to make sure you were alright.'

'Fine, fine. Don't you be worrying about me now.' He felt uncomfortable, seeing her standing there, dressed in her night attire. He wanted her to go, but he didn't want to appear rude so he said: 'Did you manage to find something to eat earlier?'

'Yes, thank you, Mananga gave me some soup. It was quite pleasant.'

'Good, I am glad you had something. You need to build up your strength.'

'Yes, I want to. Is there anything I can do to help you Mr Craig?'

'Me? Gosh no. I think you should be getting back to your room. I will be turning in shortly myself, as soon as I have finished my cigar. Off you go now, good girl. Try to get a good night's rest as tomorrow is going to be a long day for all of us.'

She left, her bare feet dragging on the wooden floorboards as she walked off the veranda.

Anthony took another puff of his cigar and downed the rest of his port. He had noticed how Mabel had taken to appearing out of nowhere like this from time to time. It made him feel uncomfortable. Isabella's sister, Celia, had recruited her in England, to come and work as Isabella's maid. It had worked out initially, until she got malaria a few months ago. She had been in hospital for six weeks and had never been the same since. Anthony sometimes wondered if the malaria had affected her brain in some way. He had heard the high temperatures that went with this affliction could adversely affect the brain.

If only Isabella could get back to her old self again. He was sure she would be much better at knowing how to cope with Mabel's odd behaviour.

*

The household was up at five on the morning of their departure, packing the last of their possessions before the trek to their new home. It was a mild February morning, still the height of summer. There had been no rain for over a week which was a great relief to everyone. Their journey would be much easier without having to negotiate mud and puddles on the rough dirt roads. The dawn sky was clear, and the tops of the trees were beginning to gleam with the first rays of sun. The birds' calls were still loud and varied, as they continued the dawn chorus they had started more than an hour before.

Anthony stood on the veranda, both dogs sitting at his feet. He felt happy and excited at the prospect of what lay ahead. His initial reservations and fears had disappeared as this day had drawn closer. He could now only see this change in their lives as positive in every way.

Mananga and the gardener, Hlabano, appeared at the bottom of the steps leading from the veranda onto the driveway.

'Can we move the table from inside, Baas?' Mananga asked.

'Aye yes, go ahead. Then you need to get the beds. Is everything else in order? Did Somani manage to catch the mules?'

'Yes Baas. We good here. The mules good with Somani there. We have everything ready soon.'

Anthony was relieved to hear this. The mules were often difficult to catch, especially when they were fresh and flighty in the cool of the early morning.

'Good,' he said. 'I am setting off for the new house shortly, and the Missus is going to have breakfast with Mrs Weir. You must have everything ready by the time she gets back. Then she and Miss Mabel will ride in the carriage while you take the cart. I will be waiting for you at the other house.'

They nodded as they moved into the dining room to collect the table.

Anthony went to say goodbye to Isabella. He found her in the bedroom, putting her nightwear into a large leather suitcase.

'You will be pleased to hear the mules have been caught and harnessed,' he joked.

She smiled. 'Well that is a relief. I would not have liked walking to Sunrising with this big, old, heavy suitcase.'

He saw the tea tray on the floor next to her bed and bent to pour himself a last cup, gulping it down almost in one go. 'So how are you, now that this day has finally arrived?' he asked.

'Good. I am pleased we are changing the course of our lives. I very much look forward to making Sunrising my home.'

'That's the right attitude, lass. Well done.' He put his arms around her, trying to ignore her immediate stiffening as he kissed her forehead. 'Indeed, we need to make a new start, and this is going to be it.'

17

Isabella could feel tears welling up. The last thing she wanted was to cry. She pushed her face into his chest, breathing in the warm, early-morning clean smell of him. 'Yes we do, and things are going to get better. I promise. I will try very, very hard. I am sorry I have been so difficult these last months.'

A pained look crossed his face, disappearing as fast as it came. 'It's alright lass, it has been equally hard for both of us, and we have each dealt with it in different ways.' He tightened his hold and kissed her forehead again, then released her. 'Come, see me off, I need to be going now. There is much to be done at Sunrising before you all arrive.'

He picked up his hat and coat from the last remaining chair in the dining room as he walked outside. Somani was standing at the bottom of the steps holding Gunner's reins. He passed these to Anthony as he was getting ready to put his foot into the stirrup. He pulled himself into the saddle, saluted Isabella, who was standing and watching from the top of the steps, and then turned towards the gate, catching up with Somani who was running to open it.

'Shoo, Shoo.' Somani waved his arms at the dogs to stop them running after Gunner.

Anthony cantered through the open gate and down the dry dust track for a hundred yards or so before reining Gunner to a standstill. He stood in his stirrups and turned around, to take one last look at the house. Somani was walking round the side with the dogs chasing each other as they followed, but Isabella had disappeared. He sighed. The last few months had been terrible, and he knew this house would always be a place of sorrow for them. He just hoped the new owners would have better times than they had. Isabella's withdrawal had made everything that much harder; they couldn't have carried on this way for much longer. He sighed again, sat down in his saddle and kicked Gunner in the ribs, giving him some rein as they set off at a swift canter down the dirt road to their new life.

*

Isabella walked back into the house as soon as Anthony had passed through the gate. She went to her room and poured tea into the spare cup on the tray, and then carried it down the passage and out of the door to the rondavel that had been Mabel's bedroom. She knocked.

'I brought you a cup of tea, Mabel.'

'Um, thank you Madam,' Mabel could not hide her surprise as she opened the door to take the cup. Mrs Craig had never brought her tea before.

'I wanted to make sure you were up and ready,' Isabella felt compelled to explain, seeing the look on Mabel's face. 'The kitchen is almost packed but I did tell Mananga to keep a loaf and some butter aside for your breakfast. Give the others whatever you don't eat.'

'Thank you, Mrs Craig, but I'm not hungry.' She stood in the doorway, holding the cup, her long, lank hair still loose. Isabella ignored the sulky expression on her wan face.

'Now, now, that will not do. It is going to be a long day, so please, do eat something. I am going to walk over to the Weirs at seven to have breakfast with Mrs Weir. When I get back we will be on our way. While I am gone please go round the house and make sure nothing has been left behind, no curtains in any windows, or anything else. I'll see you when I get back.'

Isabella wondered what the time was as she went back into the house. She resolved she still had a while before the Weirs expected her. She knew what she needed to do one last time. She went down the passage and into the end bedroom, the one that was always kept closed, except for the times she went into it. She shut the door behind her,

19

walked to the opposite wall and slid down onto the floor. The room was empty, but she closed her eyes and remembered how it had been until recently, when it was full of nursery furniture. She was sitting in the exact spot where the crib had been. She recalled all the happiness, and then all the sadness, she had experienced in this room.

'Good bye my precious little boy,' she whispered. She felt a lump in her throat as she wiped a tear away.

She pulled herself back onto her feet and left the room, not closing the door behind her.

*

Mabel returned to her rondavel after eating some bread and butter in the kitchen as Mrs Craig had suggested. She looked about her empty room to make sure there was nothing left behind. She was glad she was leaving this place. She had never liked this hut, even though Mananga had told her round houses were better than square ones, as there were no corners to trap spirits. Well her bedroom might not have any corners, but she felt the spirits trapped in the house. It had become a very sad place for all of them since William had died.

She had heard that the new house, Sunrising, was one of the grandest in the settlement and she hoped her life would improve for the better once she lived there. She wondered how Mrs Craig would be. She had changed since William had died, and the person who was the most affected by her change was Mr Craig. He was such an agreeable person, so manly, yet kind too; he did not deserve to be treated coldly by his wife. Mrs Craig did not know how lucky she was, with everything in her life. Mabel thought of her now, enjoying a delicious breakfast with her know-it-all friend, Mrs Weir, while she was left eating bread and butter on her own and making sure everything was packed. Mabel did not want to be treated like this anymore. She hoped she could find a better life for herself once she got to Sunrising.

*

Isabella had discovered from the first day she came to live in Bulawayo that mules were troublesome creatures. They moved too fast when they knew they were homeward bound, and hardly moved at all when they were leaving home. Isabella's mules were now in the interesting position of being pointed towards their new home, but not knowing this, they were kicking up their usual fuss and trying their best not to stay put.

She and Mabel were sitting in the Spider; the light, two-wheeled carriage Sir James had given the Craigs when Anthony agreed to become his partner. Harnessed to this Spider was Queenie, supposedly the best behaved of the Craig's mules, but she was obstinately refusing to budge. Isabella lifted her whip and lashed it across Queenie's rump yet again, but still she would not move.

Somani was having the same trouble with the four mules attached to the cart he was going to drive to Sunrising. Mananga, Hlabano, Trigger and Archie sat amongst the furniture packed onto the cart, waiting for the mules to move. Anthony always stated that Somani was 'good with mules', but why he should think this Isabella could not fathom. In her opinion he had lost both the mules, and then himself, on far too many occasions. If Anthony could see how they were playing up now, Isabella thought, under Somani's so-called control, he would surely change his mind.

It had not helped that the new owners of the house, the Colquains had arrived with their own cart and mules while she was breakfasting with Muriel. These mules were still harnessed to their cart, while the heaviest pieces of furniture were being offloaded. Trigger sat between two boxes, but Archie started racing about in the back of the cart, barking at everything that was going on. Mr Colquain came out of the house to see what the commotion was about.

21

'I see you are still here, Mrs Craig,' he said. 'Would you like me to try and shift that old girl for you?'

'I am very sorry to be such a nuisance but yes please, I cannot get her to move one step.'

'Mm, let me first get my mules out of sight. That may be what is causing the problem.' He glanced around, then yelled, '*Fani....Fani, tata lo mahach lapaside.*' Fani looked at him blankly. '*Tata lo mahach lapadside checha,*' he said, even louder and with more authority.

'Sorry Baas?'

'*Lo Mahach, lapaside. Checha.*' He swiped one of the mules on the rump and it jumped forward, jerking the whole cart. '*Checha, Fani, checha.*' Fani finally understood what was being asked of him. He removed the harness joining the mules to the cart and, with enviable ease, led them around the corner.

'Thank you Mr Colquain,' Isabella called, as Fani came back and began pulling Queenie towards the gate.

The other mules followed, dragging the cart behind them. When they were all out of the gate, with Fani shut it behind them.

'Well thank goodness for that,' Isabella said. 'I thought we would never get out of there. Oh my, I did feel embarrassed. Whatever did Mr Colquain think?'

Mabel pursed her lips and said nothing. She was secretly delighted the mules had been so difficult.

Chapter 3

FROM the moment they drove through the gate and glimpsed the house for the first time, Isabella knew she had found her destiny. How odd, she thought, I have never been here before and this house does not even belong to me. But she could not shake this feeling; in fact it grew stronger as they meandered up the drive towards the house. The surrounding vegetation was dense, with long grass and clumps of thick bushes making it difficult to see the house properly until the drive swung around and swept towards the L shaped front. What struck Isabella most when she got up close were the verandas; they wrapped around the house like the wide rim of a hat.

'Oh my, has this not got great potential?' Isabella said, looking about in wonder.

Mabel did not think so at all; in fact she was surprised by what she saw. She had heard so much about Sunrising from other people, who described it as the one of the grandest houses in the whole area, she had expected much more. But looking at it now, she did not think it was anything compared to the houses where she had been in service in England. However, she thought it best to say nothing. Judging from the look on Mrs Craig's face, she was obviously pleased with what she saw.

They came to a halt in front of a short flight of steps leading onto a veranda, with a large wooden door beyond. The veranda was edged with waist high wooden rails, painted white, and wooden pillars from the floor to the roof. There was trellising either side of all the entrances and a gable above the main door. Other doors leading onto the veranda had large wooden shutters on either side, like sentries standing at their posts.

'Can you imagine how picturesque this is going to be once we sort out the garden?' Isabella said, but again Mabel was unable to imagine anything of the sort. 'Sir James knew what he was doing when he built this house, didn't he?' Isabella continued, unperturbed by Mabel's lack of response. 'Just look at the lovely lattice work on the veranda in front of that door.'

Mabel was saved from saying anything by the appearance of Anthony at this very door. He looked happy and relaxed as he called to the dogs. They jumped off the cart and bounded up the steps to greet him, before rushing back down again to explore the immediate vicinity, Trigger lifting his leg against everything he could, and Archie trying to copy him.

'Welcome everyone,' Anthony said, coming down the steps and holding out his hands to help Isabella off the Spider. 'I'm sure you must be feeling tired after that long trek.'

'Yes, I am stiff after sitting on this hard, little seat for so long,' Isabella answered, reaching for his hands and jumping down. She stretched her back and shoulders.

Everyone else disembarked and another black man appeared from no one quite knew where. 'Ah, just the man we need,' Anthony said on seeing him. 'This is Moses. He's been working here since Sir James built the place. He can show you all where you need to go, including you Mabel. He knows which room will be yours. As for all the furniture we have brought, I told Moses to store it in one of the outhouses. There is so much furniture here already, you will have to go through everything and decide what we will use. But come with me now Isabella, I want to show you around.'

They walked up the steps together, with Isabella pausing at the top to look about, before going through the front entrance and into the hall. There was a big, round table in the centre of the room and doors leading off in various directions. All these doors were open so, as she stood there, she could see into the drawing room, the dining room and the library. The rooms were spacious and cool, protected from the outside heat by the veranda. She breathed in the cool ambiance of the place as she removed her gloves and hat and put them on the hall table.

Anthony noticed the strange look on her face. 'Are you all right? Is there something not to your liking?'

She did not know how to explain the peculiar way she felt about this house, indeed she did not want to. Surely he would think it odd, as she had only just walked in, so she kept to mundane observations instead. 'I am well pleased with everything so far. This house is very grand and Sir James has some beautiful pieces of furniture, from what I can see here.'

'Aye, that he has lass. But come. There is something in particular I want to show you. Follow me.' They went through the drawing room and out of the large French door on the far side, leading onto the widest section of the veranda, facing west. It overlooked an open grassy field with a seasonal stream running through it, about fifty yards from the house. There was water in it now, after the good rains they had had. 'So how's that for a view, lass? The sun will be setting soon and it will be even better then.'

'Oh, yes, for sure. It is wonderful even now,' she said, standing next to him and taking in the scene in front of her. 'I'll paint this one day,' she murmured. She could not have said anything better, as far as he was concerned, and he found her hand and squeezed it in appreciation. She did not stiffen this time.

'But there is something else I want to show you. Come.' He pulled her to the rail along the edge of the veranda and peered up the

25

stream, searching for something. 'Ah, there they are, they haven't let me down. Look.'

She followed his finger, trying to make out what he was pointing at. It took a moment for her to find them, but she gasped with delight when she did; a herd of impala further up the stream. Some were drinking while others stood about, then skipped towards the water to take a drink, while those that were there jumped away. Anthony and Isabella stood and watched them, saying nothing.

Eventually Anthony broke the silence. 'Moses tells me they are here all the time, and sometimes there is other game too. Warthog, kudu, zebra even.'

'How exciting, and how lucky we are. It is so much wilder here than at our old home, which was in a built-up area in comparison. I know you had told me this, but I hadn't quite comprehended it.'

'Aye, indeed. It is wilder than what we are used to.'

'And that noise Anthony? Is it guinea fowl I hear?

'Aye yes. There are flocks of them out there lass. Look see, there are some.' She looked towards where he was pointing. Beyond the stream, black shapes running around in the long grass.

'Oh yes, I do so love their call.'

'There are some dangerous animals too, mind. Lion, hyena, and jackal for instance. You will hear jackal most nights. Lion and hyena less often, Moses tells me.' He stopped, noticing the concerned look on Isabella's face. 'Don't worry, Moses has told me how to keep them away. He says that all I need to do is fire off a few shots with my gun every evening and they won't come near the place.'

'Well you will enjoy doing that,' she murmured. 'Maybe you could do it further away this time so that the rest of us do not get scared away too. And of course you cannot shoot your gun near these impala, otherwise they will soon make themselves scarce too.'

'I will go to the far end of the property. I know you don't like the sound of my gun too close.' He took her hand again. 'But come, let me show you more.'

They walked back through the drawing room and the hall and down a passage. She admired the pillars either side of the passage entrance.

'That way,' Anthony said, stopping for a moment and pointing further down the passage, 'goes to Sir James's wing. I'll show it to you another time. This way,' he said, leading her to the right, 'goes to our rooms, and all the other bedrooms in the house.' There were various closed doors leading off the passage. 'This is ours,' he said, opening the last one.

'Oh my, it's so spacious,' Isabella said when she walked in. 'I am amazed Sir James was able to build a place like this. It makes our previous house seem so small and pokey now.'

'Well it was. I never had the money to build anything better. Lucky for us, Sir James did. All the windows, doors, ceilings and floorboards were sent up by train, apparently. But what do you think of the furniture I had Moses put in here? It makes our old furniture seem very poorly, don't you think?'

'I've always appreciated what you did; making our furniture from all those old packing cases.'

'That's kind of you, but I won't be in the least offended if you don't use any of my homemade stuff. However, that is for us to decide another day. In the meantime, let me go and fetch a cup of tea while you freshen up. There is cold water in the jug on the nightstand. Do you want me to get Moses to bring you some hot water from the kitchen so you can have a bath?'

'No, don't worry. It is warm enough tonight. This cold water will do, thank you. But maybe you can go and check on Mabel while you're there?'

27

'Good God, yes, I had completely forgotten about her. She will not know where anything is. I'll be back shortly with your tea, lass, as soon as I've sorted Mabel out.'

*

Mabel stood on the porch outside her bedroom watching the men offload the remaining pieces of furniture, which they were putting in a corrugated iron hut, not dissimilar to her rondavel back at the old house. This one was being used as a storeroom. Well at least I am not sleeping in there, she thought, although she had not been impressed with the room Moses said would be hers. It was dark and airless, with just one small window which faced the wrong direction. While the main rooms in the house faced westward and had a magnificent view, her room faced eastward and her view was of the storerooms, the kitchen hut and the stables beyond. There was a second room next to hers and she wondered whom they would be employing, if anyone, to stay in there.

Her spirits lifted when Mr Craig came down the passage looking for her. Just like him to be more concerned about me than his wife, she thought. She had not enjoyed, one bit, having to ride all the way from Hillside with Mrs Craig, who kept trying to draw her into conversations she was not interested in having.

'Ah there you are Mabel, I see Moses showed you your room. I hope it is adequate for you.'

'Thank you Mr Craig.' She glanced at him. 'Um, yes thank you.'

He stepped into the room and looked about. 'It is getting a little dark now, I see. I am not sure anyone will have thought to put out the lamps. Would you mind going over to the kitchen and getting someone to do it? Maybe Moses knows the routine. We need lamps set everywhere so we are not fumbling around in the dark.'

'At least we have a near full moon tonight, so it won't be pitch black outside.'

'So true Mabel. It will help us tonight, when we don't know our way about this place, but we will still need the lamps.' As an afterthought he added, 'will you join us for dinner? I cannot imagine what Mananga will have rustled up, but I am sure Moses will have helped him find something for us to eat.'

Mabel was tempted to join them, there was nothing she would have liked more than to have her dinner with him, but she did not want to endure Mrs Craig again. 'No, I think I'll just stay in my bedroom, thank you.'

'Well make sure you get something to eat from the kitchen. We can't have you starving yourself. Which brings me to another point; there is a room next to this. You may care to make it into your parlour and then you could take your meals in there when you want time on your own. Why don't you take a look around the storerooms tomorrow and pick out some furniture you may like to use in there.'

As always, Mabel was touched by his thoughtfulness. He was standing next to the window staring out of it, and she was near enough to stretch out her hand and touch him. She was just thinking how much she wanted to do this, when he looked back at her and she averted her gaze.

He cleared his throat, and for a moment she thought he had noticed the longing in her eyes. But then he said: 'Well you know where the latrine is, don't you, you've found your bearings I hope?' She almost burst out laughing, this question being so far removed from what she had been thinking and hoping.

'Oh yes, I know my way around, thank you,' she managed to answer. 'Let me go and check on the lamps for you now.'

*

Isabella went into her dressing room and started undoing her buttons and loosening her clothes; she was hot, dirty and dusty and it would be good to have a refreshing wash. She would have loved a soak in a bath, but she didn't want to trouble anyone to bring the bath and fill it with hot water on this their first night. Anthony returned with a tray of tea and two paraffin lamps. He put the tray and one lamp on the dressing table in their bedroom and brought the other lamp through to the dressing room. He stopped when he saw Isabella's bare back, and he wondered if he should leave. They had not been intimate since William had died, and he knew she might be uncomfortable with him seeing her naked again. But she continued washing her body, her face, her neck, her arms, not showing any discomfort with him being there. He stood watching her until she reached for her towel.

'You feeling better now?' he asked.

'Oh yes, much.'

He went back into the bedroom and poured them both a cup of tea, but when he handed it to her, instead of taking it, she put it back onto the dressing table and reached for him instead.

Chapter 4

A MONTH after the Craigs moved into Sunrising, Sir James Brooke came to stay for the first time. Initially he planned on renting rooms at the Club, but when Anthony heard this, he insisted otherwise. Sunrising belonged to Sir James, and it was full of his possessions. There was nowhere in Bulawayo he could feel more comfortable, and the Craigs would not relax knowing he was in Bulawayo and not in his own home. He had a wing for his sole use, and the house was big enough and rambling enough for everyone to keep out of each other's way if they wanted.

He arrived at Sunrising amidst great pomp and ceremony. Anthony and Isabella were waiting in the drive to greet him, along with all the servants, dressed in their smartest clothes for the occasion. They knew he was a flamboyant character, so they were not surprised to see his elegant carriage, drawn by four horses, coming up the drive towards them. However, they were surprised when it stopped and a smartly dressed African man sprung, almost in one leap, from the top seat and ran round to the side of the carriage and opened the door for Sir James. He climbed out of the carriage, and the African man bowed with great gusto, first towards Sir James but then turning and including everyone gathered there. They all stood and stared at this spectacle, which was spoilt only by the dogs that started sniffing him with great interest.

'Mr and Mrs Craig, I am so pleased to see you both,' Sir James said. 'However, can I ask you to stop your dogs from being so rude?'

Anthony burst out laughing and moved forward to give his old friend a warm handshake. 'Wonderful to see you, Sir James,' he said.

'Mrs Craig, Isabella, do you mind if I call you this? It's been so long. How delightful it is to be with you now, and in this wonderful setting. Truly delightful.' He kissed her outstretched hand and then turned and glanced at the garden. 'I see you have been working hard here.'

'Yes, we have spent many hours in the garden Sir James; our efforts have been helped by the good late rains we've had this season,' she said.

'I look forward to taking a turn with you in the next few days, but first, let me greet the servants.'

Sir James glanced down the line of bowing servants, their eyes averted, arms hanging at their sides. He ambled down the line as Anthony introduced each in turn; Somani, Mananga, Hlabano.

'Ah, dear boy.' Sir James said. 'Such interesting names everyone has. You are going to have to go through them all again with me as I cannot remember them in one go.'

Moses was at the end of the line. '*Nkosi, Nkosi,*' he said, stumbling forward and dropping to his knees.

'Ah, Moses, how are you old man?' Moses bent further, his head nearly touching the floor. 'Up you get old man, I cannot speak to you when you are like that.' Moses pulled himself up, but still could not look directly at Sir James.

Mabel stood separate from the other servants at the bottom of the steps. She too held her head down and only glanced at Sir James when Anthony introduced her.

Finally they were able to make their way into the house, and it was now Isabella's turn to feel anxious. In the time she had been living at Sunrising she had done what Anthony had suggested. She had gone through the whole house and all the storerooms, choosing the pieces of furniture she wanted and arranging and rearranging everything until it met with her satisfaction. The only section of the house she had not touched was Sir James's personal wing, which Moses had assured her was the way Sir James wanted it. It had been a very rewarding time for her, transforming the house to suit her tastes, but now that the owner was here, she felt self-conscious and nervous in case he did not approve.

She need not have worried. 'Isabella, my dear, this house looks superb,' he said as soon as he entered. She had placed a copper jug full of Flame Lilies, picked from the grassy field in front of the house, on the round table in the hall. He touched these lightly as he put his hat and gloves on the table. 'Ah, my favourite flowers, you clever girl.'

'Come through to the western veranda. Isabella has made this a most comfortable recreational area,' Anthony said. They walked through the drawing room, Sir James glancing at everything he passed. The veranda beyond the French door was now furnished with deep armchairs, a three-seater sofa and various tables.

'Absolutely delightful Isabella,' he said, when he saw what she had done.

Mananga appeared with a tray of tea and shortbread. 'Will you take some refreshment, Sir James?' Isabella asked.

'Oh yes, I am parched, but please, not Sir James. It is far too formal for us.' He sank into one of the armchairs and took his pipe from the pocket of his jacket, banging it on his hand to loosen the old tobacco in it. 'I had always envisaged using this veranda as an outside sitting room, just as you have made it Isabella. Very well done to you.' He paused to light his pipe as he looked at the view.

33

'And this superb vista, how I have missed it while I've been away. I intend spending many hours sitting out here enjoying it. Hopefully our explorations won't take up too much of my time, Anthony, so I can do this. Do you still see wild animals out there?'

'Indeed we do,' Anthony said. 'Impala there all the time.'

'Oh good, they have always been here, ever since I had this house built. I am glad they still are.' He bent forward to take a sip of his tea before leaning back in the chair again, his pipe still in his hand. 'Before we go any further, I need to thank you both for inviting me to come and stay at Sunrising with you when I am in Bulawayo. It means a great deal to me, being here again.'

'We are just glad we can reciprocate, for everything you have done for us,' Anthony said.

'I believe our partnership is going to be a mutually beneficial arrangement. I could not have been more delighted when I received your cable, finally accepting my offer. It took you long enough, dear boy. I was beginning to give up.' He winked at Isabella as he said this. 'I do recall I made my first offer shortly after Rhodes's funeral back in April 1902, so what's that, nearly 3 years ago now?'

'Well the bank kept me busy, and I needed the security of a monthly wage then.'

'We are going to do well with The Mining and Exploration Company, Anthony, you need have no fear about that.' He lit his pipe again, and then exhaled, the smoke making small circular clouds around his head. He waved his hand to clear them. 'But, tell me, how is everyone in Bulawayo? How is our good friend Mrs Heyman, whose house I do recall we met at?'

'We have not seen her for a long time as we have not done much entertaining since, since,' Isabella bit her lip.

'Quite, quite, I am so sorry. A terrible time for you both. Such a tragedy.' He inhaled again, glancing from Isabella to Anthony, feeling uncomfortable he had opened old wounds 'Oh yes, Mrs Heyman,' he went on. 'Her parties are always so entertaining. They are even talked about in Cape Town.'

'I can well imagine, as she goes to a great deal of effort,' Isabella said. 'If I remember rightly, at the party you are referring to, she had arranged musicians as well as Indian jugglers for our entertainment.'

'Indeed she had, but my main recollection of that evening is the frogs in that dratted fishpond of hers, and how loudly they croaked. We could hardly hear ourselves think over the noise they made, let alone listen to the music or appreciate the jugglers. Do you remember this?'

'Oh yes, it was funny. I am sure they are still driving her mad every year.' Isabella had a sip of her tea and then continued. 'That's the problem with us English folk living out here; we fail to understand that it is not like England. In England, a fish pond may attract a few midges at the most, but here it becomes a hive of activity for many species other than the fish it was built to house; a breeding place for frogs, mosquitoes and heaven only knows what else.'

'Exactly. We try to recreate England here, and it just does not work. Which makes me recall the pond I had built in this garden. What has become of it?'

Isabella blushed. 'I have fallen into the same trap as Mrs Heyman. I have filled it with water and put fish in it. I have seen a bird, that Anthony tells me is called a Hamerkop, fishing from this pond, but so far we still have most of the fish and no frogs.'

'Good, because the fish will eat the mosquito larvae. We will have to wait and see how the frogs behave during frog breeding season though.' He was stopped from his musings by the reappearance of Gonda, who gave them another deep bow, ending with a flourishing wave of his right hand as he bent so low that his nose nearly touched his thighs. 'I have made everything ready for you, *Nkosi,*' he said, when he resumed normal standing position.

Besides making Sir James's belongings ready, he had freshened himself up too. His travelling clothes had been smart, but now he was wearing a black butler's suit with long tails, buttoned over a crisp white shirt. His shoes were so shiny they almost reflected the view, and he had snowy white gloves on, matching his shirt and making a startling contrast to his dark, shiny skin.

'Thank you Gonda, I will be there shortly. But while you are here, let me introduce you properly to Mr and Mrs Craig. Mrs Craig is the lady of the house and will be calling on you for as much help as I will.'

'Very good *Nkosi,* very good *Nkosikas* Madam.' He bowed again.

'I think that is all for now, thank you Gonda. I will come through soon to dress for dinner.' He waited for Gonda to leave before continuing. 'He has been in my employment for over fifteen years now and has become my right-hand man, butler, serving man and general factotum. You will find him a great benefit to have around, Isabella.'

'If his appearance is anything to go by, I am sure I will.'

'Exactly. He came to England with me, where he stayed for two years, learning the ways of the servants in the great houses there. He has come back to Africa with a professionalism that one does not find amongst the domestic staff here.'

'How very interesting, and I know what you mean. I try, but struggle, to get decent work out of the men who work for us,' Isabella sighed. 'They're alright in the garden, when they are given specific jobs, but some of the housework seems to be quite beyond them.'

'Well, we will get Gonda onto them straight away. I am sure he will be able to raise their standards in no time.' The amused gleam came back into his eyes. 'I may try to get him to refrain from all that bowing though,' he said.

*

These boys behave like animals, Gonda thought, as he stood outside the kitchen hut, listening to the antics going on within. He couldn't understand what they were saying, as he had been born and brought up in the Cape and therefore did not speak their language, but he had a good idea of what was happening. Someone must've broken something and there were screeches of laughter; very similar to the sound of excited baboons, Gonda concluded. They were obviously now trying to hide the crime. He listened with irritation to the banging and clattering of pots and pans. These boys don't know how to work properly in a household, Gonda thought; they do not understand the importance of this work. Even in the few hours he had been here, he had noticed how shoddy things were, if you looked carefully enough. The water used for washing the dishes, for instance, had not been changed from the beginning of the wash to the end and was so dirty by then it was surprising that anything would be clean after being in it. And they had broken one plate and one glass, not including the one that had just been broken now, and instead of putting them aside and telling Madam, they were hiding them. And then the stealing: oh yes, he had noticed them shoveling food into their mouths when they were cooking, and then again when they had brought the leftover food back to the kitchen after the meal.

Mananga appeared now at the kitchen door Gonda was standing behind, patting something in his jacket pocket. His face dropped when he saw Gonda. He didn't know what to make of this man. He was black like them, and yet he was different. They couldn't speak to him, other than in English, and he was dressed much more smartly than they were. And then there was their accommodation. They all lived in mud huts in the compound, but he had been allocated a four-corner house, built for him, Moses told them. He did not know of any other black men living in four cornered houses.

Mananga nodded to Gonda as he passed him, wanting to get back to his hut in the compound without being delayed.

Gonda entered the kitchen. Somani and Moses were still talking loudly to each other, but they shut up when he appeared. Gonda walked across the kitchen to inspect the coolbox. The fabric and coals surrounding it were bone dry. He opened the lid to feel the butter dish inside. It was warm. He turned to Somani. 'Wet this cloth and make sure it stays damp always,' he said. 'You need to have a bucket of water nearby always so that water can be poured over the coals often. Whose job is it to do this?'

Somani and Moses looked at him. 'It is not our job,' Somani eventually answered.

'Then whose job is it?'

'We do not know, maybe Mananga's.'

'Well Mananga has enough to do, improving his cooking; this can be your job from now onwards,' he said to Somani. 'Go and fill a bucket now, so that you can wet the coals and the cloth before you knock off tonight.'

Somani thought about refusing, but then decided it would be easier to just wet the cloth and not argue about it. He could see that this man and the new master were close so it was probably best to just do what he said

Chapter 5

MABEL left the house through the French door leading from the dining room onto the veranda. She crossed the veranda and went down the back steps, stepping carefully onto the dusty ground. The rains had ended, and any grass that had grown around the house during the rainy season was beginning to dry out. Mabel liked getting up early and going for walks along the banks of the stream running at the bottom of the property. It still had water in it from the late rains, but it would not be long before this dried up too. She never went too far though, for fear of wild animals and snakes, but she would go just far enough so that she was out of sight of the house. She always went early, in the hopes that she would come across Mr Craig, whom she knew also left the house early most mornings. She had begun to fantasize that he would find her alone in a secluded area, and that he would grab her, and push her against a tree, and they would kiss passionately. Ah, if only. She could no longer pretend to herself that she was not obsessed with him; she could not stop thinking about him. She had tried transferring her fantasies onto Sir James. At least he was single, but he just did not attract her like Mr Craig did. For one thing, he was much too old for her, at least forty, she was sure, and secondly, he was too grand. Every morning when he saw her he would say: 'and how are we today, Mabel?' in his oh so fancy accent, but she knew he had no interest in how she was. However, Mr Craig was different. Even though he was posh too, he didn't make her feel insignificant. When she first realised, back at the old house in Hillside, that Mrs Craig had become cold towards him, she felt sorry for him, but then pleased, because she thought that he might turn to her for his pleasure. That's when she started wishing Mrs Craig would pack up and leave, just like some of the other wives had done when the going got tough. That's when she started dreaming of replacing Mrs Craig in Mr Craig's life. They wouldn't have to worry too much about social etiquette. She had heard all sorts of stories about men taking up with other people's wives, and even native women, and she planned that they could be discreet for as long as it was deemed necessary.

But now, since they had moved to this house, she noticed that Mrs Craig was showing him more affection. She had even worked out that they were sleeping in the same bed again. She struggled to hide her disappointment as she noticed them talking and laughing together. She hated it. Mrs Craig was one of those women who always got everything she wanted, while she, Mabel, was constantly being overlooked. She didn't think this was fair. She had come out to Rhodesia to try and make a better life for herself, just as Mrs Craig had, but while Mrs Craig had managed to catch herself the best looking man around, and to move into the grandest home in the area, she, Mabel, was expected to be nothing more than her lady's maid. Well, at least she managed to get out of most of the chores they expected of her, but she still disliked being here with Mrs Craig around. However, she did not know how she could escape this situation. She did not want to go back to England, where she knew her prospects would be no better, but at the same time she did not know how to go about finding another position for herself in Bulawayo, without the Craigs finding out. And besides all this, if she left, it would mean she would not see Mr Craig again, something she would hate.

Mabel walked towards the stream, lifting her skirts so they wouldn't get wet from the heavy dew on the longer grass. She glanced in the direction of the stables, and as she did this, she realised there was something strange going on. Her initial thought was that the horses were lying down, but then she knew this could not be. She walked towards the stables, to have a closer look. When she saw the horses close up, it looked as if they were dead. Her heart sank and she felt shaky. She clapped her hands and shouted to see if any of them would move, but none did. Then she noticed Mr Craig's horse, Gunner, standing in the corner looking sweaty and shivering, but the rest were on the ground and motionless, as far as she could make out. She glanced towards the field beyond the stables. The oxen, mules and dairy cows grazing there all looked happy enough. It was just the horses that were in this bad way. She picked up her skirts and ran back down the path towards the house, through the hall and down the passage towards the Craigs' bedroom. She knocked on their door, something she would never usually dream of doing with both of them still in there. There was no answer, so she knocked again, more urgently this time, and called out, 'Mr Craig, I'm sorry to bother you, Mr Craig.'

He opened the door, still buttoning up his shirt and smelling of shaving soap. She could see Mrs Craig sitting up inside the mosquito netting that surrounded their bed.

'What on earth Mabel?' Anthony said.

'Ah, Mr Craig. You need to come. I think the horses have died, or most of them anyway.'

Anthony's face went ashen. 'What?'

'The horses.'

He took off, leaving Mabel to shut the bedroom door and follow him back to the stables. When she got there, she found him standing and staring, stunned at the catastrophic sight before him; five dead horses, and his own Gunner going the same way.

'God almighty, I can't believe this,' he said when he saw her. 'Somani, Hlabano, where are you?' he shouted. 'Where are you? Come quickly,' he yelled in a panic, but then his voice cracked, and Mabel thought for a moment that he was going to start crying.

James came running from the house, looking dishevelled, having been alerted by Isabella. He stopped in his tracks when he saw what was going on. Hlabano and Somani appeared from the compound and came and stood next to him, clucking in sympathy.

James knew what the problem was. Horse sickness; he'd seen it before. One minute the horses appeared healthy, and the next they were dead.

'I can't believe this,' Anthony repeated. 'Yesterday they were all fine.'

'That's what horse sickness can do. Those little insects that have been flying around have obviously got to them. We try to prevent them with these buckets of smoky fires we have all over the place,' he said, kicking one of the buckets next to him, 'but sometimes it's not enough.'

Anthony walked up to Gunner. 'Ah, how hot you are, poor boy,' he said stroking him.

'There is a chance he may still live, as he has not succumbed to it yet. Maybe we'll be lucky with him.' He beckoned Somani towards them. 'Walk him to the barn. Keep him quiet and sheltered there, with lots of fresh water and maybe he'll pull through. Lead him slowly Somani, he'll be very weak. Hlabano, take some of those smoky buckets with him to the barn, we don't need any more flies attacking him.'

Anthony checked each of the other horses, and noticed that the little mare James had recently bought for Isabella was still alive, although she was lying down and trembling. James shook his head. 'No, she is too far gone, I'm afraid. Go back to the house and get your gun, Anthony, so that we can put her out of her misery. While you are there can you tell Gonda to get everyone out here? We're going to need all the help we can get, clearing up this mess. We will have to burn all the carcasses as soon as possible; otherwise every predator in the vicinity will be prowling around here. We are going to have to gather all the dry wood we can find in the bush to use for the fires.'

*

Bright yellow flames leapt into the air as the fires sought to devour the dry wood. The wood crackled and shifted as the thicker pieces turned to smoldering embers, and just when it was starting to die down, more wood was thrown on top to reignite the flames. The fires needed to be as hot as possible. They were using one of the ox carts to go and collect dry wood from further afield. Isabella watched what was going on with a mixture of curiosity and disgust, standing a distance away on the back veranda of the house. She found it too hot to go any closer; but also, she did not want to be any nearer, knowing what was underneath each roaring fire. It was like being at a funeral pyre. Smoke billowed and swirled, finally blowing in the opposite direction to where she was standing. There was a lot of shouting and yelling, but she couldn't make out what anyone was saying above the roar of the flames.

She could bear it no longer. She went inside the house and into the library. The best way to try and cope with what was going on outside was to busy herself, she resolved. She had not written to her sister for a few weeks and she knew poor Celia would be desperate for their news. She sat down wearily at the desk in the corner, the leather padding on the seat of the chair creaking under her. She opened the roll top and smoothed her hand over the surface, making sure there was no dust. She still couldn't believe how dusty their homes always were here in Rhodesia, compared to England. From the top drawer she took out the personalized writing paper Celia had sent from England, to mark the occasion of their move. Despite the way she was feeling, she could not help appreciating, as she always did, what Celia had had printed at the top of each sheet of writing paper.

Mrs Anthony Craig
Sunrising
Bulawayo
Matabeleland
Southern Rhodesia

She could imagine how this address must have ignited Celia's romantic illusions of Africa. She wondered what she would make of the tragedy they were going through today, but resolved she did not want to bore her with all of this. She needed to tell her about Mabel, and how difficult and useless she was being these days. She felt bad about this, as it was Celia who had recruited her. She had glowing references from her previous employers, but she had not lived up to these. Well, they could not have accounted for a bad bout of malaria. Isabella needed Celia's advice on how they could get themselves out of the arrangement they had made with her. She felt she could not give her notice. What would the poor girl do then, so far from home and with no family?

'My dear Celia,' Isabella wrote, but then she could not decide where to start telling Celia about her "Mabel woes". As she sat there, thinking what to write, she stared blankly at the painting above the writing desk. She noticed that it was crooked and, still deep in thought; she stood up to straighten it. It would not straighten, so she lifted the corner to peek behind it and see what was preventing this. She looked, and gasped with horror. There was a snake wrapped around the wire on which the painting hung. She stared at the snake, and the snake stared at her, just for a moment. She dropped the corner and fled from the room, her heart beating so hard it felt like it would burst her chest open. She stopped in the dining room and tried to calm herself. She wanted to get someone to come and dispatch it, but she knew she could not do this while they were all so busy burning dead horses. She could see everyone beyond the stables, walking about, cutting wood, stoking the fires. She could not disturb any of them now. She was relieved to see the dogs down there, lying under a tree, watching all the activity. The last thing she would have wanted was for either of them to be in the house with a snake lurking about.

She went back into the hall and closed the library door, then pulled her coat from the coat rack and rammed it against the bottom of the door. She could not bear the thought of the snake slithering around the house and no one being able to find it. Despite barricading it in the library, she still did not want to be in the house anymore, so she resolved to make herself useful and see if she could rustle up something for lunch. Mananga was too busy cutting wood for the fires to prepare something for them.

In the kitchen hut she found a loaf of bread baked the day before. As usual, it hadn't kept well, but it would have to do. As she opened the wire door of the cool box, to take out the tin of butter, she noticed that the material surrounding it was bone dry. She felt the coals, wedged between the two layers of wire that made up the sides of the cool box. A few pieces were damp, but most were dry. She took the pail from where it was standing next to the door, lifted it and drizzled water over the top of the cool box, letting the water soak into the material. She was always asking the kitchen staff to do this, but of course they kept 'forgetting' unless she or Gonda checked up on it.

Isabella could not find anything interesting to put on the sandwiches she intended making, so she went down to the kitchen garden to see if she could pick some tomatoes or a cucumber. Although there was a thick fence made from cut thorn scrub around it, the kitchen garden attracted every passing wild animal in the vicinity, not to mention more insects than she had ever known existed before. However, it was their only source of fresh vegetables. She found a tomato, just starting to ripen and only slightly stung, and decided it would do. As she bent to pick it, a waft of smoke billowed passed her, the pungent smell of flesh and burning hair making her gag. Suddenly the air was filled with this disgusting smelling smoke. The wind had changed direction and was now blowing towards the house and gardens. Will this day ever get better, Isabella asked herself as she went back to the kitchen to prepare the sandwiches.

*

James sat on the western veranda smoking his pipe and drinking a whisky. The sun was just going down, but he could not appreciate the sunset today, as he usually did. What a God-damned awful day it had been. They had started lighting the fires well before midday, but even now, they were still raging, although Anthony was the only one left checking them. This was going on near the stables, behind the house, but the air was filled with smoke and the stench of burning hair and flesh. It is almost beyond endurance, James thought, exhaling, as if trying to dissipate the stink with his pipe smoke.

Isabella came onto the veranda, holding a scented handkerchief to her nose. 'Oh my, this smell. I cannot get away from it. It is making me feel sick.'

'I know, but there is nothing we can do about it. All I can say is that those carcasses must be pretty well incinerated by now.'

Isabella shuddered.

'This is the problem with having horses here, I'm afraid. It's why many people prefer mules or donkeys. They are so much hardier in many ways. But come now, Mananga has brought out the drinks tray. How about a stiff whisky this evening?'

'Yes. I think I will have one tonight, to calm my shattered nerves.' She took the glass he handed her. 'Thank you. At least it appears that Gunner is holding his own. I cannot bear the thought of him not pulling through after all this.'

'I think he will. He would have died by now, I believe, if he was going to. Some horses do manage to survive, and afterwards they build an immunity to horse sickness, so we won't have to worry about him getting it again.'

'Then maybe we should just keep him and go back to having those wretched mules for the carts.'

'Absolutely not; I enjoy riding horses as much for sport as for transportation, and we cannot let something like this make us live in fear of it happening again. That's one of the problems with living in this part of the world, Isabella. We must toughen ourselves up in so many different ways. There are diseases here that we never had to encounter in England, to mention nothing of the wild animals and, dare I say it, the snakes.'

Isabella glanced at him. When he had come in during the afternoon, she had told him about the snake in the library. After much discussion, he had instructed Somani to hold the painting out from the wall with a stick while he fired at the snake and killed it, leaving some pellet holes in the painting.

'Yes, Isabella, I know it was frightful having that snake behind the painting like that. I'm sure there have been other equally frightening situations and there will be more to come.'

Somani appeared at the end of the veranda with the tray of paraffin lamps. This had become his evening chore; to walk around the house with the trays of lamps and set them in

47

designated areas. They watched him as he went about his job, moving from the veranda and into the drawing room.

'Well maybe I should go and see if I can be of any more help to your husband,' James said, draining his whisky glass and banging the contents of his pipe into an ashtray, before setting it on the table in front of him. 'I will see you for dinner, Isabella.'

*

Mabel stood at her bedroom window looking out towards the stables and the fires raging beyond. She could just make out Anthony's form, moving from one fire to the next as he tossed more wood onto each. Then he would shift logs about with a long wooden pole, still trying to keep them as hot as possible. He must be exhausted; she thought, he had not stopped all day. Every time she thought of him, still doing up his shirt buttons in the morning, and then, how his voice had broken, almost near to tears, when he first saw what had happened, she felt her heart shift in her chest. She wished she could go down there and help him now, maybe take him a glass of cool water or a damp towel to wipe his face, anything to make herself useful to him. If it weren't for his spoilt wife and scary Sir James she would have been with him all day.

Chapter 6

WITH all the horses dead, except Gunner, transport was a major concern. Usually James and Anthony rode to the MEC offices in town on their horses. Sometimes, on the rare occasion when the weather was foul, they used James's closed in horse-drawn carriage instead. But all this was impossible now.

'The sooner we buy new horses, the better,' James said. 'I need to put the word out post haste. I do not think we can harness those troublesome mules to my carriage. It will take days for them to get used to drawing it and by then, hopefully, we will have replaced the horses.'

'We could use Isabella's Spider, except she's arranged to meet Muriel Weir at the Grand Hotel for their weekly cup of tea together,' Anthony said.

'Well, I don't want her to have to cancel that,' James said. 'This place still reeks of burnt carcasses, and she needs to get away, as much as we do.'

'Exactly. Of course there is the ox cart, but, although Bulawayo's roads are supposedly wide enough to turn spans of oxen in them, I don't want to try my hand at it,' Anthony said with a wry smile. James had bought an ox cart, with its accompanying span of sixteen oxen, for their mining expeditions.

'Absolutely not. Could you imagine the bellowing from those beasts while they're waiting around for us all day? We'd struggle to get any business done.'

'We could try the ox cart, with less oxen.'

'True, but I think it may just be best to take the mule cart instead. I never thought I'd say this, as I find those mules tricky, but I think they are our best bet for the time being.'

Despite everything that had happened, Isabella found the sight of the two men trotting down the drive in the mule cart very amusing. Usually they looked so stylish, galloping back and forth on their horses, so to see them, cramped on the hard, wooden bench of the mule cart used for menial chores, was a sight to behold. How the mighty have fallen, she chuckled to herself as she went inside to prepare for her own outing.

*

Gonda always accompanied Isabella when she went to town in her Spider. She knew she could travel alone, but she always worried that something would go wrong and she would find herself stranded in a secluded part of the route with no one around to help her. But besides this, she enjoyed getting to know Gonda better. He always dressed in his smart travelling clothes for their trips to town, and, unlike Mabel, he always made polite conversation with her. So she learned that he had been born in the Karoo, and that his parents had died when he was very young; he was not quite sure how old. He then lived with his grandmother, but she had wanted him to start working as soon as possible. She knew someone who worked in Sir James's house in Cape Town, and it was through this man that he first came to work there.

'Sir James has always treated me good,' Gonda explained on their first trip. 'He taught me that if I work hard, I do well. He took me to England to learn how to work properly in a household.'

'And what did you think of England?' Isabella asked.

'Very good, Madam, but very cold. I like it there, but I was pleased to come back.'

'And where did you work in England?'

'In Sir James's family home, Madam. It was a very good position. Their house is very smart. Much smarter than Sunrising, or even Sir James's house in Cape Town.'

'And how did you find the other servants who were working there?'

'Good, Madam, although some of them did not like me at first.'

Isabella could imagine this. When she was growing up they only had three servants in their home, but she, Edward and Celia sometimes used to go and stay with their wealthy cousins in their grand house in Wiltshire. She often used to hear her aunt complaining about 'the politics' of the servants' hall.

'And now that you are here, how do you find working at Sunrising, Gonda?'

Gonda pursed his lips for a moment. 'Those boys there, they are starting to learn to work better, Madam.' He flicked Queenie's rump with his whip.

'You are doing a good job at teaching them.'

'Thank you Madam.' He pursed his lips again but said nothing. Isabella wondered if they were giving him a hard time too. Then he said: 'I don't mind not being friends with them,' and she knew this must be true.

They arrived at the Grand Hotel and Gonda stopped the Spider near Muriel's mule cart. Unlike Isabella, Muriel did not feel the need to have anyone accompany her there. She had tied her mule's rein to the hitching post outside the hotel.

Isabella walked into the cool foyer of the hotel, removing her hat and gloves. She ran a hand over her hair. The manager, Mr Scott-Rodger, was standing behind the reception desk. 'Ah, greetings Mrs

Craig. Mrs Weir is already waiting for you in the dining room.'
Isabella braced herself. She knew Muriel would want to know every
detail of their tragedy.

*

'I know it is not good timing, after what happened,' Anthony said
later, when they were having dinner, 'but an important investor is in
Bulawayo and we would very much like to have him here on
Saturday.' He took a mouthful of his soup before continuing. 'Do
you think you could arrange a dinner party at such short notice
Isabella?'

They had entertained regularly before William became sick and
died and Isabella had always enjoyed it, but that was months ago,
and she worried that she may have lost her nerve after everything she
had been through. Then she thought of Gonda, and how much easier
he would make it for her. As if he was reading her mind, Gonda
appeared at the dining room door, followed by Hlabano, who was
now being groomed to be their headwaiter. Isabella glanced at
Hlabano as he leant forward to remove her soup bowl. She had not
noticed before the maroon fez he was wearing, and she wondered
where he had acquired it. She observed him more closely and was
pleased to see that he was looking much smarter all round. She knew
this must be Gonda's influence.

'I think a dinner party would be most enjoyable. Who is the man
you wish to entertain?'

'He is Mr Gordon Forsyth. He used to spend a great deal of time
in Bulawayo in the 1890's but has not been here since. However,
James wrote to him, telling him about the MEC, and he's very
interested in investing. He's staying at the Club, but we thought a
dinner party at our home would be a pleasant way to get to know
him better.'

Many would consider that in actual fact they had a "dinner party" every night at Sunrising. Before James came to stay they had had a simple evening routine, but, since his arrival, their evenings had taken on a more formal tone. Now they dressed for dinner, and they followed a strict evening ritual. Drinks on the western veranda, followed by a three-course dinner in the dining room. Afterwards, Isabella would leave the men to their cigar and port while she went to the drawing room for coffee. Often she would play a game of solitaire while she waited for them to join her, and then after coffee they would retire. Isabella enjoyed these evenings, the pleasant conversation, the white linen tablecloth, the glistening silverware, the shining glassware, the many candles and lamps. She spent much of her day planning for their evenings; the food, the flowers, and she had even visited Mrs Sanders, the best dressmaker in Bulawayo, to have more evening gowns made. So yes, she decided, she would be able to cope with a larger dinner party, and she liked the idea of it.

'What is Mr Forsyth like, and who should we have with him?' she asked.

'He is an intriguing character,' James answered. 'He worked with Rhodes and Jameson, and that ilk, in the diamond mines in Kimberly and made his fortune there. He's quite a bit older than me and never been married, as far as I know. You may find him a little eccentric when you first meet him, Isabella, but once you get to know him I am sure you will agree that he is a most charming gentleman, always postulating about his great love for Africa, shooting, hunting, and everything it has to offer. With this in mind, Anthony, I was thinking we should ask everyone to stay the night here. But we could suggest Forsyth gets here earlier, which would give us time to go out with him and shoot a few birds before dinner.'

'As long as you are back in time. I do not want to have to entertain our other guests alone,' Isabella said.

'Of course, lass,' Anthony said. 'As for whom else to invite: Forsyth was telling me today that he had been to the Heymans for a musical evening last week and had met Sir George and Lady Chapman there. We could invite all of them?

'Oh dear,' Isabella said, 'I cannot start competing with Mrs Heyman. The entertainment she always manages to arrange; I would not know where to start. Do not forget, her parties are legendary in Bulawayo.'

'Ah, but you forget,' James said, 'we have the advantage of Gonda. She would give her eye teeth to have someone like him, I have no doubt.' He paused, as if considering Mrs Heyman's good teeth, and then he continued. 'I don't think you need worry too much about entertainment, Isabella, although a round of charades at the end the evening won't go amiss, if you want to do something.'

'How about the Fletchers?' Anthony suggested. 'I would like to get to know them better. They live on a property not far from here. It used to be the Umguza Hotel. I am interested in finding out more about what they are doing there now.'

'Ah yes, I remember Muriel telling me that Philip once went to the Umguza Hotel. It is quite close to the Umguza River, I believe,' Isabella said. 'He and a whole group of men rode their bicycles there, if I recall.'

'I do believe I remember that occasion,' James said. 'There was some concern that the cyclists would ride into a herd of wild animals and not be able to get away in time. As it was, they all arrived there quite safely and had a grand old party to celebrate. But it is a pity the house is no longer being run as a hotel. Bulawayo is fast becoming such a busy town, with more and more people arriving every month, needing accommodation. I believe the Fletchers call their property Umvutcha.'

Isabella rang the bell and Gonda reappeared, walking solemnly in front of Hlabano, who was carrying a heavy tray. He walked around the table with his tray while Gonda offered food from each of the serving dishes. When this was done Hlabano scuttled from the room, while Gonda walked around the table again, filling the wine glasses from a crystal decanter. He put the decanter on the side table and was about to leave too when a blood-curdling scream, followed by a crash, shattered the peace of the evening.

Everyone froze.

'My God, what, what on earth?' Anthony stammered, scraping back his chair and running to the door leading out of the house to the kitchen hut. James followed behind. They stood at the door, trying to adjust their eyes to the darkness outside when James suddenly jumped back and slammed the door closed.

'It's a hyena,' he gasped. 'I caught a glimpse of it as it slunk under the kitchen window. Did you see it? Quick Gonda, close that other wretched door.' The French door leading onto the veranda had been open all the while. 'Anthony, where is your gun? We need to shoot at that bugger.'

'In the library, I'll fetch it now.'

Isabella gasped. 'But what about the men in the kitchen? Won't it attack them?'

'The door is closed, they should be safe inside.'

'And what about Hlabano; he would have been outside?'

'I believe the crash we heard was him throwing the tray, with all our serving dishes on it, at the hyena. I'm sure he jumped straight through the kitchen door after that. Don't you worry; he'll be safe.'

Anthony returned with his gun and went to the window facing the kitchen hut, looking out. 'I can't see anything. Wretched animal; it's too dark.'

James came and stood next to him. All they could make out was the dull lamplight shining from the window of the kitchen hut. It would be impossible to see the hyena again, unless it walked under this window, as it had done before. James fetched Anthony a chair to sit on while he waited. He went back to his place at the dining table. They sat and they listened. No one talked in case they missed hearing something. The room was heavy with silent anticipation. They could not even hear the crickets chirping outside now that the French door was closed.

'Scavenging bastard,' James eventually said. 'I wonder how many there are. I only saw the one, but I wouldn't be surprised if there are more.'

'We could all relax if I could just kill one. That would scare any others away,' Anthony said.

'Definitely my boy, but that might just prove impossible on this dark night. And besides, hyena are notoriously wily animals. I think the best thing you can do is fire into the air. That should make them run for their lives.'

'But Anthony never fires from the dining room window, James,' Isabella gasped. 'It will sound like the Boer war starting up again. Mabel will get the fright of her life.'

'Can't be helped. Block your ears lass. Are you ready James?'

'Fire away.'

He shot and reloaded, shot and reloaded, shot and reloaded, the sound reverberating through the confined space of the dining room like bells chiming in the tower of a church. James, Isabella and Gonda pushed their hands against their ears. Trigger cowered in the corner of the dining room, and Archie hid under Isabella's skirts, shivering. Anthony eventually stopped and leant back with a satisfied look, despite the ringing in his ears. 'Right, that should have frightened them off. What do you think James? Another few shots for good luck?'

'Please, no. No more,' Isabella pleaded, leaning down to comfort Archie.

James glanced at the pained look on her face. 'That should do the trick, old boy. The wretched hyena will know they are not welcome after that commotion, I am sure.'

'Aye, I have not been firing off any rounds of ammunition these last few afternoons, like I usually do. I've been too busy worrying about Gunner, and what had happened to the rest of the horses.'

'I believe they were attracted to the smell of the carcasses. We may have thought we had burnt them to a cinder, but the hyena could probably still smell something, being the scavengers they are.' James relaxed and took a sip of his wine, an amused expression crossing his face. 'But, where were we before this interruption? Ah, yes, our dinner party, and who we should invite.'

'James, how can you?' Isabella exclaimed. 'How can we have anyone here, with hyena lurking about? Imagine if this had happened when we had a houseful of guests?'

James and Anthony began to laugh at the thought of this, and once they started they could not stop. They're just like exhilarated schoolboys, Isabella thought, who've got the better of the school bully. As she watched their excitement and mirth, she understood the reason they lived in Africa. They thrived on the unpredictability of life here.

Chapter 7

JAMES went to look for Isabella. 'Ah, there you are. Would you like to join us on our ride when Mr Forsyth gets here?' he asked, on finding her in the vegetable garden. 'You need to try out your new horse.'

'I will, at some stage, but I am still haunted by what happened to the other horses.'

'Yes, it was most unfortunate, but we do have to move on. We were very lucky that Mr Holdengarde had those horses to sell. I did not enjoy using that rickety old mule cart for my transportation.'

'No, mules are not your style, James.' Isabella smiled at him. 'However, besides still feeling so upset about what happened to the horses, I cannot go riding anyway. I have to oversee the preparations for our dinner party tonight. These are under control, but there are still many last minute touches that need to be dealt with before the guests arrive. I will not be able to do any of this if I am out gadding on my new horse.'

'Indeed, true.'

'And in fact, I had better go and see how everything is going in the kitchen now.'

She made her way to the kitchen hut and was happy with what she found there. The eggs, to be curried for the starter, had been boiled and were cooling in a pan of water, and she could smell the aroma of baking bread above the usual smoky kitchen smell. Mananga's cooking had improved in recent weeks, and his bread, when fresh, was always delicious with lots of butter. She had managed to buy a dozen tins of butter in town that week, and she intended using most of these to make everything as tasty as possible. Anthony had caught five good sized bream in the Umguza River the day before. These had been filleted in the morning and were sitting in the cold box, waiting to be pan fried in butter once the guests arrived.

'How is the guinea fowl casserole coming along, Mananga?' she asked, walking to the stove and taking the lid off the pot. The meat had been stewing all day so that it would be tender, but the leeks and carrots, picked earlier from the kitchen garden, would only be added later. She took a spoon from the drawer and tasted it. 'Mmm, you've added enough salt and pepper, and it tastes delicious. Well done.'

'Good Missus.'

'Don't forget to mash the sweet potatoes with lots of butter, and whatever happens, do not overcook the beans.'

'No Missus.'

'What about the pudding, is it ready yet?'

Muriel had given Isabella a recipe for Venetian Rice, saying it was a 'must have' pudding. She and Mananga had tried it a few days before, and the men had sampled it for dinner later that evening. It was such a hit she had elected to serve it at their dinner party, along with her favourite, banana cream. Somani had milked the cow first thing in the morning, and the kitchen was noisy with the burring of the separator as he separated the cream to have with their bananas and Venetian Rice.

'It is good too, Missus. Cooling now.'

Gonda stood near the door, listening and watching while Isabella inspected the food.

'Madam,' he said, clearing his throat as he always did, 'please come and check the dining room now.'

59

He followed her as she left the kitchen hut and made her way
to the French door leading into the dining room. As she walked
around the table, she touched one of the crisp napkins that had
been twisted into an elaborate, birdlike shape and put into a
shining wine glass. 'Goodness,' she could not help exclaiming.
'Who did these amazing napkins?'

'It was I, Madam, although Hlabano set the table. He is
understanding the art of housekeeping much better now.'

'Well the napkins look magnificent. Indeed, the whole table is
superb. Please tell Hlabano how happy I am. All I need to do is
cut some flowers and put them in a bowl in the middle of the table,
and then it will be complete.'

'And if you can unlock the storeroom for me, Madam, so that
I can get out some more candles. The ones we had in the kitchen
are finished.'

'Of course.'

Gonda cleared his throat again. 'One more thing Madam; I
have also done these.' He reached into his jacket pocket and
brought out some cards. 'Can I put them on the table too Madam?
They used to do this sometimes, at Sir James's house in England,
on special occasions.'

Isabella took the cards and looked at them. He had written:

Curried egg with bred
Pen frid fish in butter
Ginnie Fowl stue and vehgetable
Bahnana cream and rice

She almost choked, so touched was she by his attempt at writing
out the menu. She took a moment to pull herself together.

'Oh my, this is so impressive. Who taught you to write, Gonda?'

'I have taught myself, over many years, Madam.'

'Well you have done an excellent job. There are a few words that are not spelt quite right, but I can help you correct them, if you like.'

'Yes please, Madam.'

'Come with me to the library so I can write them down, and then, yes, you must put these menus on the table for our guests. They will be of great benefit to them.'

*

Anthony took the watch from his pocket and looked at it. 'Where on earth is Mr Forsyth? We agreed that he would be here by two thirty, and it is now after three. We will not be able to do all the things we had planned if he doesn't arrive soon.'

James took a final gulp of his tea and put the cup back onto its saucer. 'I believe he would have telephoned if he wasn't coming. He is obviously detained elsewhere and will arrive nearer dinnertime.' He got up and stretched. 'Well, I vote we wait until four and if he hasn't come by then we go anyway. I want to try out the new horses, and we may be too tied up to do it tomorrow.'

Isabella's heart sank. She still felt shy when she was alone with strangers, and she knew they were often delayed when they went out riding and shooting in the bush. 'Please don't go for too long.'

'We won't lass. We'll take a quick turn about the property and be back in good time to welcome the guests.'

At four they set off, with Mr Forsyth still not having arrived. Isabella stood at the top of the steps and watched the horses trotting down the drive, Trigger running after them. Archie squirmed in her arms, desperate to go also, but he was still too small to go for a long run, even though he did not think so. Once the horses were out of sight she put him down. He took off towards one of his favourite places; the fishpond. He had once spotted a lizard there, and since then he spent a great deal of time trying to find it again. She smiled at the sight of him, tail in the air, wagging, as he scrabbled in the grass surrounding the fishpond. Isabella went down the steps and across the drive to take a closer look. She gazed into the water. It was murky and green but had attractive lilies growing in it, and the greedy Hamerkop had not eaten all the fish yet. She wondered if they should knock it down before the frogs became a nuisance.

'Ahoy there, I have arrived!' a yell startled Isabella from her thoughts about frogs and fishponds. She looked up to see an elderly gentleman marching up the drive, almost as if he was marching at the front of a military parade. Behind him was an African man, carrying a heavy looking bag and struggling to keep up with the speedy pace. Isabella knew this must be their missing guest, Mr Forsyth. Archie took off down the drive, barking. 'Hush,' the man said, bending over and allowing Archie to sniff his hand, before proceeding. When he reached Isabella he clicked his dusty boots together, as if coming to attention, and she was again reminded of a soldier in a parade. She was half expecting him to salute. He did not, but instead said: 'Mr Gordon Forsyth, Madam, finally reached his destination. Are you perchance Mrs Isabella Craig, mistress of Sunrising?' He removed his hat and smiled, his teeth flashing under his bushy, grey moustache, a stark contrast to his bald head.

'I am indeed. We had almost given up on you Mr Forsyth.'

'Madam, Madam, what a journey I have had. Who would have thought that it would take so long to travel just three miles? My sincere apologies for arriving so late; I pride myself on punctuality, but I'm afraid this has been an exception.'

'Oh my, are you quite all right, Mr Forsyth?'

'Indeed I am, despite a somewhat harrowing experience.'

'Why don't you come in and take some refreshment?'

'I would like that, indeed I would, and then I can tell you my whole story.'

She looked behind her and saw Gonda hovering in the background. 'Is Mr Forsyth's room ready, Gonda?'

'Aha,' Mr Forsyth interrupted. 'This is my man, Kenneth, with my dinner suit in that bag. Perhaps he can be shown my room so that he can air my suit. I intend making a smart appearance at your dinner table tonight, Madam. And in the meantime, I can follow you in search of the refreshment you are offering.'

Isabella could not help smiling. She could see what James meant by "eccentric". 'Come with me, I am sure there will be a fresh pot of tea on the veranda.'

Once he was settled with a cup of tea in his hands he launched into his story. 'Madam, what a day it has been. I lunched at the Club, where I am staying, and immediately afterwards readied myself for a prompt departure. My good man, Kenneth, was ready outside with the Cape cart and mule, so at one thirty we were able to leave, just as I had planned. Well, we had gone but half a mile down Main Street when it came to our attention that the left wheel was making a strange noise. We stopped and took a look and established that the wheel nut was loose. Obviously we did not have the means to fix it, but I found a piece of wire on the floor of the cart. I threaded this through a hole in the axle and wheel. We thought this would rectify the problem, but, by Jove, were we wrong. When we got to the stony crossing over the Amajoda Stream the wheel came clean off. It got stuck in a blasted rock, excuse my language, and the next thing we knew, the cart was rolling onto its side. How neither of us was injured is beyond me.'

'What a fright you must have had.'

'Oh yes, indeed, but such a relief that we were not hurt. It would have been a different story altogether if we had broken something, because we would then have had to wait for someone to come our way, and heaven only knows when that would have been.'

'Well quite.'

'But as it is, we were able to walk at a good pace here, me guiding the way, and Kenneth bringing up the rear, carrying the bag with my dinner suit.'

Isabella could not help smiling again. 'Well at least you have reached us. Maybe you would like something stronger after this ordeal, now that you have quenched your thirst with that cup of tea.'

'Indeed I would. A whisky and soda would not go amiss.' Isabella got up to pour it from the drinks tray, which had already been put in its usual place on the table near the door. 'A magnificent view you have here, Madam, over this vlei.'

'Vlei, Mr Forsyth? What is a vlei?'

'It is an Afrikaans word describing this type of open, grassy land which I am sure must be marshy during the rainy season.'

'Oh yes, it is a little. I have never heard that word before, but I will use it from now onwards.'

'There are quite a few words derived from Dutch, which are infiltrating the English we use in this part of the world.'

'I will look out for them. But tell me, Mr Forsyth, what have you done with your Cape cart and mule.'

'We left the cart exactly where it went over. We did try to shift it but it was too heavy for just the two of us. As for the mule, we removed the harness and tethered her to a tree, giving her enough rope to drink from the river. I was going to ask your husband if I could use a horse to go back and fetch her.'

'Oh yes, I do not think it would be good to leave her there after dark, in case of wild animals.'

'Exactly my fear, Madam, but Mr Craig and Sir James are not here it appears?'

'No, they still went on the ride they had planned to do with you. But do not worry, I will ask our gardener to take one of our mules and go and fetch yours. We just need to tell him where to find it.'

*

Mabel pulled at a curl on Isabella's head a little harder than she needed. There was no doubt about it; she thought, Mrs Craig had lovely hair; just another thing she found irritating about the woman. Obviously she couldn't help it, but that didn't make her feel any better. When she first came to work for the Craigs she used to do Mrs Craig's hair every time they went out for dinner, or had guests around. Mrs Craig always used to tell her how talented she was at hair dressing. She quite liked this compliment to start with, but now she just found it patronizing, especially as her own hair was so plain in comparison. Mrs Craig was lucky; although her hair was not exactly blonde, it had natural streaks that made it seem lighter than it was. This lightness was enhanced by the natural curls she had. As for Mabel's own hair, it could only be described as 'mousy brown', and, if she didn't want it to look greasy, she had to wash it every day. However, while Mrs Craig had someone bringing her water (cold, hot, whatever she wanted) every evening, she had to lug her own water to her room if she wanted to wash her hair. Sometimes she could get Moses to do it for her, but not often.

'Would you mind not brushing quite so hard, Mabel, you will give me a headache at this rate,' Isabella said, interrupting her thoughts.

'Sorry.'

'Is everything all right? You seem so deep in thought. Are you feeling better these days?'

'Not like I used to be Mrs Craig. I am still very weak.' She was not going to tell anyone that she was as strong as she had ever been before she had malaria. If that happened they would be expecting her to work like a slave from dawn until dusk, and she had no intention of doing this.

'Well take care of yourself and hopefully you will make a full recovery soon.'

'Yes, I will. I have started going for long walks. These seem to be helping.'

'Are you not afraid of wild animals?'

'I have seen nothing that scares me yet. I believe Mr Craig's shooting keeps animals away.'

'Good, well I'm glad to hear this.'

In fact, her walks weren't that long. She had found a large, shady tree upstream, well out of sight of the house, where no one else would go, and she had taken to spending hours every day sitting there. Sometimes it got a bit boring, but at least it was better than sitting in her room, trying to think up excuses as to why she could not work. There was a family of ducks that she often used to see swimming on the water if she kept quiet enough. She found she was entertained watching them.

The door burst open and Mr Craig walked in, pulling his shirt from his breeches and undoing his buttons. He stopped dead when he saw Mabel in their room. Mabel blushed, seeing him in a state of half undress like this.

'Hello Darling,' Isabella said. 'Mabel is just finishing off my hair. She won't be long and then you can freshen up. I'm very relieved you are back in time.'

*

The Chapmans and the Heymans travelled from Bulawayo in their carts together, arriving at Sunrising just as it was getting dark. Gonda was waiting and showed them to their rooms, informing them that drinks would be served in the drawing room at 7.30. The Fletchers arrived at that time. They were not going to spend the night as they did not live far away, and with the moon nearly full again, they would be able to see their way home later.

Mr Forsyth was soon in his element, regaling everyone with a colourful account of the "torrid time" he'd had in getting there earlier.

After some time, Isabella left her guests and went to make sure everything was ready in the dining room. It looked superb; with an abundance of lit candles enhancing the white tablecloth and shining glass and silver. She had planned with Gonda to bring the first course through at 8.15. She was about to go back to her guests when she happened to glance at herself in the mirror above the dresser and noticed that her hair was coming down. She looked at herself, stunned. She looked ridiculous, with the coil on the top of her head falling to the side. Thank goodness she had seen it then, and hadn't sat down to dinner like this. She rushed back to her bedroom and tried to repair it as best she could. While she did this she could not stop herself from wondering if Mabel had pinned it loosely intentionally, so that it would fall down.

She pushed this mean thought from her mind.

'By Jove, how different Bulawayo is now, compared to how it was when I was last here twelve years ago,' Mr Forsyth boomed, as Isabella walked back into the drawing room. All her guests sat, or stood in silence, as if in awe of him, while he held forth. 'Oh yes,' he continued, 'at that time there were *Impis* hiding everywhere, trying to kill us whenever they could. You can't blame them, I suppose. Their king, Lobengula, had signed the mineral rights over to us after being duped by Rudd and his men. My good friend, John Moffat, was part of that team, you know, sent with them to butter up the old boy, because his father, Robert Moffat, had been friendly with Lobengula's father, Mzilikazi. Well, when Moffat realised how Lobengula was being deceived, he was not happy with Rhodes, not that Rhodes gave a jot. He felt Lobengula had been paid enough, with the monthly rental of 100 pounds, the 1000 rifles, 10 000 rounds of ammunition, and of course that darn steam boat.'

'Whatever happened to the boat?' Sir Charles Fletcher asked.

'The King never did get it. How Rudd and his men ever thought they could get a steam boat up the Zambezi River and above the Victoria Falls, heaven alone knows,' said Sir George Chapman.

'By Jove, but those rifles and ammunition proved to be a nightmare when they rebelled again,' Mr Forsyth boomed. 'All those natives running around, trying to shoot at anything that moved. Thank goodness they didn't know how to use them properly, and they were no match against the Maxim guns of course.'

'I can imagine,' Sir George said. 'But tell me Mr Forsyth, if you do not approve of Rudd's treatment of Lobengula, why have you changed your opinion now, which surely you must have, if you want to invest in mining yourself.'

'Well of course my man. When you look at how things have developed since then: the houses; the roads; the railroad; the telephones. You cannot help but be impressed. If we don't do it, someone else will. The abundant opportunities this place has to offer; the opportunities that no one was making use of before. Just consider, Mzilikazi brought his crowd here in 1838, was it? Just fifty odd years before us, and what did they ever do to develop the place? You tell me, what?'

Mrs Heyman cleared her throat.

'Exactly, my dear, exactly.' He downed the remainder of his whisky and would have continued if Isabella had not taken this opportunity to interrupt.

'Dinner is served in the dining room. Mr Forsyth, may I have the pleasure of being escorted into dinner by you?'

His face puckered with surprise. 'Aahem?'

Isabella held out her arm. He looked at it and cleared his throat.

'Madam, I would be delighted.' He flashed a broad smile. 'I assure you, the pleasure is all mine. He strode across the room to take her arm. 'All mine, indeed.'

As if on cue, the dinner gong boomed from outside the dining room door.

Chapter 8

THE more people invested in the Mining and Expedition Company, the more they were able to expand. They needed to finance their expeditions into the countryside to find new areas to mine, they needed to excavate these areas and check how mineral rich they were. They needed to employ geologists, engineers, miners, office staff, cooks and cleaners. With investment, the company grew rapidly.

James and Anthony rode at the head of their latest expedition. They picked their way along a narrow bush path. The going was slow so that the ox cart, laden with all their equipment would not get left behind as it struggled through the thick, rough bush. They had left home before dawn and they were feeling hot, tired and grimy now. But they still had a lot to do before they could rest.

'Has Isabella any regrets about the way your lives have changed since you agreed to join me?' James asked, trying to take his mind off the dreariness of their slow pace.

Anthony hesitated. He knew she still found many aspects of her life challenging. She was not over the death of their baby, and never would be, but, besides this, he knew it was difficult for her being alone so much now that they kept going off on their expeditions, he knew that although she was very fond of James, it was difficult having him living with them. And he knew that she found it difficult being so far away from her female friends.

'She doesn't complain. She loves living at Sunrising. Who wouldn't?'

'Ah yes, and what a magnificent job she has done, making it into such a comfortable home. I am so grateful to her for doing this, and for allowing me to share it with you. It is just the sort of home I envisaged when I built it back in the nineties. How I enjoy being able to entertain there the way we do now.' Since the dinner for Mr Forsyth, they were now entertaining regularly; mainly men who wanted to invest in the MEC, but Isabella was making plans to start inviting her friends from Hillside to come for weekend parties.

Whenever they went on their expeditions they had to carry a great deal with them, not knowing how long they would be away, what they would find on the way, or if they would be delayed at any stage. So they had the ox cart stacked with heavy canvas tents and thick wooden poles, canvas beds, chairs with wooden frames and sturdy wooden tables. James even insisted on taking his copper bath, in which he bathed whenever they camped near a river and they could use river water to fill it. This bath had a lid and in it they stored their steel cutlery and enamel crockery and cups. They had a gang of ten men to drive the carts, and set up and take down the camps. Mananga had been commandeered as the camp cook, and he drove the mule cart, which usually carried all the food and bedding. Besides cooking, Mananga had also become a very useful interpreter whenever they needed to discuss anything with the local people. James and Anthony could use some native words and phrases, but they were unable to have an in-depth discussion with anyone.

Their newly employed geologist, Mr Robert Browne also joined them on their expeditions; a reserved man in his early fifties who had little to say beyond the suitability of the terrain for mining gold.

James reined in his horse and stood up in his saddle to get a better idea of where they were. The rains had finished now, but the grass was long and dry as it waved in the breeze. They were riding down a gentle slope and they could see a low hill in the distance. 'When we get to the bottom of this incline we'll leave everyone behind and you, Mananga and I will proceed to Chief Khumalo's village. From what I have been told, I believe the village is not too far from here.'

'Right,' Anthony said. 'I checked last night and the gifts we have for the chief are easily accessible in the mule cart.'

'Chief Khumalo is a pleasant chap. I've met him before, but not here of course. I believe he moved his people to this area in 1903 after the drought we had that year, probably because he couldn't find enough grazing for his cattle where he was then.'

'Well he won't be having any problems here. There appears to be plenty of grass.'

'Exactly.' Their mundane trudging was suddenly broken. 'Bloody hell,' James cried, his horse shying. Lying in the path was a fat, blubbery snake, the chevron pattern on its body almost camouflaging it. 'Bloody puff adders. Thank God I saw this one when I did, otherwise my horse would have stepped on it, and that would have caused no end of problems for us. I cannot abide the way they will not get out of the way.' He took his pistol from the holster around his waist. 'Brace yourselves everyone; steady your animals while I shoot.' The sound of the shot ricocheted around them and their horses winced, despite being used to having weapons fired from them. The mules pulling Mananga's cart jumped and strained against their harness. 'We had better get a move on so that we reach Chief Khumalo as soon as we can,' James said, putting his gun back into its holster, 'in case anyone there thinks they're about to be attacked after hearing that gun shot.'

*

71

They walked their horses through the village, the mule cart following behind. This took some time as the village was spread over a good-sized area. Chief Khumalo was a relative of the late King Lobengula and descended from the Ndebele tribe. As such, most of the huts were of the beehive type, domes of varying sizes, made of grass matted together with thin ropes cut from the bark of trees. However, there were some pole and *dagga* huts too, with loosely thatched roofs, many blackened from smoke rising through them. A dusty, smoky smell hung in the air. As they walked, they nodded to women, standing at the doors of their huts, or sweeping around them. The women stopped this as they passed, grass brooms in hand, staring at them, not knowing what to expect. The children were less scared. Many began to follow them, at first slowly and quietly, but then one shouted and waved the stick he was carrying, encouraging others to run alongside them, kicking up dust with their bare feet, their only covering being small skirts made of animal skins that covered their crotch area. A group of young girls, coming from the bush and carrying wood on their heads, bare breasts bobbing, scurried behind the nearest hut, giggling as soon as they saw them.

The chief sat on a wooden stool under an *indaba* tree near his homestead, watching them as they came towards him. He was surrounded by his elders, also sitting on wooden stools in the shade of the large tree, with the younger men standing nearby. Chief Khumalo and his elders were also wearing skirts made from animal skins, although more substantial than the ones the children wore. Thin strings made from skin were tied around their ankles and wrists, and the chief shifted the animal skin cape on his shoulders as if it was suddenly too hot.

'Woa,' James said, pulling his horse to a standstill a good distance from the tree. He got off and handed the reins to Mananga who had stopped the cart behind him. Anthony did the same, and they walked towards the chief and his entourage, taking their hats off and carrying them.

'Ebrookie,' Chief Khumalo said, recognizing him. He stood up as James moved forward to shake his hand, bowing.

'Chief Khumalo.' He motioned to Anthony. 'My *mhgane*, Mr Craig.'

The chief mumbled to a man standing next to him. James put out his hand to shake his. '*Salibonani,*' he said, and the man said something he could not understand. He and Anthony went down the line of elders, greeting each in turn. They had learnt from their first visit to a native village that they were expected to take a long time meeting and greeting the elders. They could not hurry this long-standing tradition.

Eventually the greetings were over. James took his handkerchief from his pocket and wiped his face. Although it was autumn and the weather was cooler than it had been of late, he felt hot and sweaty after shaking so many hands. He walked to the cart to get some of the gifts they had brought. Mananga untied the tarpaulin and started to roll it back while James felt inside for the gun: a new rifle for the chief, plus one hundred and fifty rounds of ammunition. The chief turned the rifle over in his hands as soon as James gave it to him, clucking as he did this. He felt its weight and checked its length.

'Not Martini Henry rifle?' the chief noticed.

'No, this is called a Short Magazine Lee Enfield rifle.' James spoke slowly. 'A SMLE or Smelly.' He glanced at Anthony, winking. 'It is a better rifle than the Martini Henry.' Mananga translated, as James pointed out the magazine and five round charger clip. 'It goes bang, bang, bang, bang, bang and not bang, reload, bang reload like the Martini Henry.' He pretended to do the bolt action reload the chief would be familiar with, making everyone burst into confused laughter. James realised he would have to show them how the rifle worked.

'Tell him I will teach him how to use this rifle, if he wants,' he said to Mananga.

'*Uzaku fundisa ukubulula umbhobho,*' Mananga said to the chief, who nodded his head in agreement.

'Tell him this rifle will make a lot of noise. We need to go somewhere where it won't be dangerous shooting it.'

'*Uyenzaumsindo umkhulo.*'

'*Yebo,*' the chief answered, and everyone around him nodded their heads in agreement. He wanted to go off immediately for his shooting lesson. James looked about, trying to decide where they should do this. He remembered an appropriate looking place, back the way they had come, where there were two low hills forming a small enclosure. He hadn't seen any huts near there. Again he had to ask Mananga to suggest this to the chief, saying it was not far for them to walk. The men and the children joined in the slow, sombre procession to this place. When they got there Mananga warned everyone to stand well back while James went forward with the chief. He showed the chief how to stand and hold the rifle. He took the rifle from the chief, took off the magazine and removed five rounds from the ammunition belt around his waist and loaded them into it. He clicked it back onto the rifle with some difficulty, then took his stance. He pushed the rifle into his own shoulder and pretended to shoot, ramming it into his shoulder each time an imaginary bullet went off. He put the rifle down and rubbed his shoulder, pretending to grimace while he did this, hoping the chief would understand that it was going to kick, and this could be painful. He then picked up the rifle again, steadied himself in a more exaggerated fashion than he would usually do, and shot one round at a nearby tree in front of them, again magnifying the kick and how painful it was. The crowd behind them started jabbering, with some children running back towards the village, until their curiosity got the better of them and they came back to resume watching, hands rammed over their ears to muffle the impending noise. James put the gun into the chief's hands. The chief waved it around precariously, with James steadying it and shaking his head. The last thing they needed was for the chief to have an accidental discharge and for someone to be shot. The chief readied himself, as James had done, and after some hesitation pulled the trigger, twice, so that two shots went off in quick succession. He had never shot a gun that didn't need to be reloaded before shooting again, and he got such a shock he nearly dropped it. James had to reach out to ensure this didn't happen. The chief clutched his jaw in surprise, before letting out a great bawling laugh. James laughed with him, and then the chief indicated he was ready to try again. This time he kept his chin well out of the way, and he only pulled the trigger once. He smiled at James, then fired again. When all five rounds in the magazine had been shot, James showed him how to replace them, and then he went through another five rounds. James filled the magazine for the third time, but the chief indicated that his ears were ringing with the noise and he'd had enough. James unclipped the magazine and they began their slow stroll back to the *Indaba* tree with the mule cart near it.

Barrels of salt and sugar were removed from the cart, along with mounds of blankets. Finally, when all the presentations were over, they were invited to sit down on wooden stools and drink water from calabashes while they discussed, through Mananga, the reason for their visit; to discover if there was gold in the area.

*

They left the village three hours later. By now it was late afternoon and they would not have time to travel anywhere else that day. The chief had said they could camp the night where they had stopped. The next day they would set off to the place that the chief had agreed they could excavate, a good ten miles from where they were.

They sat next to the fire drinking whisky before dinner, exhausted after such a long day. They listened to the sounds of the evening, the men talking as they sat around their own fire, fifty yards or so from them, crickets chirping nearby, a nightjar calling, drums beating in the distance. Suddenly the talking at the other fire stopped, and both Anthony and James turned in that direction to see why. It was too dark to see anything. They could hear some murmuring, and then Mananga appeared with two young men holding a wooden bowl with eggs in it. They set the bowl on the dirt in front of the fire.

'These boys, they have brought you these eggs from the chief,' Mananga said.

They were so surprised by this gesture they did not know how to respond at first.

'Well I never,' James said. 'Please tell the chief *'siyabonga'*. We will enjoy eating them for our breakfast tomorrow morning.'

Chapter 9

ISABELLA sat at her dining room table trying to look interested. She was having dinner with a man by the name of Bert Robinson, whom Anthony had asked to come and stay at Sunrising while he was away, 'just in case something goes wrong,' he said. She stifled a yawn, thinking how much easier it would be to deal with any crises alone, rather than having to listen to Mr Robinson's inane waffle night after night. One of his problems, she decided, was that he spun his stories out so much she found it hard to believe anything he said.

'There was nothing I could do, you see Mrs Craig, except sit in the tree and hope the lioness would not come after me.'

'I can quite imagine, Mr Robinson, it must have been a terrifying experience for you.'

'Well, I took it in my stride. I climbed as high as I could, and then waited for the dawn light. However,' he wiped his mouth with his napkin and was about to continue when Hlabano came into the dining room with his tray.

'Would you like to help yourself to some more, Mr Robinson, before Hlabano clears the food away?' Isabella asked.

He glanced at the serving dishes on the tray. 'Oh yes, rather.'

He spooned more casserole and rice onto his plate. 'So where was I? Oh yes, the lioness; it was angry that I had shot the other two. Thankfully it had cubs waiting in the bush, not fifty yards from my tree, and one of these started mewing, almost like a kitten. This distracted her and I took my opportunity. I scrambled down the tree, I grabbed the biggest log I could find, and I hurled it at the dastardly creature. I then walked away. Never run from lions, Mrs Craig. Always walk, otherwise they will think you are prey and attack you.'

'Please,' Isabella started. She was about to say, please, no more of your ridiculous talk, but then she felt a pang of sympathy for him, watching him shovel the last of his casserole into his mouth, knowing he was eating better at her table than he ever ate elsewhere. 'Ah, please, Mr Robinson,' she said instead. 'Can I ring the bell for the pudding?'

'I would be delighted, Mrs Craig,' he said, as she steeled herself for more stories.

If only Mabel had agreed to join them, she thought, at least this would have diluted things for her. Or maybe not, Mabel was still as unfriendly as ever.

*

Mabel could not have been more excited with the way her life was changing. She found it difficult to hide her glee, although she made sure she did when she was with anyone from Sunrising. The last thing she wanted was to be given a whole list of things to do right now, in her final days at Sunrising, when she had so much else on her mind. Oh yes, indeed, her final days at Sunrising. She could still not believe her good luck. She had met a man; a young, good-looking man and he wanted to marry her. Percy Brown. He was her saviour. Since she had met him she had not given Mr Craig a passing thought.

They had only known each other six weeks, but they were going to be married next week, and she could hardly wait. He worked for the Matabele Laundry, which was not that far from

Sunrising. One of his jobs was to watch over the Indian men employed to wash the laundry in the Matsheumhlope River. She had come across him on one of her walks. He had been asleep in the soft grass on the banks of the river, while the Indian workers scrubbed and rubbed and spread the clean washing out to dry further down the bank. He woke up just as she was trying to slip by without being noticed. He lifted his hat from his face, and she was surprised to see how handsome he was, making her feel embarrassed and awkward so that all she could do was scurry on down the path. But, when she came back later, she found he was still there, sitting under a tree right next to the path this time, smoking a cigarette. The Indians appeared to have gone.

'Morning Miss, enjoying your walk?' he asked, drawing on his cigarette.

It took Mabel all the self-control she could muster to act calm and collected. 'Thank you, yes, although it is a little hot now. I need to get back to the house to cool off.'

He immediately jumped up and ran to the river where he took a handkerchief from his pocket, dipped it into the water, wrung it out and brought it back to where she was standing. 'For you to wipe your brow, Miss,' he said. Mabel was so surprised she could do no more than stand and stare, first at the handkerchief, and then at him. He misinterpreted her hesitation. 'It's alright, Miss, it's clean.'

'Yes, of course, thank you,' she said, taking it and wiping her forehead.

'So where do you come from Miss? I was not expecting to meet a lovely lady on the banks of this river.'

'Well actually, I live and work at Sunrising. I go walking around this area quite a bit, but not usually this far up the river.'

'Blimey, so you come from that fancy place, hey. What is it like there?'

'It is a beautiful house full of beautiful furniture, but the people who live there are snooty, if you know what I mean.'

'Oh yes, there are a lot of snooty people in this town. I wasn't expecting such snootiness when I chose to come out here from England. Why don't you sit down so we can chat for a while?'

Mabel felt like she had met a kindred spirit. She sat down. 'Yes,' she said, 'some of these people weren't even minor aristocrats in England, but now they are here they think they are special, when in fact we should all be the same, don't you think?'

'Exactly.'

'The 'lady' of Sunrising is Mrs Craig, and she treats her dog better than she treats me. And as for this one African boy they have working there! His name is Gonda and even he thinks he's better than me, and everyone in the house allows this.'

'Ah no, now that is too bad,' he said, reaching in his pocket for his packet of cigarettes. 'Fancy trying one of these, while you tell me more?' he asked.

*

Isabella had suspected for a while, but now she knew for certain, that she was pregnant again. She was pleased she was on her own (except for the tiresome Mr Robinson), when she came to this realization. Outwardly, she appeared much better since moving to Sunrising, not spending as much time as she used to pining for her William, but now that she knew she was pregnant she felt uncomfortable with the idea of replacing him. She was glad that Anthony wasn't around, in case he picked up on these negative feelings she was having and thought they were inappropriate. They were, but she could not help it. She resolved she needed to talk to someone, and the best 'someone' would be Muriel Weir. She could wait till their weekly tea at the Grand, but sometimes other ladies joined them, and then she wouldn't be able to discuss her worries without the whole of Bulawayo finding out. She decided she needed Muriel to herself when they next met. She went to the library to telephone her.

'Ah Isabella,' Muriel sounded breathless, shouting into the phone. 'This telephone instrument, I'm still getting used to it. Hold on; let me change ears. Maybe that will be better. I cannot hear you at all.'

Isabella laughed. 'It is because I have not said anything except "hello". I have been waiting for you to give me a chance to talk.'

Muriel laughed too. 'Oh dearie me, it's going to take me a while to get used to talking to someone down this strange little trumpet. You're lucky, you've had yours for a while.'

'Well let us be quick then. I just wanted to say I need to talk to you about something when we meet this week, so please don't ask anyone else to join us, if you don't mind.'

'Oh dear, I've already asked Lady Chapman. Can I put her off do you suppose? Oh dear, no I don't think I can, without appearing rude.'

'Alright then, I'll have to talk to you about it another time.'

'No, no, why don't I come out and visit you tomorrow instead? We keep saying I should come and see your beautiful home, but we never do it.'

'That would be splendid. I'm still on my own with the men off on yet another of their expeditions. Well actually, I am not alone as I have a Mr Bert Robinson staying here, supposedly looking after me.'

'Bert Robinson. Good Lord, he's hardly good company. That man tells the biggest stories in the whole of Bulawayo.'

'I have noticed Muriel. Believe me, I have noticed.'

Muriel arrived mid-morning the next day, this time getting her man to drive her in case something went wrong on the way.

'I can't wait to have a look at everything here,' she said to Isabella as she alighted from her cart. 'What a magnificent looking place. You have not done it justice when you have described it to me.'

'I'll show you around and explain all that I have done since we moved in, but first, let us go and have some refreshment.'

They settled themselves on the veranda, and Hlabano materialized with a tray of tea. A gentle breeze blew over the vlei in front of them.

'Ah, you are so lucky to have this wonderful view, Isabella,' Muriel said. 'Those impala I can see in the distance must be such a delight to watch. They look almost tame.'

'Absolutely not, they run away if anyone goes anywhere near them. I have forbidden Anthony to shoot on this section of the property, just in case the noise scares them off forever.'

'Quite. Anthony has always been far too active with his gun for my liking. Thank goodness Philip doesn't share the same passion.' This had always been a standing joke with them, going back to Anthony's springhare-shooting days at Hillside.

'It is lovely here Muriel, and of course to live in a house like this in Bulawayo is such a privilege, but I do sometimes wish it was a little closer to town. Three miles is a long way, I can't just 'pop in' and see my friends like I did when we lived in Hillside. I do miss not having friends close by.'

'Yes, I can imagine it gets lonely for you at times.' She took a sip of her tea. 'But tell me, what is it you want to talk about?'

'Well,' she said, 'well, I wanted to tell you I am pregnant again.'

'Oh Isabella, how incredible. How wonderful. How delightful. I wondered if it was that. I hoped it was that. I am overjoyed by your news.' Isabella stared at her friend, surprised by her jubilation. It wasn't that amazing, surely? 'You see, one of the reasons I am so happy is because I am expecting too. I was going to tell you this week, funnily enough. But isn't this the most wonderful coincidence, that we will be having babies at the same time? Just imagine, they can play together, they can go to school together.'

The Weirs had been married for longer than the Craigs, and this was their first child, so it was something for them to celebrate. Suddenly Isabella felt better about her own pregnancy. Suddenly she was comfortable with the idea. She was very pleased she had not expressed any of her reservations.

'But of course it will be harder for you, Isabella. I can understand that. None of us will ever forget your darling little William. This is going to bring it all back for you, and it will be difficult, I can see that.'

'Yes, it will be hard.'

'You will never get over losing poor William, Isabella. You just have to accept it.' She took another sip of her tea. 'Maybe a new baby in the house will make Mabel change her attitude towards you.'

'Yes, that would be nice. I'm at my wits end with her. But, speaking of Mabel, you've just put a wonderful idea into my head. I'm going to write to my sister, Celia, in England and ask her to come out and help me with the baby. Celia was the one who recruited Mabel in the first place, you will recall. But how much nicer it would be to have her here. You'll love her, Muriel. She's so calm, so sensible, and I know she has always wanted to come and visit me here. She lives with my father, and life gets a little boring for her. When I came out here for the first time in 1898, to help my sister-in-law with her new baby, Celia was deeply envious. She would love an excuse to come.'

'Oh, to have family around, that's one thing I do miss about being here, my family.'

'Me too. I was sad when my brother and sister-in-law moved to the Cape. But having Celia here would make up for that.' She leaned forward to check if there was still some tea in the pot. 'Now, let us have another cup of tea shall we, and then I will give you the grand tour of Sunrising.'

*

Later, when Muriel had left, Mabel knocked at the library door. She knew Isabella was in there and she found her sitting at her desk, pen in hand, writing paper spread in front of her.

'Ah, Mabel. Speak of the devil. I am just writing to my sister, Miss Braithewaite, telling her that you are better but still not fully recovered.'

Mabel stared at her with the closed, sulky expression she had perfected in the last few months. 'I need to speak to you Madam.'

'Oh yes, is something the matter?'

Nothing could be further from the truth, Mabel thought gleefully, but she was certainly not going to tell Mrs Craig. 'No, I just came to tell you that I will no longer be working for you from, um, from the end of this week.'

'What?' Isabella's eyes widened in surprise.

'I will no longer be in your employment, Madam.'

'But, but, why ever not?'

Just like Mrs Craig, Mabel thought, to think that everyone's lives must revolve around her. And now she was expecting her to tell her everything.

'But what, what are you going to do? Where are you going to live?' Isabella frowned, confused.

Mabel knew that she would have to say something.

'Well, as a matter of fact, I'm getting married.' She had to suck in her cheeks to contain her amusement when she saw the look of surprise on Mrs Craig's face. For a moment it seemed she was going to fall off her chair from the shock. Typical of the woman, she thought, to think that she, Mabel, was incapable of attracting a husband. She regained her surly expression.

'But, who on earth, what on earth, where have you met anyone? I mean, you never go anywhere. Whenever I ask you if you want to come to town with me you decline.'

Mabel looked at her feet. She was now starting to feel irritated. Why should it be so amazing that someone wanted to marry her? 'He works for the Matabele Laundry. Can I be excused now?'

Isabella drew her breath. 'Actually no.' She put the lid onto her pen and laid it on the desk. She folded her hands together on her writing paper before looking at Mabel again. 'Now, just remember. You are our responsibility. It is because of us that you are in Rhodesia. You have been sick for a long time. We have all been sympathetic and understanding. We have told you we want to help you, any way we can. With all due respect, you have not been very helpful back.' Mabel was about to walk out, but thought better of it. 'So now you waltz in here and state you're off to marry someone; I think I am entitled to a few more details than you are giving me.'

'All right then. His name is Percy Brown, he works for the Matabele Laundry, which, as you know, is not far from here. We met when I was out walking. He is a very charming man. He has asked me to marry him. He has found a house for us to live in, in First Avenue. We are getting married on Monday. Is there anything else you need to know?'

*

Isabella sat at the dinner table, deep in thought. She was more upset than she would ever let on that Mabel had behaved so badly towards her. She could not understand why. As far as she was concerned, both she and Anthony had treated her well, trying to include her in the household, being more than sympathetic when she became sick, had hardly asked her to do anything since (which had irritated her, but she had managed to keep quiet about it). And now this? To be treated like this, in this cold and indifferent way. She could not help it that Mabel was employed to be her maid. Mabel had been a maid in England, so what was so wrong with being a maid here too? There were lots of women who worked as maids and were happy to have the position. That was just the way society worked.

She stared at Bert Robinson as he sat eating his chicken pie. Thankfully he was not prattling away in his normal fashion, but it suddenly occurred to her that he worked at the Matabele Laundry too, and she wanted to find out more about Percy Brown.

'So you know Mr Percy Brown from the laundry, do you?' she asked.

He looked up from his pie, wiping his mouth with his napkin. 'Percy? Oh yes. He's in charge of the washing department. He hasn't been there very long, not as long as me. I think he came to Bulawayo a year or so ago.'

'How interesting. And, and, the two of you are friends?'

'We meet for a few pints at the Exchange Bar, when we are in town. I don't believe you will have been to the Exchange Bar Mrs Craig. It's in Main Street, opposite that grand establishment Mr Willoughby is building. Yes, that is surely going to be the grandest building in Bulawayo when it's finished. Even grander than the Exchange building and the post office.'

'Indeed it will be, and no, I have not been to the Exchange Bar. Did you know that Mr Brown is getting married?'

Bert looked surprised. There were so few single women in Bulawayo, it was always quite an event when a bachelor managed to find someone to marry.

'No, I didn't know that. Maybe he had a girl back in England and she's coming here to marry him?'

'No. The girl he's marrying is much closer to home than that.' He looked at her, confused. 'Mr Brown is marrying our Mabel; Mabel who works here.'

'No!' he gawked. He had met Mabel a few times since staying at Sunrising. He had tried to engage her in conversation, but she was usually aloof with him and scuttled off to her room whenever he tried to talk to her. 'Well I never. But, on saying that, Percy is a good looking man. I can understand that women would be attracted to him.' He scraped the last of his chicken pie onto his fork and put it in his mouth. 'Well I never.'

Isabella was more intrigued than ever. She resolved to go with Somani to the Matabele Laundry next time he took the washing there. She was eager to see what this Mr Brown was like for herself.

'Have you finished? Can I ring for the pudding?'

Chapter 10

ISABELLA told Anthony about Mabel as soon as she could after his return. 'What a surprise,' he said. 'But, it is the best thing possible. I was starting to wonder what on earth we were going to do with her, having her hanging around the place, doing nothing, yet still feeling obliged to look after her. Although,' he continued, touching Isabella's arm, 'considering your other news, maybe we could do with her services again. Maybe a bairn would get her back on track.'

'Maybe, maybe not. I think, all in all, her getting married is a much better solution.'

'Aye, you are right.'

'And I have come up with an equally 'better solution' for when our baby arrives. I have written to Celia, asking her to come out and help. Now isn't that just the best possible idea?'

'Aye, lass. That would be wonderful for you, for all of us.'

'Exactly so. I have written to her, but must be patient while I wait for her answer. That's one of the problems with living here, being so cut off from the rest of the world and having to wait so long for mail. And then, of course, she will have to do something with Papa. She can't just abandon him. I've suggested she ask his sister, Aunt Elizabeth, to take over while she is here.'

'From what I remember of your Aunt Elizabeth at our wedding, she is a most formidable woman. Indeed, your father would be kept on his toes by her.'

'Aunt Elizabeth is very capable. I am sure she will be able to deal with him much better than Celia, to be honest.'

'I have no doubt.'

'Going back to Mabel, I still cannot understand why she has been so cold towards me all these months. I just wish I knew.'

'You can't lose any sleep over it lass. I think the best thing is for us to go through our storerooms and find a nice piece of furniture for her as a wedding present, and then we can wash our hands of her.'

*

'I don't suppose you've told Isabella about our latest, well, what we can call it, project, venture. I'm not quite sure?' James asked, as they sat down for dinner that night.

'No, I thought we could tell her together.'

'Ah, now what?' Isabella asked.

'We are going to acquire a piece of land,' James said.

'But I thought that's what you did all the time.'

'Yes, we do. We peg ground for mining. But this is different. This land is going to be for, well, farming, I suppose, in the end. To start with we will use it for recreation.'

'Recreation? What do you mean by recreation?'

'Shooting, hunting, you know, that sort of thing.'

'But you do that here, don't you?'

'Well sort of, but not to the same extent. Remember Sunrising is near Bulawayo. I know you think we are out in the sticks, but we aren't really. And with every passing week, it gets less and less wild. I know you don't think this, what with that hyena incident not so long ago, and monkeys always breaking into the kitchen, and baboons stealing vegetables from the garden, but that sort of thing will be happening less and less. It's even going to be difficult to keep our impala in front of the house in the not too distant future.

'But this land we've been looking at, Isabella,' Anthony continued, 'now this place we are going to acquire, it is wild and totally undeveloped.'

'You mean there is nothing there?'

'A man by the name of Tate has been living there since the1880's I believe. He lives in some pole and *dagga* huts. Other than building the huts he lives in, he's done very little else, except plant an orchard near the river. Oranges. So there is just him, the few African people who live with him, and nothing else. Just wild, wild, wilderness, both the terrain and the animals. We wouldn't be going there if there were people living all over the place, I can assure you.'

'But, where are all the other African people? I always find it strange that we see so few, other than those who work for us.'

'They live in their villages,' James answered. 'They practice subsistence agriculture, and they are, to a large extent, nomadic. Once they have utilized the resources in a certain area they move away. Just consider, Isabella, while we are here building permanent structures, like brick houses, railroads and bridges, they build grass and mud huts that are not made to last. Our cultures are very different. While we are looking to develop, they are looking to survive. It must be this way; otherwise surely they would have done more over the centuries?'

'It is difficult to estimate the population,' Anthony continued, 'as they are illiterate. All statistics are 'word of mouth', but the population is small in comparison to the vastness of the land. Life has been cheap up until now, what with them warring amongst themselves, famine and disease. Most of the population does not survive until old age. Of course this is changing, now that proper medicine is being introduced. Just think about Mabel. She would have died from malaria if she had not been treated with all that quinine. That is what has been happening here for centuries. That is why populations move about so much. Even the people living in this area now, many of the tribes only arrived in the last fifty years or so.'

'They did do a census of the European population last year,' James said. 'They found there to be 12600 whites, with just under half living in the towns. As for the African population, it is impossible to be as exact, because of the reasons we've just been discussing, but it is believed to be somewhere around 600 000 people in total. This is a very small number when you think about how huge this country is. That's why there seem so few people about.' He took a sip of his wine. 'But, we are digressing. The main thing, as far as we are concerned, is that there is this vast tract of land that has no one and nothing on it, and we would very much like to utilise it. Mr Tate is not well and wants to go back to England to see his family again. He is more than happy for us to take it off his hands.'

*

Isabella kept herself busy, planning for all the changes that were going to occur in her life. She had received a reply from Celia saying she would come out in September, in four months' time; there was a lot that needed to be done before then.

The top of her list was to prepare a room for the baby. This was a priority, mainly because little William's room had become such a place of sadness in the months before and after he had died. She could not help being afraid that the same thing might happen again, and she wanted to try and face this fear by having a room that would be a happy and positive place. The bedroom next to theirs was the obvious room to make a nursery. It had been a guest bedroom up until now, but had only been used once in the time they had been living there, when they had given their first grand dinner party. Isabella had had a look around the room. It was similar to theirs, just smaller, but it also had an adjoining dressing room. This would be useful if they elected to bring a nanny out from England, although she was reticent about this after the trouble they had had with Mabel. But the rooms could do with a lick of paint, she concluded, and she needed someone to do this.

'My brother's brother has a brother who needs work,' Moses told her when she enquired who among their workers would be able to paint the room.

'Is there no one here already who is capable?'

'No, Missus. They are all too busy.'

'Well can you get this man, your brother's brother, or whoever, to come and see me in the next few days.' She had learnt long ago that it was better not to try and understand any African relationships. A 'brother' did not necessarily mean someone who shared the same mother and/or father.

'Yes, Missus,' Moses said.

This man arrived later that very day. Isabella was amazed that the message had got through so quickly, when so many of the other messages she sent with her servants seemed to be delayed for days. As soon as she met him, she knew he was a cut above average. His name was Mangeni.

'I worked for relatives of Mr and Mrs Duncan in Suburbs, Missus. I was there from 1898 until 1903. They only dismissed me because they chose to go back to England. I went back to live at my village, but I cannot pay the hut tax, and that is why I want work again.'

The 'hut tax' had been introduced by Rhodes in the 1890s; to ensure that at least one person from every household went out to work, so that they had the money to pay this tax.

'I see. Did you ever paint when you worked for the Duncans?'

'Just once, Missus. I may be a little slow when I first try it again, but I will soon remember. I also want to work, Missus,' he added, 'because we like to have the things that you have. The clothes and the pots and pans. We can't have them if we don't have money. It is good to work so we can earn money.'

Oh yes, Isabella concluded, this is the type of worker I like having around.

Mangeni was indeed a little slow with his painting to begin with, but was soon working well. It did not take long to do the nursery and adjoining room, and afterwards, Isabella thought up other jobs for him to do. Somani usually did the day-to-day laundry, the things that weren't sent to the Matabele Laundry, but Isabella elected to try Mangeni at this job instead. She was tired of the way Somani managed to destroy even the hardiest of their things. Unsurprisingly, Mangeni was soon doing the laundry much more efficiently than Somani had ever done. Somani was sent back to working in the garden instead.

*

Isabella elected to go with Mangeni on his first trip to the laundry with the sheets, towels and the curtains she was going to use in the nursery. She did not need to go, she was just being inquisitive. She had still not met the mysterious Mr Percy Brown although he and Mabel had been married for two weeks now. Isabella had found a very comfortable sofa in the storeroom to give her for her wedding present.

Gonda had delivered it to their new home in First Avenue. She had been tempted to go with him, but then decided her inquisitiveness would be too obvious.

But now it seemed she was in luck. When they arrived at the Matabele Laundry they saw that bags of laundry were being loaded onto the cart to take down to the river for washing. There was a youngish man overseeing this, and Isabella decided he must be Mr Brown.

'Ah, we've arrived just in time, I see,' she said to Mangeni. 'We need to go straight to that cart there, Mangeni, where they are loading the laundry. Over there,' she pointed. 'Correct, well done,' she murmured as they approached the laundry cart. 'Good morning, Sir,' she said to the young man standing next to the cart. 'We are from Sunrising, and our laundry needs to be done post haste. Can I be so bold as to ask you to load it with the rest, so that we can have it back soon?' She gave him her most charming smile.

He lifted his hat, revealing a full head of thick, blonde hair. 'At your service, Madam,' he said. Oh yes, Bert is right, she thought, if this is Mr Brown, he is indeed pleasant looking. 'We can deal with your laundry straight away, if you can just get the paper work done in the office over there. We will wait for you.'

Isabella skipped into the wrought iron rondavel with a sign saying 'Matebele Laundry' next to it. She had met the owner, Mr Sarsons before, but he was still surprised to see her. This wasn't surprising since she had never brought the laundry before. Most people in her position sent their servants.

'Well, well, Mrs Craig. Good morning. To what do I owe this honour?'

'Hello, Mr Sarsons. I'm only here because I have a new laundryman and I wanted to show him where you were,' Isabella lied. 'Your man outside asked me to come in here to deal with the paperwork.'

'Ah, you mean Mr Brown. He is in charge of washing. Well of course, we just need to write down what you have brought, so we can make sure you get it all back. Do you have a list, Mrs Craig?'

'Oh dear, I believe I have left it at home,' she said, pretending to search her pocket.

'Never mind, we can go through your laundry as we transfer it to our cart.'

They walked back to the carts together. Mangeni had already opened their laundry bags and was pulling out the sheets and towels.

'Mr Brown, this is Mrs Craig, the mistress of Sunrising.'

'Oh, Mr Brown,' she said, feigning surprise, 'But this is such a pleasure to meet you. I have heard about you from your new wife, Mabel. She worked for us when she first arrived from England.'

She held out her hand for him to shake. 'Pleased to meet you, Madam,' he said.

'And how is Mabel? We hope you are settled comfortably in your new home.'

'Oh yes, we are indeed, and thank you very much for the sofa you sent round for us. I believe Mabel is going to write a letter of thanks.'

'We hope you enjoy this wedding gift, Mr Brown, and please, we hope that we will see you and Mabel from time to time.'

'Thank you, Mrs Craig. You are too kind. Now, we need to count out your washing, and as it is such an emergency, I can make a special delivery when it is ready.'

'I would appreciate that very much,' she answered.

*

Anthony found Isabella in the nursery with Mangeni who was standing on a wooden stool hanging curtains while she watched. She had found a table and two comfortable armchairs in one of the storerooms, which she had placed in this room, but they still had to buy the baby furniture. It was a shame they had given away all the stuff they had had for William, the wicker crib and new perambulator Anthony's parents had sent them at vast cost. But she had not been able to stand the sight of them after William died. They brought back bad memories for Anthony too, and he had not spent nearly as much time nursing the baby as she had.

'That laundry is becoming very efficient I see,' he said. 'I believe it was just yesterday you sent all those curtains down there to be washed.'

'Ah, yes, I met Mabel's new husband, and he was happy enough to bring the clean washing back as soon as possible.'

'Hardly necessary, as the baby is only due in November, but I'm sure you are delighted, as now you can get on with your decorating.'

'Exactly.'

'I wanted to tell you that there are two men staying at the Club. We have been talking to them about investment, and we thought it may be an idea if they come and stay here on Sunday night, as we intend taking them to see some of our mining claims the following day. We can make a very early start on Monday morning if we all leave from here.'

'That should be fine. Do you want me to invite anyone with them?'

'No, I think it will be best if they come alone, so we can talk business for most of the time they are here.'

'I will be going to town tomorrow for my weekly shop so will look for something special to feed them.'

'Thank you.' He walked to the door and was about to leave when he remembered something else. 'Oh yes, I almost forgot. I've asked

Bert Robinson to come and stay again, so he can look after you while we are gone. We'll be away until Friday or Saturday.'

Isabella's face dropped. 'Oh no! You didn't?'

'What do you mean? What's the matter?'

'He is such a bore. I cannot bear having to listen to his inane chatter for days on end again. I wish you'd asked me before you went and did that.'

Anthony glanced at Mangeni. He didn't like having a rift with Isabella in front of him. 'Mangeni.'

'Yes Baas.'

'Please go and ask Mananga to make us some tea, and take it to the veranda. You can finish hanging those curtains later.' Mangeni got down from his stool and left the room. 'Now Isabella,' Anthony continued. 'What's the matter with you? I didn't know you disliked Mr Robinson, you never mentioned anything to me before.'

'It's not that I dislike him, as such. I just don't much like having him around. If you had asked me I would have suggested I stay here alone. It would be so much easier for me. I do not think having Mr Robinson here would make any difference if there were a crisis. You have to understand, while you are off, out and about on your adventures, I am sitting here alone, often feeling quite lonely and bored, and having that little man around makes it a whole lot worse, because I cannot even relax and read a book, or go to bed when I want, unless I behave very rudely.'

'Well, first of all, we aren't exactly off on 'adventures', as you put it. We are working. Second, I did not realise you got lonely when we went away, but if you do, I would have thought that having Mr Robinson here would have helped with that. Third, if you are bored, then why don't you go to that paint shop, C H Naake, I believe it is called, on one of your jaunts to town? Buy some paints, brushes and canvases and start painting again. And fourth, I will feel uncomfortable knowing you are here alone.'

'But I am not alone. I have got Gonda and Mangeni and all the others.'

'Yes, but they are not in the house with you.'

'Well, please, please, can we just try it this next trip. Please let me try staying here without Mr Robinson.'

'I do not want to leave you here alone. Maybe I can look around for someone else. Someone more entertaining, it seems you need.'

She ignored his sarcastic tone.

'However,' he continued. 'We will be going on another 'adventure' just a few days after returning at the end of next week. Why don't you come with us? We are going out to that property we want to buy. We will go for two or three days. If you come with us you can see what it is like for yourself, and you can also see just how 'adventurous' it is, camping in the bush.'

Isabella did not hesitate in answering him. 'Yes, thank you, I would like to join you. I have only been on one camping trip since I have been living here, when we went to the Matopos Hills with the Weirs. I enjoyed that very much so I cannot see why I will not enjoy this too.'

'Because it was much easier to get to the Matopos than it is getting to this new property,' he said. 'You will find the journey very tough going.'

'I am sure I will cope.'

'Well, suit yourself.'

'I will thank you.'

He did not want her to come in her condition, but he had given her an invitation and she had accepted it. He did not want to back track now.

'Good,' he said. 'Well that's settled. Next week it is then,' and he left the room.

Chapter 11

GONDA tapped on the bedroom door. Isabella woke up startled, confused by the noise, as it was still dark in the room. Then she remembered; they were going on their adventure today, and she felt a surge of excitement at the thought of this. Anthony did not stir in the bed next to her so she drew back the mosquito net and got up. She pulled on her dressing gown and shuffled to the door, opening it as Gonda was about to knock again.

'Good morning Gonda,' she whispered, amused by the surprised look on his face. She could not blame him; this was the first time she had ever opened the door to him and his morning tray of tea. He murmured a greeting as he set the tray down on the chest of drawers just inside the bedroom. Isabella left the door open so she could make use of the dawn light coming through the east facing passage window to pour the tea and see her way around the room.

'Good morning Darling,' she said brightly, putting Anthony's cup on his bedside table and pulling back the net for him to reach it.

He shifted and stretched, before opening his eyes. 'My God, Isabella, what on earth are you doing, wandering around the room so early?'

'Just pouring our tea. I thought you said you wanted to make an early start. I woke with Gonda's knock and thought there was little point in delaying.' She took a sip of her own tea before going into the dressing room and opening the curtains. The weather was cooling off now, with winter on its way and the daylight hours shortening. She had packed some warm clothes for their trip, although she knew that while the mornings and evenings would be cool, it would be hot at midday.

Isabella had been longing for this trip ever since Anthony invited her to join them. She found her life frustrating in some ways, always remaining at home while the men were away on their expeditions. She often thought back to when she was young, when she used to imagine Thomas Baines' exciting life as she stared at his painting above the fireplace at her family home in England. Her life in Africa had never quite lived up to her expectations; she hoped it would this time. She had even bought some canvases, and she intended doing some sketching.

*

The sun was just rising when they rode out of the gates and up the dust track towards the Umguza River, and the eastern horizon was glowing in silent anticipation of the sunshine-filled day ahead. Isabella sat next to Gonda on the bench at the front of the mule cart, while Anthony and James rode their horses and the dogs ran behind them. Isabella breathed deeply, smelling the dampness of the morning dew on the tall, dry grass. Gonda glanced at her.

'It's all right Gonda. I'm just enjoying the morning sounds and smells,' she said.

'Yes Madam. It is very fresh now. We always like to get up early. Today we have many hours to travel.'

By the time they were passing Umvutcha the sun was well over the distant horizon. Once it had shown the top of its head, it quickly made a full appearance. Isabella glanced towards Umvutcha house to see if any of the Fletchers were out and about, but she could see no one. Not long after Umvutcha the road dipped and they soon found themselves crossing a dry riverbed, the horses and mules having to pick their way over the rocks, with the cart lurching as the wheels kept jamming into crevices.

'We have to cross this river twice more before we get to our destination,' Anthony shouted as he came alongside the cart on Gunner. 'It meanders a great deal, and if we tried to follow its course our journey would take much longer. At least it is dry at this time of the year, but you will find the journey getting more difficult from here on.'

Isabella looked at the mules, already struggling to drag the cart over the rocks. As soon as they climbed out of the riverbed she knew what he was talking about, with the path deteriorating in every way. They turned off the road and followed a track, but this track became narrower until it was no more than a path, winding its way through thick, scrubby bushes, many with large thorns on their branches. Gonda had to keep clipping the mules' rumps with his whip to get them to push their way through the bushes, pulling the cart behind them. Branches whipped back after the mules had pushed them, scratching Isabella and Gonda as they sat on the forward bench.

'Do you want to lie in the back Madam?' Gonda asked.

'Good gracious, no,' Isabella said, adjusting both her hat and coat to give her more protection.

However, when Anthony came up alongside them again she couldn't help ask; 'Are you sure this is going to work?'

'Aye, we've got some axes, and if necessary we can chop away bushes and branches. However, I think the dogs should come with you in the cart now. Archie is going to be exhausted.'

Trigger jumped in on command, but Archie had to be lifted by Somani, who was sitting at the very back of the cart. They were taking just the mule cart on this journey, as they were going for only a few days, so there was little space for anyone or anything else on the cart after all the camping equipment and food had been loaded. However, Somani had made a small place to sit. Trigger tucked himself in next to Somani, but Archie insisted on walking across the tarpaulin covering the equipment until he got to the front bench, where he wedged himself between Isabella and Gonda. The further they proceeded with their journey, the more wild animals they encountered. Impala, kudu, wildebeest, zebra, even some giraffe, although most animals took off and disappeared, before they got close. They reached the second river crossing around mid-morning. They had to go down a steep embankment into the dry riverbed, the mules bracing themselves to control the heavy cart behind them. Large rocks rose above the sand, but there were still some pools of water. They made slow progress with the mules struggling to pull the cart through the thick, soft sand. Finally they got to the other side, where the bank rose sharply upward again. Majestic acacia trees, growing on the bank, stretched their branches over the river bed.

'I vote we stop here and have our breakfast before making the mules attempt the climb out,' Anthony said. 'We can relax in the shade of these trees, and let the mules and horses drink from one of the pools.'

The wooden box containing the food for breakfast had been stored behind the seat. Gonda was chief cook and camp hand on this trip as Mananga had gone on leave to his native home. Gonda started readying everything for breakfast, while Somani took the harnesses off the mules.

'Let's go for a short walk down the riverbed to stretch our legs,' James suggested. The dogs took off, sand flying from their feet as they ran.

When they returned to the breakfast place Gonda had put out camp chairs, and on a table he had set plates, cups and the food they had packed for their breakfast; hard boiled eggs with bread and butter. He had lit a fire amongst some rocks and had a kettle balancing on this fire.

'What a lovely place this is,' Isabella said, settling into one of the chairs. 'What are those magnificent trees on the bank?'

'They are called acacia galpinis,' James said. 'We have some growing at Sunrising, surely you have noticed them? Although I don't think any are as big as these.'

'Yes, you are right, I recognize them now. How silly of me not to notice.'

'When we get to our destination you will see well established galpinis like these ones. There's a whole forest of them following the river course, and we will camp in this forest, near the river. That's where we camped last time and it was most pleasant.'

He stopped talking.

Somani was screeching, standing next to one of the pools with the mules and pointing at the water.

'Oh my God. Quick Anthony, your gun.'

'What?' Anthony leapt to his feet, grabbing the weapon.

Both men belted across the sand towards the pool.

'What's going on?' Isabella asked Gonda, who was standing next to the fire.

'A crocodile, Madam, in the pool.'

Isabella stood up to get a better view of the pool. The water was still and dark, but she could see no evidence of a crocodile. However, Somani continued to jabber to James.

'The crocodile, Madam, it has taken Trigger. They cannot see him now,' Gonda said.

'Oh no,' Isabella gasped, blanching. She looked around in panic for Archie. He was standing near the men, next to the pool.

'Let me go and fetch your other dog, Madam,' Gonda said, desperate to get closer to the action.

Somani began to wail.

103

'Shut up Somani,' James said. They all stared into the water. 'Nothing. Not even a ripple on the water. It must have grabbed Trigger and then sunk to the bottom of this pool.'

'Bastard,' Anthony said. 'Who would have believed it?'

'Why don't you fire into the water?'

'I'm sure he'll be dead by now,' Anthony replied, his voice breaking as he spoke.

'Fire anyway, just in case.'

Anthony did this, numerous times. They all stood and looked at the water, hoping for something miraculous to happen. There was nothing.

James put his hand on Anthony's shoulder. 'Sorry old boy, he was a good dog.'

'Yes, he was.' Anthony turned and walked back to Isabella, staring at his feet moving through the sand.

Isabella started to sob.

No one felt like eating any more.

*

They finally arrived at the galpini forest James had spoken of in the early afternoon. They were on a section of flat ground at the top of a small cliff overlooking the river. The acacia trees formed a cool, shady canopy, underneath which thick, long grass grew.

Anthony dismounted. 'This is exactly where we camped last time,' he said, 'hence the flattened grass just here. And this is where we had our fire,' he continued, kicking the old embers. 'I think it best we set up camp here again. By the time we've finished setting up the tents it will be nearly dark, so we will have to show Isabella around tomorrow morning.'

'While you do this, I will ride over to Tate and let him know we are here,' James said. 'I don't want him to see our smoke and wonder what's going on. It's less than half a mile to his huts so I won't be long.'

Isabella went to the cliff edge and looked over into the river below. Anthony came alongside her. 'Now don't you worry lass. No crocodile will be able to traverse this cliff. I know what you are thinking.'

Isabella had to smile, despite everything. 'Yes, I am now worrying about Archie.'

'He knows something untoward happened and must be wondering where his friend is, so I think he will keep close to us. Put him on a leash if you are still worried.' He paused. 'It was a horrid thing to happen. I was terribly fond of that dog.' His voice cracked and tears welled up.

Isabella felt for his hand. 'Me too. I am so sorry Darling. I feel quite sick at the thought of losing him like that.'

He squeezed her hand. 'That's what the bush is like here though. We always have to take great care when we are in it. It is not like tame and gentle England. We will hear a lot of activity from the wilds tonight: jackal; maybe lion; maybe hyena; and all sorts of other screeches, grunts and calls. But we will keep close to the fire and then shut ourselves into our tents later, and we should be safe. 'He squeezed her hand again. 'Come now, there is much to do getting our camp ready.'

*

The camp began stirring at first light. Isabella was surprised she had slept so deeply in her narrow canvas camp bed. She woke to the sound of Gonda moving the logs about in the fire pit near their tent, reigniting the embers. The acrid smell of wood smoke soon filled the air. Archie had slept in their tent, and Anthony dressed and then took him out. Gonda had hung a canvas wash bowl from a wooden stand in their tent the night before so they could wash themselves before retiring. Isabella took her time washing from this bowl again in the morning before changing into her day clothes. The water was cold, but she felt better for her wash afterwards.

James and Anthony were sitting on camp chairs next to the fire sipping tea when Isabella made an appearance. She felt a surge of excitement for what lay ahead, despite what had happened yesterday.

'Have some tea Isabella, and then we'll go for an early morning walk down the river while Gonda makes our breakfast. Afterwards, I suggest you relax here while Anthony and I go for a ride around the property. We need to have a better look at the place, and we can only do this on horseback. I don't think you should spend too many hours in the saddle in your condition. We'll take you for a shorter ride this evening so you can get some idea of what the place is like.' James had brought a pony back from Mr Tate yesterday evening for Isabella to use while they were there.

'That will suit me. I've brought a canvas and some pencils, and I'll try my hand at sketching. It is so beautiful here amongst these majestic trees. I feel quite inspired.'

They picked their way through the long grass trying to find a place where the riverbank flattened enough so they could climb down into the dry sandy riverbed. It would be much easier walking in the sand than through the thick grass. Isabella had tied a piece of rope around Archie's neck and he strained at this, breathing with difficulty as he pulled against it.

'Stop it,' she said, yanking at the rope, but he would have none of it and she found herself being dragged along much faster than her normal pace. She was just thinking of asking Anthony to take Archie when she became aware of a more pressing problem. Itchiness. She was wearing a long skirt, petticoats and stockings and grass seeds of varying sizes and shapes were sticking to her underclothing. She was suddenly desperate to pull everything off and give herself a good scratch. She glanced at James's retreating back and wished he was not there so that she could do just this.

'I'm sorry,' she said, stopping abruptly. 'I'm going to have to return to the camp.'

Both men turned to see what her problem was.

'The dog?' Anthony asked, but then a smile, spread across his face. 'Ah ha. I know what your problem is.'

'No you don't. I just need to get back. Archie is too small to be walking through thick bush like this.' She tried to nod at him, not wanting him to start talking about her underclothing in front of James.

Anthony walked back to her, still smiling. 'Very well lass. Let me take you back and then James and I can carry on without you and the dog.'

'Thank you, I would appreciate that.'

As soon as they got back to the camp she rushed to the tent and tore her clothes off. It seemed as if the grass seeds had stuck to everything and it took her a very long time to pick them all off. How she wished she had thought about what she needed to wear before they came here. She would have gone to Mrs Sanders and had a pair of breeches made. That would have given Anthony something to smirk about, but at least she would have been able to join them.

*

Later, Isabella sat in a canvas chair finishing the sketch she had been working on. It was of a particularly tall galpini growing on the opposite side of the river to their campsite. She looked at her sketch, trying to see if there was any detail she still needed to include. Although she had brought paints with her, she now intended painting it when she got home. She had not expected them to be camping quite so rough. She made one or two more adjustments to her sketch before concluding she had done enough for now. She got up and stretched. Archie, who had been lying next to her, jumped up too, ready for action. Gonda and Somani were sitting just out of sight, at their own fire, and Isabella could hear them murmuring to each other. Every now and then they threw sticks and stones at any monkeys in the trees that tried to venture close, while Archie barked at them. Isabella felt restless and wished her men would return. She looked at the sky, trying to determine the time by the placement of the sun. About two, she guessed. It would be another hour or more before they got back. She did not feel like sitting there any longer, waiting for them to come back. On the spur of the moment she asked Somani to saddle up the pony so she could go for a gentle wander in the immediate area. They had brought her side saddle especially from Sunrising. Oh how she wished she had a pair of breeches, she thought again, and a proper saddle. At least she would know for next time.

She would not go far. Hopefully by the time she returned the men would be back too. They could have a cup of tea and then take her on the longer ride they had promised earlier.

Archie tugged at his rope and barked when she set off, Gonda having to hold him so he wouldn't break loose. She considered taking him but then thought the better of it. She would not go far, but she felt quite possibly there could be some wild animals which she did not want him to encounter, not after what happened yesterday. She walked the pony through the bush, taking in the sights and sounds. She could see some easily recognizable hills in the distance and she used these to get her bearings. The pony seemed to know its way about and she gave it its head. After walking for a short while it stopped and whinnied. Isabella was surprised when she heard another horse whinnying back. They continued and the bush opened into a clearing, with four or five pole and *dagga* huts scattered about. Two dogs ran out of one of the huts and started barking. This must have alerted the people living there because a young boy came out of one of the huts. He stopped when he saw

Isabella, and she gaped in surprise at him. He must have been ten to twelve years old, with coffee coloured skin and dark, tightly curled hair. He had striking blue eyes. Isabella had seen many people of mixed race in the Cape, when she had passed through on her way to and from Rhodesia, but none since she had been in Rhodesia. The boy and she stared at each other, and then the boy said: 'Hello, and how do you do?'

Isabella was even more shocked that he could speak such good English. 'Well, hello,' she stammered. 'What is your name?'

'I am Toby Tate,' he replied.

'And I am Isabella Craig.' She surprised even herself for being so informal, and blushed.

Toby Tate didn't notice. 'How do you do,' he replied.

Their introductions were interrupted by a man coming out of another hut, putting on his jacket and combing a hand through his thinning blond hair. Isabella noticed he had piercing blue eyes also, just like the boy.

'Mr Tate?' Isabella asked.

'Indeed, and you must be Mrs Craig.'

'Yes, I am sorry to have stumbled on you like this. I gave your pony its head, and it found its way home.'

'Not a problem. It's Toby's pony. Maybe you would like to come in and have some tea with us.' As he spoke a black woman appeared at the hut door, holding a toddler on her hip.

Isabella was intrigued. 'Thank you, yes. I would like that very much.'

Chapter 12

FOR much of their journey home from the camping trip, Isabella sat on the front bench of the mule cart, deep in thought. She could not stop thinking about her conversation with Mr Tate and the predicament he was in; she had never encountered a situation like his before, but now she had, she could see just how difficult it was for everyone involved.

'You feeling alright?' Anthony called, noticing how distracted she was when he rode alongside the cart.

'Yes. Absolutely,' she said, but as he cantered ahead of them again she felt uncomfortable, wondering what he was going to say about her with Mr Tate. She looked at Archie, wedged between her and Gonda again and stroked his head, wishing her life could be as simple as his. Even with his friend now gone, he still appeared as content as ever.

Mr Tate had confided in Isabella and she wanted to help. It had seemed the natural thing to do at the time, but now, when she thought about it more clearly, she realised the others would not approve. At first she was unsure how she could make it work, but, during the course of the long, slow journey home, she came to the decision that she would get Mangeni to assist her. Mangeni was like Gonda: she could communicate with him and depend on him in a way that she could not with the others.

But when they got back to Sunrising she was in for a shock.

They arrived late in the afternoon and Mananga, Moses and Hlabano were in the drive waiting for them. They busied themselves unpacking the cart while Anthony and James took their horses to the stables. Isabella collected her hand luggage and went into the house, shivering as she walked in. The weather had changed during the day. Now there were dark clouds and a cold wind. She decided the house needed warming with fires in the bedrooms and drawing room. She would love a hot bath too, but did not want to worry anyone to fetch hot water when they were all so busy. The most she felt she could ask for was to have the fires made and lit in the fireplaces. She went to the kitchen to ask Mangeni to do this, as she had noticed he was not in the drive with the others. The kitchen was empty, but the kettle was boiling on the wood stove, so she made a pot of tea and took it to the drawing room to wait. But she felt agitated and cold and could not relax. She went back to the kitchen to see if Mangeni had made an appearance but found Moses there instead, stoking the wood stove.

'Ah, Moses, where is Mangeni? I wanted to ask him to light the fires.'

Moses looked shifty. 'He has gone, Missus.'

'Gone? Gone where?'

'Back to his home.'

'Home?'

'His home far away.'

Isabella was confused. 'What do you mean Moses? He is supposed to be working here.'

'He doesn't want to work here anymore Missus.'

'What? Why ever not?'

Silence from Moses, just another edgy look.

'Moses, what is going on?'

'Eh, Missus.' He glanced out of the door, his face twitching.

'What? Tell me what is going on. You found him the job. He told me he wanted to work so he could pay his hut tax and buy things for his family. He was doing so well, but now you tell me he has gone.'

'Mangeni has big problems Missus.'

'Goodness. Oh dear. What problems?'

Moses looked out of the door again. 'Missus,' he said in a quiet voice. 'He has been *loyaed.*'

'What? What's that?'

'*Loya* Missus. Mangeni left because Somani went to see the witch doctor and he has *loyaed* Mangeni. If Mangeni stay here he will die.'

'Sorry, I don't understand. What do you mean?'

Moses stared at his feet.

'Moses?'

'Missus, it is like this. Somani sees that you like Mangeni more than him. He is unhappy about this because he has worked for you for many years and Mangeni is new. But you remove him from his laundry job. You make him work in the garden again while Mangeni does the jobs Somani likes to do. Somani does not want Mangeni here because of this, so he asks the witch doctor to put a, a curse on him.'

'I beg your pardon?'

'Somani, he, umm, he, eh.' Moses could not explain the situation any clearer.

'But, I still do not understand. Somani was with us on our journey.'

Moses fidgeted with the pocket of his jacket. He glanced at Isabella and then looked away.

'He went to see the witch doctor before.'

'And, and Mangeni knows all this?'

'Ah, Missus, since you have been gone, Mangeni, he has been very, very sick. He left this morning, otherwise he was going to die.'

'So Mangeni believes that Somani has the power to make him sick?'

'No Missus. It is the witch doctor. Somani paid the witch doctor.'

'And he did this because he thinks I have been treating Mangeni better than him?'

'Yes Missus, he liked taking the washing to the laundry, but you stopped him from doing this and sent Mangeni instead.'

'But why did he not just come and talk to me about it? If it meant so much to him why did he not just ask me if he could take the washing to the laundry?'

Moses stared at a place behind Isabella, saying nothing.

'So if Somani chose to have a curse put on Mangeni, what is there to stop him putting a curse on all of us? Or at least Gonda? He must see that we treat Gonda differently from him.'

'The witch doctor, he does not have the power to do this to you because you are a white madam Missus, and he can't do it to Gonda either, because Gonda has spent many years in the white man's country, so he cannot be *loyaed* either.'

'But it works on the rest of you?'

'Yes Missus.'

What could she say? These superstitious beliefs were foreign to her way of thinking. She stared at Moses, with a growing sense of unease and discomfort, trying to imagine what it must be like to live your life believing others have the power to destroy you through witchcraft, simply because they are jealous of you. She shook her head and left the kitchen. As soon as she was out of the door she found herself running back to the house. She wanted to get away from him and what he had been saying. She went to her bedroom, crawled into bed and pulled the blanket over her head and she started to sob. She felt tired, cold, and depressed by what had transpired, both with Trigger a few days before and now this. Africa is a harsh place, she concluded. She hated the idea of them all plotting and planning against each other, in relation to the way she treated them.

Eventually she pulled herself together and got out of bed. It was dark and the wind was even colder. She found her warmest coat and put it on, going outside to look for Somani. She found him standing next to the stove in the kitchen, his hands held out to the fire.

'There you are Somani. I want you to get the bucket and fill the bath in my bedroom with hot water. Is there enough water? No? Then fill those kettles and put them on the stove. While you are waiting for them to boil, go to my bedroom and light the fire, then light the fire in the drawing room and in Sir James's room too. By the time you've done that the water should be hot enough for the bath.'

Somani looked surprised. It had been a long day and he was about to knock off. The last thing he wanted was to do all these chores now.

'I would ask Mangeni, but he has disappeared. Do you, by any chance, know what has happened to him?'

Somani did not hesitate. 'No, Missus.'

'Well, you are going to be very busy now he is no longer here.'

She went back to her bedroom, closed all the windows and huddled in the chair next to the fireplace. Somani arrived with a shovel full of hot embers and put them into the grate. She did not want him around for any longer than necessary, so she told him to go and light the other fires. She threw twigs and a log into the hearth and pumped the bellows. The embers sparked and caught light, immediately making the room cosier and more comforting.

Anthony found her still sitting in the armchair next to the fire when he came through to change for dinner. 'Are you sure you are all right?' he asked. 'You have been very quiet all day.'

'I am feeling a little low, so I think I'll relax here tonight. But do not worry about me. Somani is going fillingl the bath, and afterwards I will go to bed.'

'Well if you don't mind being left alone, James and I have a lot to discuss tonight before we have our meeting with the British South Africa Company representatives tomorrow about purchasing the property.'

He left the room after changing, excited and motivated about his next venture.

His good mood had not changed the next morning when he and James set off for town on their horses. Unlike Isabella, who woke up still feeling agitated about Somani and the *'loya-ing'*. She considered giving him his notice, and sending a message to Mangeni that it was now safe to come back, but then decided this may cause more problems. After wandering around the house for some time, unable to shake her uneasiness, she unfurled the sketch she had done on their trip and tried to find a place to start working on it. The clouds had not lifted, making the house dark, and it was too cold to sit on the veranda and paint. She eventually established that the nursery was the lightest room in the house, and she was thankful to finally lose herself in her painting, spending most of the day doing this.

*

James and Anthony visited the British South Africa Company offices to discuss what was referred to as the alienation of the property to them. The BSAC owned most of the land in Rhodesia, since the defeat of the Matabele king, Lobengula, in 1893, and after initially assigning most land for mining, they were now looking more and more into agricultural development. The men came home in high spirits, and, as soon as dinner was finished, they settled next to the fire in the drawing room with a large, hand drawn map of the property.

'I count my blessings that we live in this country in these times,' James said as he unrolled the map onto the coffee table. 'Just think of the opportunities we are being afforded. However, on saying this,

I'm not sure we are buying land for farming in the right part of the country. The climate in these parts is not conducive to cropping, or indeed anything too intensive, as far as I can make out. There just is not enough rain. Now if we were in Mashonaland, we would be trying our hand at tobacco farming. Many have started growing this crop and are doing well with it.'

'So why don't you look for a place there instead, James?' Isabella asked.

'Because. I am most attached to this part of the world, and I am particularly taken with the property we are going to acquire. And of course, we intend carrying on with the MEC too. All this is in Matabeleland.'

'What are you going to do with this new property then, if it is not good for growing crops? You mentioned something about using it for recreation and the like, when I asked you before.'

'Yes, well I was just being facetious then. I apologise. Now that we have looked into it more carefully, we know we have to do something with it; indeed we will be under pressure to develop the land. It appears this country does not have the gold resources they originally thought it might, so the BSAC now wants to expand agriculture significantly. Their shareholders in England are calling for some return on their investment, you see. Anthony and I have put a lot of thought into it recently, and we're considering cattle breeding. The breeds that you find here are rangy, runty animals for the most part. We are thinking of importing pedigree animals from England and seeing how they fare. There is so much land here, there must surely be an opportunity to develop a cattle industry.'

'Of course it is not going to be easy,' Anthony continued, 'because of all the diseases cattle get, mainly tick borne. Rhodes tried to bring cattle from Australia, 2000 head I believe it was. He thought they would be hardier coming from that part of the world. They were shipped to Natal, and were supposed to walk up here, but not one animal survived. All struck down by disease. It was a bad blow for him, being the man he was and hating to fail at anything.'

'However, vaccines have advanced since then,' James said, 'and we will look for a hardy, meaty breed that can cope with these harsh conditions, with the right treatment. I intend returning to England in the next few months, and going around various cattle studs. I need to research what will be the best breed to bring back here. I was always interested in animal husbandry when I was a boy, growing up on our farm in Wiltshire. I very much look forward to getting back into it.'

Anthony tossed the remainder of his cigar into the fire. He sipped his port and then leaned forward to trace his finger on the map. 'This property has the Umguza River running through it, which in turn has many tributaries. The grass along the river bank is thick, lush and sweet. If we can overcome the tick problems, I believe cattle will thrive here. We are lucky there is so much unutilised land.'

'The next time we go out there, Anthony, we need to look for a place to build some huts for ourselves,' James said. 'We can burn down the ones that Tate has been living in when he leaves.'

Isabella's heart began to race. She needed to tell them what she had done and this was her cue. She took a deep breath. 'But you can't do that. What about the people living in them?'

'We told you before; Tate is going back to England. He has no interest in that property anymore,' Anthony said.

'I know. But I am talking about his wife and children.'

'His wife? That's not his wife.'

'Maybe not legally, but they do have two children. Surely you noticed that?'

'Of course. I haven't spoken to Tate about them, but I should think they will go back to her family. That's what happens most times in these cases, I assume.'

117

'Well actually, I did speak to him about his situation. He told me he needs to go back to England, but that he will come back as soon as he can. He told me his woman's family does not want her back. They never approved of their union in the first place.'

'Well they should have thought about that before they got involved in all of this, do you not agree? It is not our concern Isabella. I am sure they will come up with some plan.'

'He is very worried about it, Anthony. Besides all of this, his son, Toby, appears to be a very intelligent young boy. Mr Tate has taught him to read and write, and he shows great interest in books. He even read something to me when I was there, and I was most impressed. Mr Tate pointed out that he would be out of place in an African village, where none of the other children have any concept of reading or writing.'

'Again Isabella, I do not think this has anything to do with us. Mr Tate has created these problems for himself, by taking on a woman like that, and it is he who needs to decide what to do about them.'

'I'm afraid I see it differently. Since meeting them and talking to them, I have been thinking a great deal about us Europeans coming and settling here. I understand the tremendous opportunities this country has to offer, that have never been utilised before, but at the same time I can see that we are destablising what was already here.' Isabella took a deep breath. 'We can try to pretend we are not, but we are, and Mr Tate's predicament is just one small result of this. So, when he told me his story, I assured him that they could remain where they were and that we would make sure they had what they needed until he gets back from England. When this happens he intends finding another place for them to all live together.'

Anthony looked at James and then back at Isabella. 'I cannot believe you did that, without even consulting us.'

'Well I did. It did not seem like such a difficult thing for us to do, when I was talking to him.'

'Oh, Isabella. It's going to cause all sorts of problems. I wish you had not interfered like that.'

'I am sorry, but I could see they needed help.'

'Well, what is done is done,' James interrupted. 'We could go back to Tate and tell him they cannot stay after all, but I believe that would make Isabella very unhappy. It is true, it will not be difficult letting them stay in those huts. As far as the rest is concerned, we'll have to make some sort of plan.'

'Mr Tate said he will leave us money to buy everything they need. I had thought I could get Mangeni to take it out there, whenever necessary, but now he's gone that plan won't work.'

The room was silent. James and Anthony stared at the map.

'I'll do it, 'Anthony eventually said. 'I will have to go out there a great deal in the next few months. I can take what they need.'

'Thank you,' Isabella said. 'You are a good man.'

He grunted, and then turned his focus back on his map.

Chapter 13

MABEL huddled under the blankets on her bed, staring at the sofa the Craigs had given them for a wedding present. As much as she disliked that boy, Gonda, at least he had delivered it, she thought, and not one of the Craigs. She would have been overcome with embarrassment if either of them had been here and seen what she was reduced to; living in mud huts, no better than the natives. The sofa was the only decent piece of furniture they owned. Percy had promised they would go to Haddon and Sly and buy more furniture, but of course this had not happened, just as Percy had promised they would only live in the huts for a few weeks. Well, that was two months ago, and it looked like they would be in these huts for a good deal longer. When he asked her to marry him, he told her he was building a "comfy lickle house in Ist Ave", as he put it. This had been true, he was building a house in 1st Avenue, but after starting it, the building had almost come to a standstill. One room was near completion, and they could sleep in this, but the rest of the house was no better than a building site. They still had to cook in the huts, the smelly, smoky mud huts, and there was nowhere to relax, other than the room they used as a bedroom. When the weather was fine they could sit outside, but not when it was cold or wet like today. Their neighbours, the Pingstones, had also been living temporarily in huts while their house was finished, but their building had progressed at a good rate.

When Mabel first met Percy, sleeping on the banks of the Matsheumhlope River, ostensibly overseeing the Indian laundrymen doing the washing, she thought there was a certain rebellious charm in what he was doing (or not doing). But now she thought no such thing. Now she knew Percy was simply lazy and had no ambition. This caused her great concern, because, if he were left to his own devices, they would probably remain like they were for many years to come and she could not bear the thought of this.

Mabel turned around to face the wall and pulled the bedclothes over her head. She wanted to shut out her cold, smelly, gloomy world.

She was disturbed by a knock at the door and a call, 'Yoo hoo, Mabel dear, are you there?' She knew this voice; it was her neighbour, Peggy Pingstone. For a moment she thought to pretend she was out, but realised Peggy would know better. She was such a busy body. Mabel pulled herself out of bed and went through the building site to the front door. Peggy shivered on the step, her baby on her hip and her toddler clutching her skirt. 'Hello dear,' she said. 'The weather is so foul today, and I know you have nowhere to sit. Cedric worked like a slave last night, getting our sitting room finished enough for us to move in. I've made a lovely warm fire in our hearth and I wanted to ask you to come round and join me for a nice cup of tea and a bowl of soup later. There is not much else we can do on a miserable day like today.'

'Thank you, thank you very much,' Mabel said. 'I was feeling very depressed, for sure, with nowhere to keep myself warm except my bed.'

'Exactly. Well collect your things and come over. We'll be waiting for you.'

Mabel soon felt much better, sitting in Peggy's cosy sitting room, with her hands wrapped around a hot cup of tea and her feet stretched out towards the fire.

'We've still got a lot to do with this room,' Peggy said. 'We need to buy more furniture and curtains, a rug and some mats, but at least we can use it now.' She hesitated; leaving unsaid the next phrase, "unlike you", hanging between them.

But Mabel chose not to be so reticent. She was tired of pretending.

'Oh Peggy,' she started, 'what am I to do with my husband? He's just not getting on with building our house, and I am so tired of living the way we do.'

'I can imagine. I found it most uncomfortable too, and count myself very lucky that my Cedric worked so hard to finish ours. I could not have endured living in those mud huts much longer.' She took a sip of her tea, and cleared her throat.

'The problem with Percy is that he doesn't earn much money, and right now he's spending any surplus at the Exchange Bar every night,' Mabel said.

'Yes, we have noticed.'

'I have tried encouraging him to come straight home from work, but he doesn't listen to me.'

Peggy cleared her throat again. 'May I be so bold as to make a suggestion?'

'Yes, please do.'

'Cedric and I have discussed your predicament, and this was Cedric's idea. He thinks you should go back to those people who employed you, the Craigs, and ask them to give Percy a job.'

Mabel hesitated as she digested this. 'Unfortunately, I cannot see him fitting in there, or me anymore, for that matter.'

'No, no, not to work at their house. What Cedric thinks is that you should try to get him a job working for the MEC, at one of their mines, out of town.'

Mabel stared at Peggy. She had never thought of this.

'You see, that way he'll be away from the temptation of the Exchange Bar, and besides, I'm sure he'll get a better wage, working on the mine, than he does at the laundry.'

'Yes, the laundry is a dead-end job.'

'Exactly. He'd have time off to come home every few weeks, and you could use the extra money to complete your house. You could pay a good builder to do it in a jiffy.' She sipped her tea. 'So what do you think? There would be no distractions for him, way out in the bush.'

'It is a good idea,' Mabel said, wishing she had been friendlier towards the Craigs in her final months of working for them.

*

It took Mabel some weeks to come round to the idea of approaching the Craigs about a job for Percy. She hoped she would not have to, but his behaviour had not improved, and she eventually plucked up the courage to go and see them. She wrote, asking when it would be convenient and received, by return post, a pleasant reply from Mrs Craig. It was written on the fancy writing paper she always used, suggesting she come the following Saturday morning at 10.00 am. She explained that Mr Craig would be at home then, as he was often away during the week.

With no transport of her own, Mabel had to catch a lift on the cart going to Umvutcha. The boy driving the cart promised he would make his way straight there, but this did not happen, and he ended up stopping at three shops on his way out of town. And then, when Mabel asked him to go via Sunrising and drop her at the gate, he said he could not do this, otherwise he would be late "and the Madam would be cross". As a result, she had to walk the final mile to Sunrising, and, although she did not know the actual time, she knew she was late for her appointment.

Gonda opened the front door just as Mabel was about to rap the knocker for the third time. He greeted her in his usual manner, but she imagined, just as she always had, that he was looking down his nose at her. In her opinion he had always been far too big for his boots, probably because the Craigs and Sir James liked him so much and were constantly lavishing praise on him. However, she returned his greeting and was about to step into the house when Mrs Craig's spoilt dog, Archie, ran into the hall and started barking at her, before losing interest and rushing out of the front door and down the steps to the fish pond.

Gonda took her hat and coat and showed her through to the drawing room. Mrs Craig was sitting next to a crackling fire, but when she saw Mabel she rose, with some difficulty. She was noticeably pregnant now. She came over to Mabel, holding out her hands in greeting and Mabel had no option but to put her cold hands into Mrs Craig's warm ones, feeling very uncomfortable, as she always did around her.

'Mabel, hello, goodness, how lovely to see you. Come in, come in and sit next to the fire. You must be freezing, travelling here in this horrible weather.'

It was warm and comfortable next to the blazing fire, and, as Mabel sat down, she thought about her cold, bleak hut and half built house. This is why I'm here, she thought to herself, I must keep focused on this.

'I'm very sorry I'm late,' she said. 'I caught the cart going to the old hotel, and they wouldn't come via here.'

'How very annoying,' Mrs Craig answered. 'And especially as Mr Craig has just left.' She glanced at the grandfather clock in the corner. 'He waited until 11.30, but then had to go to another appointment. He asked me to send you his regards.'

Just my luck as always, Mabel thought. 'Oh dear, because it is he I most need to speak to.' She looked at her hands, struggling to hide her disappointment.

'Never mind, if you are not in a hurry, stay a while and let us catch up. I am not sure how long he will be gone, but he might get back while you're still here. In the meantime, it will be so nice to talk with you again. Let us have a cup of tea, and you are most welcome to stay for lunch.'

It was the last thing Mabel wanted, but she did not have a choice if she wanted to see Mr Craig. She put on a friendly face. 'Thank you Mrs Craig. That would be most kind.'

'I will be back shortly,' Mrs Craig said. 'I'm not sure why no one has brought our tea; let me go and see what is happening in the kitchen and I will tell them to lay a place for you at the table.' She heaved herself out of the sofa.

Once she was alone, Mabel settled herself more comfortably in her armchair and looked about the room. She noticed a few new sketches Mrs Craig had put on the mantelshelf above the fireplace, but otherwise the room was no different from the way it had been when she lived here. It had always been one of her favourite rooms, with its comfortable armchairs and sofas, covered in pretty chintz, a grand piano in one corner (which she had always thought rather affected, as no one ever played it), the grandfather clock ticking away in another corner, the dresser on which the drinks tray was always set, the soft Persian carpet, taking up three quarters of the floor space. If she hadn't been wearing lace up boots she would have slipped her feet out and rubbed them on the carpet, just to feel its comforting silkiness. Oh dear, she thought, if only I could have just some of this; I cannot just settle for my drab life in 1st Avenue. Any misgivings she had had about coming quickly dissolved as she imagined a better life for herself once she had spoken to Mr Craig.

Mabel had to stop herself from smirking when Isabella waddled back into the room and eased herself onto the sofa again. To hide her mirth, she stared at a pile of children's books on the sofa next to Isabella.

'No, Mabel, I'm not thinking of books for the baby yet,' Isabella joked, noticing her looking at the books and trying to make small talk. 'We've acquired a property in the countryside, about twenty or so miles from here. I found these books in town for a little boy who lives out there, as he loves reading. Mr Craig is going to the property on Monday so I am packing them up for him to take.'

'Do his parents not give him books?' Mabel asked, surprised.

'His father has gone back to England, and the boy has remained with his mother. She's an African woman, you see, so it would be difficult for her to travel to England also.'

Mabel was even more surprised. How strange that Mrs Craig should be sending books to someone like that, she thought.

'He's very bright and loves reading,' Mrs Craig explained.

As Mabel considered this, she couldn't help smiling to herself. She was sure Percy and the Pingstones would think it very odd too, when they heard that Mrs Craig was sending books to a half native child in the middle of the bush. How confused was that. For the first time ever, she felt superior to Mrs Craig. She relaxed and resolved she would enjoy her time with her after all, finding out more about this peculiar new interest of hers.

Chapter 14

JAMES made plans to leave Bulawayo at the end of July. He intended travelling to Cape Town and staying at his house there, before catching a ship to Southampton. He had all sorts of excuses for leaving, but the truth was, he needed to get away from Bulawayo, and he planned on absenting himself for as long as possible. The Mining and Exploration Company was doing well, and Anthony was more than capable of running it without him. He was no longer needed in the same way he had been when they were initially setting it up and so there seemed little reason for him to stay. He had been in Bulawayo for nearly five months, and this had become a worry for him: a worry because he was beginning to feel too settled and reliant on the Craigs' company. Living with them at Sunrising, going on expeditions with Anthony, finding new areas to open mines, coming back to the beautiful home Isabella had made Sunrising; he could happily continue like this forever, and he knew this was not good. The Craigs were a married couple and he believed he was trespassing on their privacy. It might be his house, and it might be his money and influence that had initially got the MEC going, and indeed, he had asked them to join him, but now he was not sure where he fitted in.

Anthony and Isabella had no idea James felt this way. Their lives had improved so much since moving to Sunrising, it never occurred to them he was uncomfortable with the arrangement. He had no intention of telling them, but, because he knew he would be away for a long time, he elected to arrange a farewell party for himself. He called it his 'little thank you to investors and friends' party.

As it transpired, there was nothing 'little' about it; sixty men and women assembled at the Palace Hotel in Abercorn Street.

They started with drinks and canapés in the hall, with the guests standing about chatting while waiters moved around, juggling trays of clinking glasses and food-filled platters. The men looked smart in dinner jackets, and the women sparkled and fluttered in evening dresses. A quartet was set up on the dais, and the musicians played a variety of tunes.

As pleasant as everything was, it did not take Isabella long to decide she was uncomfortable standing and mingling. She took refuge in a corner, next to a potted palm, and, as soon as Muriel saw her there she joined her.

'I'm sure you're delighted James chose to throw this party here and not at Sunrising,' she said, easing herself into a chair next to Isabella.

'Oh yes, I could not have managed in my condition. I'm far too fat and awkward to be entertaining these days. Thankfully James also booked us to stay at this hotel tonight, as he thought the journey home would be too tiring for me after the party.'

'How very kind and thoughtful.'

'Yes. We arrived earlier this evening and went straight to our bedrooms to freshen up. I've never been into any of the bedrooms here before, and I was most impressed. They are very comfortable.'

'Indeed. Philip and I have stayed here once. We thoroughly enjoyed it.' She took a sip of the sherry she was drinking. 'But did anyone tell you what happened this week, here at the Palace Hotel?'

'No. What?'

'Well, a native, would you believe, was found in one of the bedrooms.'

'Sorry? I don't quite follow you.'

'You see, he wasn't a cleaner, or attached to the hotel in any way. One of the staff caught him in the bedroom and concluded he must be a thief, so locked him in the bedroom and went to call the police. He found a lone policeman in Abercorn Street, who came back to the Palace to hand cuff the alleged criminal and take him away. But in the meantime word got out, as it so quickly does in Bulawayo, that a black man had been caught in a bedroom at the Palace Hotel. With all the implications attached to such a scenario, a crowd soon gathered in the street.'

'Oh dear. Had he actually committed a crime?'

'I don't know, but the policeman still wanted to take him back to the station for questioning, and when he was leading him down the steps, the wretched man managed to break loose. He jumped over the banister, into this very hall, and ran out of the front door, straight into the waiting crowd. This took everyone by surprise, and he was able to duck his way through them and flee down Abercorn Street. They followed in hot pursuit, with the policeman bringing up the rear.'

'It sounds like a scene from a comedy drama, except that, umm, well, what can I say?'

'Exactly. Anyway, thankfully the policeman was a fast runner because the crowd managed to catch the suspect first, and, by the time the policeman got there, they were intent on murdering the poor fellow.'

'No!'

'Yes. The policeman had to wrench him from them, with the help of two other policemen who arrived at the scene just in time. He was pretty badly beaten up, by all accounts, and one of the policemen had a few scratches and bruises too.'

'Oh dear.'

Muriel's story was interrupted by a booming voice; 'Mrs Craig, what a pleasure,' as shiny-shod feet clicked in front of them.

Both ladies looked up in surprise. It was Mr Gordon Forsyth, standing as if to attention in a military parade, his bald, dome-like head glistening above his bristling grey moustache. 'Why, Mr Forsyth. Good evening,' Isabella said, giving him her hand.

He bowed and kissed it in his usual extravagant manner.

'Madam, an honour.'

'How nice to see you again.' Isabella turned towards Muriel. 'Do you know Mrs Weir?'

'I do not believe we have ever met. No, I do not think I am mistaken in this.'

'You are not,' Muriel said, 'but Isabella has told me about you, when you were last in Bulawayo and staying at Sunrising.'

'Indeed. It was a most pleasant time.' He dragged up a chair and positioned himself opposite the ladies. 'This dratted music,' he shouted, 'I can hardly hear myself think above their blasted melodies.' Isabella caught Muriel's eye and smiled. She had been thinking how pleasant the quartet sounded. Mr Forsyth pulled his chair closer to them. 'I've been living on the outskirts of Salisbury since I was last here,' he continued, 'growing tobacco. I'm building a home for myself on my farm; not a house on the same scale as Sunrising, mind you. But the climate in Mashonaland is delightful, even more delightful than in Matabeleland, and tobacco grows extremely well.'

'You are very enterprising, Mr Forsyth,' Muriel said. 'Last time you were here you were investing in mines, I believe.'

'Oh yes, my investment in the MEC is showing great returns. I am updated regularly on their progress and duly paid my dividends. The farming venture is just another string in my bow,' he said, turning around and scowling at the violin player. 'That man would do well with less strings in his bow,' he yelled.

Isabella and Muriel giggled. 'You are too funny, Mr Forsyth,' Muriel said.

He looked confused.

'We are going to start farming too,' Isabella interjected. 'Did you know this? Breeding cattle.'

'Oh yes, Sir James told me all about it, and how he is going to use his time in England to investigate the best breeds to bring back here. I will be fascinated to see what type of cow he eventually decides on.'

A gong boomed and Mr Forsyth leapt to his feet. 'Ladies, I believe dinner is about to be served. I had a peep in the dining room earlier, and I see James is a most extravagant host tonight. The table is as grand as any you would find in England and the menu looks superb, with a most enviable wine list. May I have the honour of escorting you both through?' He pushed his elbows from his sides for each lady to take one, but, dressed in his dinner suit as he was, this had the effect of making him look remarkably like a penguin. Both ladies suppressed a desire to laugh out loud.

'You are too kind,' Muriel giggled.

'Absolutely,' Isabella agreed.

*

On the very night James held his farewell party at the Palace Hotel, Mr Sarsons, the owner of the Matabele Laundry, hosted a small gathering for Percy Brown in the laundry office, adjacent to his home. Mr Sarsons was not sorry to see Percy go, finding him a congenial, but lazy fool. However, he felt it was only fair to wish him well in his new endeavour. His wife, Anna, made a punch (with perhaps a little more gin in it than was necessary), tomato sandwiches and savoury scones.

Mr and Mrs Sarsons, Bert Robinson and Percy's replacement, Sidney Jacobs, congregated in the laundry office after work to consume this fare.

'So sorry your wife could not join us,' Mrs Sarsons said, taking a bite of her savoury scone.

'Thanks, but she will be getting 'erself ready for tonight,' Percy said, 'as I am taking 'er to the Grand 'Otel for dinner and dancing. I've never taken 'er there before.'

'She will enjoy it, I'm sure. Mr Sarsons and I have attended their dances on occasion, before his knees started playing up, that is.'

I'm amazed your knees don't play up too, Percy thought, glancing at her round frame.

'Your wife deserves to be spoilt while you're still at home,' Mrs Sarsons went on. 'She's going to be dreadfully lonely once you're at the mine.'

Percy was not so sure about this. He had not told any of them that it was Mabel who found him his new job. Sometimes he wondered if she had done this because she wanted him out of the way. Whatever, he did not worry about it too much. The new job meant he would be earning twice his laundry wage. The MEC had already given him three months wages in advance with the proviso, from Mr Craig, that Mabel be given the bulk of it so she could get their house finished. He had no qualms about this either; he wouldn't have anything to spend his money on when he was stuck out at the mine for weeks on end, and, when he did come home, it would be much nicer staying in a brick house than a mud hut.

'Who would like some more punch?' Mrs Sarsons asked.

'Top up everyone's glasses Anna,' her husband said, 'and didn't I see you had baked another batch of scones? Why don't you fetch them, and make some more punch while you're in the kitchen, there's a good girl? We need to give Percy a fine send off, eh.'

'But what about Percy's plans for later? Dinner and dancing with his wife?'

'Plenty of time for that,' Percy said, grabbing the last scone before Mrs Sarsons took the plate away.

As it turned out, Percy, Bert and Sidney finally climbed into the laundry cart and took themselves back to town well after midnight, hiccupping and singing all the way. Percy rolled off the back of the cart and staggered into his yard, yelling his goodbyes to his companions.

'Sweet'art, where are you?' he called, as he fumbled with the locked door that met him. Mabel was in bed, waiting for him, and she got up to unbolt the door and let him in when she heard the commotion he was making. He reached out for her, but she dodged him as she rebolted the door and stomped back to bed without saying a single word. He stumbled after her.

'What's the matter, Sweet'art?' He said, as he flopped onto the bed beside her.

Mabel still said nothing. Percy put his cold hand inside the bedclothes and tried to fumble with her nightgown buttons. She slapped his hand and tried to push him away. He began to snore. His mouth was open and she could smell his gin-soaked breath as he let out long, low, stuttering snorts. She kicked him, but he did not stop.

*

The day after James left on the train, Anthony rose before dawn and rode out to their new property. He was sad James had gone and resolved the best way to deal with this was to keep himself busy. It was strange, going off into the wilds on his own, when he'd always ridden out with James before. He was excited about what James intended doing when he was in England: investigating the best breeds of cattle to bring back to Rhodesia. It wouldn't surprise him if James sent a cable in the next few months, telling him he had bought, and was sending out, a whole herd. James was not someone to sit around doing nothing. This made Anthony focus more sharply on what he needed to do on their property; a great deal, before they could look after any cattle on it. As he rode about the place, he looked for the best areas to graze cattle, the best places to dig wells and the easiest terrain for erecting fences. He identified a section of the river where he thought they could build a dam wall one day, and he tried to decide on the best places to build cattle handling pens.

Eventually he decided he was too hot, tired and stiff to carry on. He had been sitting in the saddle for a long time, and he needed to get off and stretch his legs. Mananga had made some sandwiches and he elected to ride up a small hill where he could eat his lunch. The hill was steeper than it appeared from the bottom and it took Gunner a while to pick his way to the top. When he got there, Anthony eased himself out of his saddle, pulling the reins over Gunner's head as he patted his neck. He looked about for a tree to tie the rein. He hadn't expected the ride up the hill to be so difficult, but long grass and rocks had made the going tough for Gunner. However, now he was here, he concluded the climb was worth it as the view was magnificent. He was surprised by this. From the bottom, it had seemed an insignificant incline, yet, from the top he could see for miles around. He noticed a good-sized rock near where he had tied Gunner and chose to climb this. There were smaller rocks balancing against it, and, after checking there were no snakes or scorpions, he clambered up these and onto the top. He felt a soft breeze and he undid his shirt buttons and took off his hat to get the most of it. Taking his grubby handkerchief from his pocket, he wiped his face and stared at the view. It was even more impressive from the higher elevation of this rock. He looked southward, trying to make out any distinguishing landmarks that would identify Bulawayo. There were none, just the flatness and the emptiness of the surrounding countryside. Nothing, except dry, greyish brown, scrubby looking bush and, further away, greener looking bush marking the river.

Anthony looked at the sky, trying to approximate the time. He was spending the night in one of Tate's huts and he still had much to do. He had dropped off a package from Isabella for them when he had arrived in the morning, and asked them if he could stay. It was too far to ride from Sunrising and back in one day. He had left his bedroll with them and, and when he got back later, he found it spread on the hard-packed mud floor of an otherwise empty hut. Tate's woman gave him porridge for supper, and they sat on wooden stools around the fire. The woman said nothing, although her son, Toby, showed great interest in him. But Anthony was too tired to talk for long and retired to his hut as soon as he had finished eating. He took off his dirty clothes and climbed into his bedroll, his mind still spinning with everything he needed to do.

Chapter 15

FOR a long time after James left Isabella found the house desolate and empty. Having him sitting on the veranda, smoking his pipe and staring at the view, or hearing him return from a shoot and going into the kitchen to tell Mananga what to do with the birds, or entertaining his friends and colleagues when they came to stay. All this had become an integral part of life at Sunrising, and there was a deep void once James had gone.

To fill her days, Isabella spent more and more of her time painting. Once she was in the routine of painting every day she felt a great sense of fulfillment. She was delighted that her art inspired her so much again. She still used the nursery as her studio, as it had the best light in the house, but she had discovered a loft above the stables, and she was going to convert this into a studio after the baby was born.

She was lucky to have her art to keep herself occupied as Anthony was away a great deal. Besides building huts for himself at the farm, he also oversaw the activities on the four mines the MEC now owned. This meant being absent from home most week nights, and even when he was back, he spent long hours at the office in town. Isabella had convinced him she didn't need Bert Robinson, or anyone else, to "look after her" when he was not home. She had Gonda and the others living close by if anything went wrong, and she rarely felt lonely because Archie was constantly with her:

snoring on a mat in the nursery while she painted; sniffing around the garden when she went for a walk in the evening; scratching under the table at mealtimes; sleeping in his basket in her room when she went to bed. As far as other company was concerned, she still met Muriel on her weekly trips to town, usually at the Grand Hotel for tea, but the Weirs had moved into a new house on the corner of Jameson Street and 14th Avenue, and Isabella sometimes visited Muriel there instead. It interested her to see what Muriel was doing with her new house and garden.

'I am overjoyed we are finally living in a brick building,' Muriel said to Isabella when she first visited. 'That rickety wrought iron place we were in before was too hot in summer and too cold in winter. This house is going to be much more agreeable, and more convenient too, so close to town, especially when baby comes along.'

Isabella was not sure she agreed with this. The longer she lived at Sunrising, the more she enjoyed living out of town; with the vlei in front of her house and the large grounds where she could take Archie for walks most evenings.

*

While she painted, Isabella often thought of her sister and what she might be doing at that moment. Celia was now on her way to Bulawayo, having set off from King's Lynn a few weeks before. She would be arriving in Bulawayo in the middle of September. As Isabella worked at her easel, she would think of Celia on her journey and what she might be experiencing right then. Isabella had made the long journey twice, but this was the first time Celia had ever travelled so far from home. First she would have to catch the train from King's Lynn to Southampton. There, she would stay at the Admiral's Arms while she waited for the ship to set sail, on a Thursday, which was the day it always departed. Her passage was on the RMS *Dunottar*

Castle, and Isabella wondered how this would compare to the *Hawarden Castle*, the ship she first travelled on when she came out by herself for the first time in 1898. Not much different she suspected, both being Union Castle liners. Isabella imagined Celia's seventeen days on the ship: salty sea breezes; walks on the decks; dressing elegantly for dinner every night; (maybe she'd be invited to join the captain at his table); stopping for a day to look around Madeira. She hoped Celia would enjoy her sea journey as much as she had enjoyed hers. Their brother Edward, and his wife, Alice, planned to meet her off the ship and spend some time in Cape Town, before taking her to their home in Victoria West, where she would stay for a few weeks. From there she would catch the train bound for Rhodesia.

For Isabella, this journey seemed to take forever; but finally the time came for Celia to reach Bulawayo.

'Which vehicle shall we use to collect Celia from the station?' Anthony asked. It was the day before her arrival and he and Isabella were walking with Archie along the dried up stream at the bottom of their garden, as they often did on the evenings when he was home. 'We could take the Spider, except there is not much space for luggage. I suspect she will have brought a great deal with her.'

'Of course, what with all the clothes and furniture for the baby, plus things for us too. She's bringing new linen, and glassware, and I'm sure she will have other presents from Papa and Aunt Elizabeth.'

'Maybe we should have Gonda follow us in the mule cart, and all her trunks can be loaded into it.'

'But why don't we just take the mule cart ourselves?'

'It's not as pleasant as the Spider. I thought a woman in your condition needed to be as comfortable as possible.'

'Not I; in Africa we women have to be hardy. You know that. I'll be quite comfortable in the mule cart.' She stopped and looked out, over the vlei beyond the stream. 'I am so excited Celia will be here tomorrow. I can hardly wait to see what she makes of all this.' She waved her hand in the air, as if making great brushstrokes on a large canvas. 'These wonderful little pom pom flowers on all the trees, for instance. They are enchanting, and their smell, ah, I am quite intoxicated by it.' 'She will probably find everything dusty and brown, coming from England.'

'Oh yes, but she will have had some experience of dust and dirt after spending time in Victoria West. I am sure that place is much dustier than here, being in the Karoo Desert. But Anthony, what about the soft pinky-grey of our evening skies, and the glowing yellowness of the setting sun shining through the long, dry, grass, and, of course, our dainty Impala drinking in the stream. Celia is going to be so, umm' Isabella was at a loss for words.

'Hot and fatigued for much of the time, I've no doubt,' he finished off for her.

Isabella dug her finger into his ribs, laughing at him. 'Stop being such a killjoy, she is going to love it.'

'But it is going to be unbearably hot very soon. October is stifling.'

'Well I've put her in the coolest room in the house, with windows that open on both sides, so she'll have a through breeze, and with just a sheet on her bed, she'll be fine.'

'Of course she will, lass. Now, let us go back to the house and have an evening drink on the veranda, shall we?'

*

Celia's first impression of Bulawayo was far from the romantic visions Isabella had been conjuring. Both Isabella and Anthony were shocked when Celia stepped shakily from the train; grey faced and bowed over.

'Oh my, what's the matter?' Isabella blurted out, as soon as she saw her.

139

'I ate something that did not agree with me and have been wretched ever since.' She clutched Isabella's arm and would not let go.

'I'm so sorry. How long have you been like this?'

'Two days.'

'But are you going to be able to travel back to Sunrising? It's about three miles from here, and we're in our mule cart.'

'I'm a little better now. It's been a nightmare on that train.'

'I can imagine.' Isabella looked about for somewhere to sit, but there was nowhere comfortable. Just hot looking wrought iron huts.

'They are going to take their time unloading the luggage,' Anthony said. 'We can't have you standing around while they do this.'

'Why don't we take Celia to Muriel's house? It's not far from here, and you can come back and fetch her things.'

Muriel was delighted when she saw the Craigs' cart draw up at her front gate, but as soon as she glimpsed whom she knew must be Celia, her delight changed to concern. The short ride from the station to Jameson Street had done Celia's condition no good, and she was feeling nauseous again. Anthony helped her off the mule cart, but, as they passed through Muriel's gate, she could help herself no longer. She clutched onto the gatepost and threw up. Everyone stood around, helpless, as she retched and spat, and retched and spat again.

'Oh my, this is too terrible,' Isabella said, stroking her back.

Anthony gave Celia a clean pocket handkerchief, and she wiped her mouth.

'Can't be helped,' Muriel said, staring at the splatters on her freshly white-painted picket fence. 'I think we need to settle Celia in my spare bedroom, with the curtains closed and a bowl by her side. You cannot think of travelling all the way back to Sunrising with her like this. When she's feeling a little better, I'll see if she can drink some sugared water, and if there is no improvement by tomorrow, I'll call the doctor.'

Isabella could feel her disappointment increasing even though she knew Muriel was right. Celia needed to stay exactly where she was, and hopefully she would start to recover.

'I'm so sorry, I, I, I....' Celia glanced at them, unable to talk.

'Absolutely no reason to apologise,' Muriel said. 'The food sold at the stations, especially after Mafeking, can be quite horrendous. I starve myself when I travel by train.'

'I'll stay while Anthony goes back to the station,' Isabella said.

Anthony turned the mule cart around in the street and headed back up 14th Avenue while Muriel and Isabella helped Celia into the house.

'So lovely and cool,' Celia murmured as they walked in. The spare bedroom was off the passage next to the front door. Muriel led them in and closed the curtains. 'You don't need that glare,' she said. 'I'll get my cook to boil water for a bath for you later, but first, I think you need to get into bed and regain your strength. Isabella, can you go to the kitchen and ask Cookie to fill the jug with water for the washbowl? I'll go and fetch one of my nightgowns, and a towel, and soap.'

When they returned Celia was sitting on the bed in just her petticoat, with her boots off.

'We'll leave you to wash and get into bed,' Isabella said reluctantly. 'I'll see how you are when Anthony gets back and before we leave.'

'Call if you need anything,' Muriel said. 'We'll be right next door.'

Anthony did not take as long as they'd expected, but Muriel insisted he have a cup of tea before leaving to go back to Sunrising.

'Fine place you've got here,' he said, sinking into one of the chairs in her sitting room and looking about the room. 'I am sorry I have been too busy to come and visit you and Philip before.'

'Understood perfectly. But yes, I think we are going to be very happy here. We find it is such a convenient location.'

'We're lucky you live here now and could come to our assistance so readily. That girl is in a bad way, and the less she moves around, the better.'

'Yes. I've put some boiled water beside her bed, for her to sip, and I'll try her with a little soup and dry bread tonight.'

'Yes, soup is just the thing.'

'You may think that, but I haven't told you what I recently caught Cookie doing, have I?'

'What?'

'I keep telling him to launder the dish towels daily, as they always seem so grimy. Well, when I went into my kitchen the other day, I found them in the soup pot, boiling away merrily. It turns out he's been doing this for heaven only knows how long. When I asked him what on earth he was doing he told me he thought this was a good way to wash them. Goodness, no wonder they were always looking so grimy.'

'Oh my,' Isabella laughed. 'Too funny. What could he have been thinking? He's not doing it any more, I hope? It would do Celia no good, having dirty dish towels boiled in her soup.'

'No, I can assure you he understood the error of his ways once I had finished lecturing him.'

They finished their tea and Isabella went to see Celia to say goodbye, but found her asleep.

'I cannot believe we're going home without her,' she wailed, as they started their journey back to Sunrising.

'It won't be for long,' Anthony said.

'Oh my, I hope you are right.'

But the following morning, when she telephoned Muriel, the news was not what she had hoped for.

'I called the doctor, who came to see Celia this morning. He said she must not be moved for at least another twenty-four hours.'

'Oh no. That's awful. Can I come and see her?'

'Isabella, think of your condition. You cannot be traipsing in and out of town every day, even in your Spider. You will bring the baby on much too early if you try.'

'But I have been longing to have her with me, here at Sunrising.'

'It will happen, all in good time.' Muriel said. 'I will let you know as soon as she's able to move. If she hadn't been on that train when she fell sick, she wouldn't be so bad.'

Two days later the doctor gave the 'all clear' and Anthony and Isabella went into town again, this time in the Spider, to take Celia back to Sunrising.

Squashed in between them in the Spider, Celia said: 'You know what has struck me the most, since I've been here in Bulawayo?'

'What?' Anthony asked.

'The birds; the numerous types, and the variety of their calls. Every morning I wake early and listen to them chirping, and trilling, and chatting, and squawking. I am enchanted by the noise they make.'

'How interesting, that you should have noticed this, above everything else.'

'They are very striking, when you have never seen or heard them before. Obviously in England we have lovely birds too, but not like here. Muriel put a large dish for them to bathe in, in the

143

yard outside my bedroom window, and once I felt stronger, I sat up and watched them coming and going all day long.'

'You will find the birds at Sunrising equally entertaining,' Anthony answered. 'Being less built up, we probably have an even greater variety.'

Isabella glanced at her husband and sister, sitting next to her, discussing birds. She knew she should be content, being with her two favourite people together, and yet she felt a strange sense of foreboding instead. She could not understand it. She tried to shake it off, focusing instead on everything she wanted to show Celia when they got home.

Chapter 16

OF the four mines the MEC owned, only Big Rock Mine was operational. The other three were in varying stages of development. Cutting roads for carting equipment at one. Molding and firing bricks for building at another. Transporting and setting up the equipment at the third. Anthony oversaw all this, as well as the operations at Big Rock Mine. They had expanded Big Rock first, because it was closest to the river, making it easiest for using a stamp mill. When they first started work in the area there had been nothing more than a rough track. This had now turned into a well-worn dust road after carting all the equipment to the mine. Bringing out the stamp mill, piece by piece, and erecting it on site; hauling out railway tracks, section by section, and laying them between the dig and the mill; towing out a steam engine to help run the mill. They were under pressure to get Big Rock operational and productive so their investors could see a return on their money. James had delivered the first ingot to the bank in Bulawayo in July, a week before he left. Anthony had delivered more since.

Anthony now sat in the mine office with the manager, Mr Henderson. They had been discussing cyanide tanks. They wanted to start using the MacArthur Forrest Process to separate finer gold from the powdered ore.

'We have to be bloody careful with that stuff,' Mr Henderson said, rubbing his sweaty face with his handkerchief. 'The mercury is dangerous enough.'

'Quite, I'll leave this article that was sent to me from England recently for you to read, and we'll discuss it further on my next visit.'

Mr Henderson picked up the paper and waved it around his head. 'I used cyanide when I was working on the mines in the Transvaal. I'll start thinking about where we can put the tanks.' He flapped the paper in front of his face, trying to stir the air in the furnace-like office. 'This heat is a real bugger. Difficult to get anyone to do a decent day's work in it.'

'At least you have the river to cool off at the end of the day.'

'Yes, we can bathe there, now all the animals have buggered off. That stamp mill is loud enough to stop a herd of charging elephants.'

'But I'm sure the tents are more comfortable in this hot weather than they were in winter?'

'No, they were bloody freezing a few months ago, and now they are as hot as hell at the end of the day.'

The lines deepened around Anthony's eyes, despite his trying not to show any irritation. It seemed there was nothing he could do to satisfy Mr Henderson. 'I am sorry about that. As soon as we get the next mine into production, we will start building accommodation here.'

'Won't be a moment too soon.'

'Aye, but we have to stick to our budget. I'm delighted you've given me another four ingots to take back to Bulawayo. It'll help make our investors happy. Well done Henderson, you are running a tight operation here.'

Anthony spent just one night at the Big Rock Mine as he wanted to travel home via the farm and spend a night there too. The men employed to build his huts had finished them, and he wanted to see how they had turned out and to pay the builders. He also had a package from Isabella to give to Tate's woman and children.

He took biscuits and biltong from the mine to eat overnight, and his hipflask full of whisky. When he got to the property he stopped off to give the woman and children their parcel and was surprised when they gave him one back, 'for Mrs Craig', the young boy explained in his earnest fashion. They had never given Isabella anything before and he knew she would be touched by their gesture. It was a long, thin package, wrapped in a torn piece of blanket, and he had to strap it to the back of his saddle. He allowed Gunner to drink long and hard from their water trough before making his farewells. He did not want to stay long with them as he was impatient to see his new huts.

There was little difference between them and all the other pole and *dagga* huts in Rhodesia, but he had a great sense of satisfaction when he first saw them. They were the first small step towards everything else he intended doing on the property. He had arranged for three huts to be built. One for him to sleep in, one to use as a pantry or storeroom and a third, which just a thatch roof over wooden poles, for a sheltered sitting area. The sleeping hut and storeroom hut were also thatched and both had walls and doors. They had all been built just a few yards from each other and faced each other to form a small circle. He jumped off Gunner, patted his neck, and then loosened the girth to remove the saddle. It felt wet underneath and smelt of sweat after so many hours strapped to the horse. He had asked the hut builders to make a small hitching post next to the hut where he would sleep, and he rested the saddle on this as he tethered Gunner to it, giving him a long rein so he could graze the sparse, dry grass near the hut. Not very appetizing, but better than nothing for just one night, he concluded. He carried his saddle into the empty sleeping hut and laid it in the middle of the floor. He took his bed roll from the back of the saddle, unbuckled the leather straps that kept it in a tight roll and spread it onto the hard mud floor, canvas side down so the sheet inside would not get dirty. He then went outside and to the storeroom hut, opening the door and looking inside. He did not expect to find anything in it so was surprised to see a pile of wood, probably left by the builders. He was glad of this as it was starting to get dark and he did not much relish the idea of searching around in the bush for firewood. He carried the wood outside and looked about for the best place to light a fire. He established this would be in the space between the sitting room and the kitchen huts. There, the prevailing wind would blow the smoke away from everything. He had become an accomplished fire builder after all the camping he had done in the last few months and it wasn't long before bright yellowy orange flames were licking into the air, throwing a warm glow onto the whole area. They soon died down, and he threw another log onto the blaze. He went back into his sleeping hut in search of his food and drink and then sat down on the ground near the fire, his back against the storeroom wall. He felt relaxed as he took a slug of his whisky and bit into a piece of salty biltong. He pondered how he could never relax like this when he was at any of the mines. There was always too much to consider and too many people wanting to discuss things with him; he sometimes felt overwhelmed by the amount of work they had ahead of them in setting up all these mines. But when he was here, on this property, everything seemed more manageable.

He relished being here.

He had received a cable from James a few days before saying he still had not made any firm decisions on what breed of cattle they needed. Anthony did not mind this. He could enjoy the place without feeling too much pressure to get everything in order 'chop, chop', a term he had noticed Gonda loved using when instructing their workers. He smiled to himself as he thought about the ever efficient Gonda and how much Isabella liked him.

A night jar called in the distance, and, as if in reply, a jackal cried further away.

That's my bedtime call, he said to himself. He got up and went to shorten Gunner's rein and make sure it was tied securely to the post. It would be a disaster if his reins came loose in the night and he went wandering into the bush. There were wild animals lurking out there. He stroked Gunner's silky nose as he said goodnight, then went into his sleeping hut, undressed and lay down on his bedroll, using the saddle as a pillow and pulling the sheet over his body. It was too hot for any other covering.

He was soon fast asleep.

*

Celia rode her horse into the enclosure next to the stables and dismounted. Somani left what he was doing, mucking out the stables, and came to get the reins from her. She patted the horse's neck, thanked Somani, and walked back to the house. She felt hot and sweaty, and looked forward to getting to her room where she could strip off her riding habit and wipe herself with a damp towel. She found the October heat draining, especially later in the day. Because of this, she had made a habit of riding or walking early, when there was still a hint of freshness from the night before. After washing and changing she went to the dining room for breakfast. She found Isabella there.

'How was your ride?' Isabella asked, looking up from the paper she was writing on.

'Lovely, as always.'

'See anything interesting?'

'The impala, of course, lots of Guinea Fowl, a Francolin, an African Hoopoe, some grey Louries and, um, let me think, what else?'

Isabella laughed. 'You are clever, the way you have learnt so many of the birds' names so fast.'

'I am fascinated by the bird life here. You should start painting them, Isabella. I am surprised you have not already.'

'I am struggling to paint anything at the moment. I feel too fat and sluggish to do anything constructive.'

'Of course, but after the baby has arrived, perhaps?'

'Yes, maybe.'

'I had a wonderful idea when I was out riding this morning.'

'What?'

'That you paint detailed little pictures of different types of birds, and I write about each: their calls; their habits; what their nests are like.'

'Oh my, Celia, it would take us a lifetime to do something like that.'

'But wouldn't it be fun?'

'Yes, it would. It is something to consider, one day, when I'm back to my old self.'

Celia patted her arm. 'Of course.' She got up and went to the dresser to help herself to scrambled egg and toast.

'I am glad you have slotted into our life here so well, Celia,' Isabella said.

'I'm loving it.'

'And the heat, it's not getting you down?'

'As long as I'm not too active between now and four pm, I can cope. That's why I love watching the birds. I sit in a chair under a shady tree, with my big hat on, and I am entertained for the rest of the day. But before I do this, is there anything I can do for you?'

'I've made a list of housekeeping chores that need to be done today. Would you mind going through it with Gonda, so there aren't any mix-ups?' She handed Celia the paper.

*

They sat in the drawing room later doing their embroidery, waiting for Anthony to return. They had delayed dinner, expecting him back in time to eat with them, but after waiting for an hour, they decided to start without him. They had now finished, and he still was not back. Both women felt worried that he hadn't returned, but they did not want to say anything. The French door was open onto the veranda, and, although the fishpond was far away, they could hear the frogs croaking loudly. Their noisy racket had started in September, 'because of the breeding season', Anthony explained, but Isabella hoped it would not go on for much longer.

'Thank goodness that fish pond isn't closer to our bedrooms,' said Celia. 'We would not get a wink of sleep with them croaking closeby.'

'I think I may ask Anthony to shoot the lot of them when he gets home. He's good at killing troublesome creatures.'

Celia looked horrified. 'That sounds a bit drastic.'

'It may be our only option. There's a lady in town, a Mrs Heyman, who had the same problem, and she lives in a more built-up area than this, in the Suburbs. She told me that once she did a little experiment. She had her gardener tie pieces of wool around the back legs of the frogs in her fishpond; to identify them from other frogs, you understand. The gardener then put all her frogs into a wheelbarrow, and wheeled them two miles away, where he dumped them in a river. You would have thought they would have been happy there, but oh no! The Heymans had a few days of peace and quiet, but then the noise started up again. It turned out they were the same frogs; they came straight back to her fishpond, as fast as they could hop. Mrs Heyman knew they were her frogs because of the wool.'

Celia wiped her eyes, she was laughing so much. 'Oh dear, that's too funny.'

'It is, but not when you have to put up with their din night after night.'

Isabella glanced at the grandfather clock in the corner.

'Oh dear, Celia, I wish Anthony had returned safe and sound. It's so unlike him. He always makes sure he is back when he says he will be, because he knows I worry.'

Celia concentrated on her embroidery. She didn't know what to say.

'I know he visited all the mines during this last week, and he told me he was going to stay last night at the farm. I can't imagine what would have delayed him there.'

151

They carried on working at their embroidery, but half an hour later Celia suggested they went to bed.

'You go,' Isabella said. 'I am not feeling sleepy. I will wait up a bit longer.'

'Are you sure?'

'Yes, don't worry about me. You go off now, dear Celia.'

'Well goodnight then. Don't stay up too long.'

'No, I won't.' But despite making this assurance, she would not contemplate going to bed. She sat in the drawing room, feeling restless. She wanted her husband with her, and she was frustrated that he was not. She tried reading, but the lamplight was not bright enough so she soon gave up. Her embroidery did not hold her attention any more. She eventually wandered outside and sat on the veranda, staring at the horizon. The night was balmy after the hot day. She could hear dry leaves rustling, and in the distance, she saw flashes of lightning. Maybe they would have their first rainstorm tonight, she thought. What a relief that would be after the heat they had been enduring. She listened to the frogs, croaking in the fishpond. They were noisy, yet there was something comforting about the sound they made. Maybe she had been overreacting when she told Celia earlier that she would ask Anthony to shoot them.

But where was he?

She went back into the drawing room and poured herself a glass of water from the drinks tray. She contemplated something stronger, to help herself sleep, but then thought of the baby.

What has happened?

Why hasn't he come back, as he said he would? He was usually good at getting back when he said he would.

She walked outside again and sat on the steps leading onto the garden. She stared at the deep, clear, star filled sky. There was nothing like an African sky at night. She heard far away rumbles of thunder, as the sky flashed with distant lightning. It was getting closer, but she doubted it would reach Sunrising tonight.

A gentle gust blew, rustling the leaves again. The breeze on her face was refreshing. She lifted her long hair and felt, with relief, the cool air on her neck.

But she soon felt uncomfortable, sitting on the steps with the baby pushing into her ribs. There was a mosquito humming around her face and hands.

She moved inside again, closing the door behind her. She sank into the sofa, staring at the painting she had propped up on the mantelpiece, dimly lit by the two lamps either side of it. The painting was a watercolour she had done of Anthony, cantering across the vlei on Gunner.

She finally fell asleep.

Gonda woke her when he came into the drawing room at dawn to remove the tray and dirty glasses. He was as surprised to find her lying on the sofa as she was to find herself there and being woken by him.

They stared at each other.

Then Isabella said: 'The master did not come home last night like we expected, Gonda.'

A look of concern crossed his face. Isabella thought for a moment she was going to cry. She glanced through the French door at the sky. It was starting to lighten from the deep, velvety darkness she had been staring at the night before. The stars had disappeared.

Then she heard what she had been listening for all night; a horse coming up the drive. Only this sounded like more than one horse, and they were going at a good pace. She rushed out of the drawing room and into the hall, her heart pounding. She pulled the front door open and ran onto the front veranda, just as the horses were being reined in at the bottom of the steps. She panicked when she saw that Anthony was not there; just Charles Fletcher and someone she didn't know. She reached behind her and clutched the doorknob to steady herself.

Charles dismounted and handed his rein to the other man. He walked up the steps just as Celia came through to the hall, tying the belt of her dressing gown around her waist. Isabella stumbled backwards into the hall and Celia put her arm out to steady her.

'What, what's the matter?' she stuttered.

'Let's go in and sit down,' Charles said. Celia helped Isabella into the drawing room and onto the sofa, sat next to her, grabbed her hand and held it in hers.

Charles stood next to the fireplace, finding it difficult to look at them. 'There is no easy way to say this, so, let me just get on with it.'

But he stopped and cleared his throat.

'I'm afraid Anthony was, that is to say, he died yesterday, Isabella.'

A look of pained confusion crossed her face as it drained of all colour.

He averted his eyes, concentrating on his hands instead; his rough, reliable hands. He did not know where else to look.

Isabella slumped back on the sofa, and Celia clutched her hand even tighter. The room was as silent as a grave.

Celia eventually broke the silence. 'What happened? Did he fall off his horse?'

'We don't believe so. We don't know what happened at this stage. He was found near the road from the Big Rock mine into town.'

'But, but I thought he had been at the farm?' Celia said.

'There is a detour from that road to the farm.' Isabella whispered. 'He told me it was quicker to come home on the road than to cut across the bush. When, when did you find him, Charles?'

'Two miners were travelling into town at about midnight. They happened to stop on the side of the road and saw a horse grazing in the bush. That's when they discovered Anthony, about twenty yards or so from the road. As my hotel was the closest place to the scene of the, of the, you know, to where they were, they came and fetched me. I rode out to check on things and then came straight here. One miner has stayed at the scene while the other has gone into town to alert the police. We still need to find out what happened, and we will.'

Isabella leant over and buried her face in her sister's lap. She remained motionless while Celia stroked her hair, feeling helpless.

Chapter 17

NEWS of the tragedy spread through Bulawayo like a wild fire. The first person to come to Sunrising to offer his support was Mr Gordon Forsyth. He was in Bulawayo at the time, staying at the Club, and he came as soon as he heard what had happened. He found a household numb with shock and pain, and he immediately took charge.

Isabella had not moved from the sofa in the drawing room, sitting and staring at the watercolour sketch she had done of Anthony on his horse, Gunner. Even when Mr Forsyth arrived, clicking his boots and twiddling his moustache in his usual way, she was hardly conscious he was there.

'Would you like a cup of tea, Mr Forsyth?' Celia asked, doing her best to cope with the difficult situation.

'I most certainly would. Thank you.'

Mananga brought in the tray and Celia poured. Isabella accepted hers without looking at her sister. Celia and Mr Forsyth exchanged a worried glance.

Mr Forsyth sipped his tea and settled himself in an armchair opposite the women. 'Now Madam, if I may be so bold. What are the arrangements for the funeral?'

This got Isabella's attention, but Celia blanched and shook her head.

'You need not worry. Sir Charles is taking care of everything,' she said.

'But Mrs Craig must have some thoughts on her husband's funeral?'

'I do, Mr Forsyth,' Isabella murmured, 'and I want to talk about them.'

'No need to worry,' Celia repeated. 'Sir Charles will give us all the details as soon as he has made the necessary arrangements. He said he would take care of everything.'

'What is it you want to discuss, Mrs Craig?' Mr Forsyth asked.

'I want him to be buried on the farm.'

'That's the problem,' Celia interrupted. 'She mentioned this earlier, but I do not know how we can do something like that. It's too far away. Even Sir Charles said it would be impossible.'

'It is the place he loved most,' Isabella said. 'He always told me the farm was his destiny.'

'We can bury him there,' Mr Forsyth said.

The room went silent.

'But, but how? Celia asked.

'I will organise it.' He took a final gulp of his tea and stood up. 'If you would be so kind as to lead me to your telephone, I need to speak to Charles first. I want to find out what arrangements he has made thus far. After that I will know how to proceed.'

Celia showed him to the library, and then returned to Isabella. They could hear his voice booming through the closed doors.

'That man is a card,' she said.

'Yes, but his heart is in the right place,' Isabella said, going to the dresser, where she knew Anthony kept his map of the farm. She unrolled it onto the coffee table, just as he had always done, and stared at it, saying nothing.

Mr Forsyth came back after some time, looking distracted, but he pulled himself together when he noticed both women staring at him.

'Excellent, excellent. Everything is under control. Everything is in order.'

'Really, Mr Forsyth?' Isabella said. 'What is going to happen?'

'Tomorrow morning I will leave before first light, with a gang of workers provided by Sir Charles. We are lucky that the days are long and the weather is warm. We should get to the farm by noon, and we will start digging the, um, the grave, straight away. We will, therefore, have it ready by the time you arrive.'

Isabella put her finger on the map. 'This is the place you need to dig, Mr Forsyth.'

He walked across the room and peered over her shoulder. 'Madam that may be tricky.' He knelt on the carpet to take a closer look. 'I am struggling to discern anything on this map.'

'I'm not sure of the exact place either,' Isabella said, 'but Anthony told me all about it. He said there's a hill, and on the top of this hill there's a big rock. He said the view of the surrounding area is magnificent from there. He was so taken with the spot, he said he could stay there forever. That is why I want it to be,' she hesitated, unable to carry on for a moment. 'To be, to be his final resting place,' she whispered.

'Quite understandable, but to find this hill, to find this rock. Madam I am not sure I will be able to.'

'Well, here is the river.' She traced it with her finger.

'Indeed.'

'And this is where Tate's huts are.'

'Yes.'

'And this is where Anthony's huts are.'

'Yes, I see he has marked that area.'

'So, in relation to all these places, maybe it will be easier than you think.'

"Well I will do my best to find it, but I cannot guarantee that it will be the exact rock on the exact hill he was telling you about. You will have to be satisfied with the place I choose. However, I will make sure it has a magnificent view, Madam. You can rest assured about that. Rhodes will no longer be the only man in this country with a view of the world from his grave.'

He left shortly afterwards, with much to organise for his trip, but he was hardly out of the door when Lady Fletcher arrived with trays of food. 'For your guests,' she explained, and it turned out there were many: the Weirs; the Chapmans; the Meikles; the Napiers; the Heymans. Even people she did not know well came to see her: the Clarks; the Paulings; the Lawleys; the Sanders, the Sarsons, the Colquains. The rest of the day became a blur of sympathetic murmurs and respectful cups of tea. There were many times when Isabella felt she wanted to scream, but she managed to sit politely and accept their solicitude.

'But what is this I hear about you going to the farm?' Muriel asked.

'Yes, I know Anthony would want to be buried there, and so that is what we are going to do.'

'Isabella, you cannot think of travelling all that way in your condition.'

'I am, Muriel.'

'You cannot. What about the baby?'

'The baby will have to put up with a bumpy ride and an uncomfortable night. We are leaving tomorrow after breakfast. We are taking Anthony with us; in the back of the mule cart. Mr Forsyth will have dug the hole by the time we arrive, so we can have the funeral as soon as we get there. And then we can go back to Anthony's huts to sleep. It is all organised, Muriel.'

Muriel's forehead furrowed with concern. She opened her mouth to say something, but then closed it when she saw the determined look on Isabella's face.

'Celia is coming too, obviously, and Felicity and Charles Fletcher, and um, Sir George. All our staff from here too. I can't think who else, at this stage. They will all have to camp as there are only two huts.'

'I'll come too,' Philip Weir said. Muriel looked at him aghast. 'You will be fine on your own for one night, my dear,' he said. 'We need to give Isabella all the support we can.'

'Thank you, Philip,' Isabella said. 'I was hoping you would offer, because now I can ask you to read from the bible and say a closing prayer. Would you mind?'

'I will be honoured. Who is going to give the eulogy? Would you like me to do that too?'

'Thank you, yes. I think Anthony would approve of that, in the absence of James and his family.'

Philip Weir and George Chapman brought the coffin from Bulawayo early the next morning. The party set off soon afterwards with the coffin lying on the back of the mule cart, under a canvas awning so that it wouldn't get too hot. Isabella sat on the bench at the front with Archie and Gonda, just like she had the first time she'd gone to the farm. She still could not accept the reality of what had happened. Everything was a bewildering, blurred dream for her. The Fletchers travelled in their mule cart too, laden with food and equipment, and Celia sat up front with Felicity Fletcher.

'How difficult all this must be for you,' Felicity said. 'First Anthony's tragic passing, and now having to traipse into the bush like this.'

'Yes, it is very different from what I am used to, back in Norfolk, but I am so relieved I am here for Isabella right now. I know she is going to need me in the coming months. Our brother sent a telegraph to say he and his wife will come to Bulawayo as soon as they can.'

'That's good.'

'Yes, and Sir James also sent a telegraph to say he will come back post haste.'

'What a blow this must be for him. They were very close.'

'I believe so.'

'Have you met Sir James?"

'Yes, he came to see me before I left England. He brought some clothes and furniture for me to bring out for the baby.'

'How thoughtful of him. I have always found him to be a most charming gentleman.'

'Yes, I thought so too.'

'Their friendship aside, he's going to find it difficult trying to replace Anthony as far as the MEC is concerned. Anthony had become an integral part of the running of that company.'

'It is a terrible blow on every level. Does Charles have any more news about what could have happened?'

'Unfortunately there was a rainstorm during the night, so any telltale footprints were washed away. I'm afraid foul play is suspected. Judging from his wounds, there was a scuffle.'

'Oh dear. I can hardly bear the thought of this. It's bad enough that he is dead, but that someone should intentionally have killed him. Please do not say anything to Isabella about this yet.'

'No, I'll tell her as little as possible. The only piece of material evidence they found at the scene was an assegai, so that tells us a great deal. But, how does one find the owner of such a weapon in a vast country like this and with so many of the local people having assegais?'

The journey was slow and laborious, but they did not take a break this time. They needed to get there as early as possible so they could get the burial over and done with before dark.

They arrived at Anthony's huts in the middle of the afternoon, where they found a hot and sweaty Mr Forsyth. He was waiting for them, and he started issuing instructions as soon as they had disembarked.

'Let us all have a cup of tea before proceeding up the hill. I have had one of my workers boil the kettle for you. And we need to unload your cart Charles, so the camp can be set up while we are away. We do not want to have to arrange our campsite when we get back in the dark. Can your men help with this, Mrs Craig?'

'I believe they want to come with us Mr Forsyth.'

Mr Forsyth was undeterred. 'That will work too. They can help with the lowering of the coffin.'

*

Isabella felt shaky as she stood next to her husband's open grave an hour later. She leant against the large rock next to the hole, looking at the top of it and imagining Anthony sitting there, his hat off, his hair blowing in the breeze, surveying the view. She did not hear a word Philip said: not his readings; not his eulogy; not his closing prayers. She focused on a fish eagle instead, soaring high in the sky above. She admired its white body and contrasting black wings and listened to its haunting cries. She was glad she had insisted on bringing Anthony here.

*

In the early hours of the following morning Isabella got up to use the bedpan, and felt wetness between her legs. She put her hand between her legs and was shocked to find herself sodden. She felt for the pot, and tried to sit on it as quickly as possible.

'Celia,' she whispered. 'I think there is something happening with me.'

Celia woke with a start. She sat up, staring into the darkness. It was pitch black and she had no idea where the lamp was, or how to light it.

'What's the matter?'

'I don't have any control, and I've wet myself. I'm afraid there is a mess.'

'Oh no Isabella, this is what I was afraid of. You had such a stressful day yesterday. It's no wonder something has gone wrong now.'

'There's nothing wrong. It's just the baby. I believe it's on its way.'

Celia's heart sank. 'But how?'

'It's alright Celia. I am not in pain or anything, and I cannot feel any contractions yet. However, we cannot wait until dawn.'

'But. Oh dear, I have no experience of these sort of things.'

'I know what we need to do. I thought about it on the journey out here, in case something like this happened. Someone needs to go and fetch Mr Tate's woman. She will know how to deliver my baby, she has delivered two of her own, with little help, I am sure. She won't have a problem helping me deliver this one. It is my second, so it should be easier anyway.'

'Oh Isabella.'

'Don't worry Celia. It will work out, but you need to get things going. I will lie here and lift my legs against the wall, while I wait for the woman to get here. Nevertheless, please hurry.'

Celia felt her way to the door and opened it, calling out to the Fletchers. She was thankful the huts were close together and she didn't have to shout, but the night was deathly quiet, and soon there were stirrings around the camp.

The first person to arrive at their hut door was Mr Forsyth.

'Whatever is the matter Madam? Can I be of assistance?'

'It's the baby, Mr Forsyth. The baby is on its way.'

For once, he was at a loss for words.

'Please can you go and fetch Tate's woman to help us.'

Mr Forsyth stood rooted to the ground.

'You will need to go as quickly as possible. Please Mr Forsyth, hurry.'

He stood, gawping a moment longer. He twiddled his moustache. He opened his mouth and closed it. Then he clicked his heels together and fled across the campsite, calling to anyone who could hear him to prepare his horse.

'There is a candle holder under my bed Celia. Would you mind finding it and going outside to light it with the embers of the fire? I am sure there will be nothing nasty lurking around after the commotion Mr Forsyth made.

Celia returned, looking around the now lit hut, trying to work out what best to do.

'I think this camp bed is too narrow to have a baby in,' Isabella said. 'What about dragging your bed outside, and then I can lie on your bedding on the floor? I am sure that will work better.'

Philip Weir appeared at the door just as Celia opened it again to try to remove the heavy wooden and canvas camp bed. He took over, taking great care not to look inside, while Celia arranged the blankets on the floor where her bed had been. She then looked around for her towel. She dipped it into the water in the canvas basin hooked on its wooden stand next to the door and wiped Isabella's sweating brow.

Isabella crawled off the bed pan and onto the blankets, lying down with some difficulty and putting her legs up the wall.

'I'll lie like this while we wait for Lokuthula,' she murmured. 'She will know best how to proceed.

Chapter 18

THE arrival of a newborn baby usually brings feelings of hope and happiness, but Isabella was incapable of feeling anything except loss and emptiness, as she dragged herself from one day to the next. She named her son Oliver Anthony Craig, but beyond this, she showed no interest in him. Celia would bring him to her to be fed, and she would oblige, like a dutiful dairy cow, allowing herself to be milked before she could be left alone again. The only living creature she showed any interest in was her Staffordshire bull terrier, Archie. He was constantly at her side, and she stroked his head and rubbed his ears, taking comfort in his presence in a way she could not from her baby.

Celia looked on in despair.

Their brother, Edward, and his wife, Alice, arrived in Bulawayo with their two young children, a few weeks after the funeral. They had not seen Isabella since they had left in 1903.

Alice went to find Isabella in her bedroom soon after they arrived at Sunrising. She found her lying on her bed, staring at the ceiling, the curtains closed, the world shut out, Archie sleeping in his basket. Alice sat down next to her, pushing the welcoming Archie away as she took Isabella's hand, rubbing it in her own.

'Isabella darling, we are so sorry about what has happened, but we are here to support you now. Edward and the children are settling into their rooms, and they will see you later. We are going to stay as long as we can.'

Isabella did not respond.

'You have a beautiful home, and a beautiful baby, and we are going to help you get through this difficult time.'

Isabella rolled over and curled herself into a ball, her back to Alice.

'I'm so sorry,' Alice repeated. She stroked her arm, not knowing what else she could do to comfort her.

After some time Isabella turned over again. 'The problem is, Alice, I'm so scared of everything now. I don't know how I can go on without him.'

'I understand. It is terrible for you, but you are young, and you have a little boy who needs his mama.'

'That's just it. The last time I had a baby, he died. It is only a year since we lost William, you know. I do not want to become attached to this one, in case he dies too.'

Alice was shocked, but she did not show it. 'I'm sure that's not going to happen. Oliver seems a strong, healthy, little boy.'

'William started out healthy too. For his first two months he was like any other baby. There seemed nothing wrong with him. That is the frightening part'.

Again, Alice did not know how to respond.

'Then one day William developed a bad cold, and he was sick for three days. We did not know what to do. We asked our neighbour, Mrs Meikle, to come round and help us treat him, as she had some knowledge of home medicines. At first her suggestions seemed to make a difference and he improved for a day or two, but then he got worse. The doctor was away at the time, but as soon as he returned we took William to see him. He told us he had asthma, and nothing could be done for him. Is that not pathetic? Everything we did was useless, we were helpless.'

'It must have been dreadful for you. But do you want to talk about this now?'

'Yes, I do. I have not spoken about it for a long time. I thought I was getting over it, until this, until this happened.'

'It is most unfortunate.'

Isabella lay on her back again, staring at the ceiling. 'He died four months later and those months were more than terrible for Anthony and me; watching the poor little mite struggling to hold onto his tiny life. It was heart breaking in every way. I became obsessed with looking after him, and taking care of him, willing him to get better. I would spend hours walking around the house and the garden with him in my arms, trying to make his breathing easier. There were times when he seemed quite healthy, and he would lie on his mat and smile at me, or gurgle contentedly. Anthony tried to encourage me to attend parties and other social occasions, but we would inevitably come home early because I was always worried about William. Finally he took a turn for the worse, and the doctor came to the house to see him, but again said there was nothing he could do. He died later that day, of heart failure. That's what happened, Alice, and I do not think I can go through it again, especially now that Anthony is, is gone too.' She began to sob. 'I cannot go through it again, Alice. I cannot. Not without Anthony.'

There was nothing Alice could do to comfort her.

*

James Brooke came back to Sunrising in the middle of November. He dreaded his return, but at the same time he was desperate to get back, he needed to get back.

He knew Isabella's siblings were staying, and he was relieved to find a full and bustling household. He had been told Isabella had sunk into a deep depression, but when he got to Sunrising he discovered she had diverted this depression into her painting, turning the loft above the stable into a studio. Her brother, Edward Braithewaite told him she was there when he first arrived, and he went to find her as soon as he had freshened up.

He climbed the stairs, his footsteps sounding heavy on the wooden rungs, and he found her standing at her easel, turned towards the opening, wondering whom it was. A look of relief crossed her face when she saw it was him.

'James!'

He strode across the room and put his arms around her. 'I am so very, very sorry,' he said, struggling to maintain control. She rested her head on his shoulder for a moment, saying nothing. Then she pulled away.

'Thank you for coming back.'

'I would have come sooner if I had been able.'

'Yes. How was your journey?'

'It felt long, which made it frustrating. But I am glad to find you busy. You have made yourself a pleasant studio here, I see.'

'I love it, although it is blistering hot some days. But I open this window wide, and I get a breeze.'

James glanced at the canvas on the easel. 'And I see you are painting the scene from this window.'

'I am pleased with it. What do you think?'

'Most impressive.'

She dabbed her paintbrush into a jar of water and continued working; painting tiny, controlled strokes, building up the shadows in the grassy vlei.

He sat down in the armchair next to the window and felt for his pipe, filling it with fresh tobacco before lighting it, blowing puffs of smoke into the room. He crossed his legs and watched her paint.

'It's certainly relaxing. I can see why you moved your studio here.'

'I was using the baby's nursery, but I obviously cannot anymore.'

'I had a brief glance into his pram when I got here. He was sleeping peacefully on the veranda, despite your family talking all around him while they had their tea. Such a dear little soul.'

'They are all very good with him. Especially Celia.'

James wanted to talk about Anthony. He wanted to ask her if there were any new leads on what may have happened, but he could see that she was fragile and that she was blocking everything out. He would need to speak to Edward instead.

He sat, smoking his pipe, watching her work for some time before he suggested they go down and change for dinner. She said she needed to finish off what she was doing.

A while later they were all on the veranda, except Isabella, having a sundowner before dinner.

'She has not had any meals with us since the tragedy,' Celia said. 'She prefers to eat in her bedroom.'

James was about to respond, when he glanced beyond Celia, to the drawing room door. Isabella was standing there. 'I've decided to join you tonight,' she said. 'Things will be better, now that James is back.'

*

But this was not the case.

Early the next morning there was a telephone call from a Sergeant Smythe. He asked James to come and see him at the Fife Street Police Station as soon as possible. James arrived mid-morning and Sergeant Smythe showed him to his office, closing the door behind him. He sat in his chair behind the desk, inviting James to take a seat too. He opened a file then closed it again.

'I wanted to inform you that we are arresting two men this morning, in relation to the murder of Mr Craig. I thought you should know, before the news gets out, so that you can inform the family. You know how this sort of news spreads.'

'I am very pleased to hear this. Who are the men?'

'A Mr Frederick Payne and Mr Percy Brown, both employed by you at Big Rock Mine. You will know them, I trust?'

'What? No. No I do not know them.' He took out his pipe and banged it on the wooden arm of his chair, loosening the tobacco. 'On consideration, I know Brown, but not Payne. He must have started working there after I left. Why do you suspect them?'

'I cannot say much at this stage. There will be an arraignment tomorrow and, if they plead not guilty, the preliminary hearing will follow in a few days. But briefly, Mr Payne was in town recently, and he told his girlfriend Brown and he were involved. She reported this information to one of our constables and we did some follow up investigations. There seems enough circumstantial evidence to take this further, hence their arrests this morning.'

James was silent.

'I want to warn you that there is going to be uproar in Bulawayo over this.'

'Why so?'

'We are a small white community here, and we like to think we have the same goal; to develop this country. It is my belief, no one wants to accept this murder was perpetrated by white men. Our community can relate to black-on-black killings, black-on white and white-on-black, but white-on-white, no! There is going to be an outcry. As you know an assegai was found at the scene, and this pointed to a black man attacking Mr Craig. No one questioned this, but they are going to have a lot to say about this new development.'

'And what of the assegai? I thought this was the main piece of evidence.'

'We cannot explain it at this stage, but, as I said before, there is enough circumstantial evidence against Brown and Payne to arrest them.'

'Everyone at home is going to be horrified by this news. Brown is married to Mrs Craig's former maid. Mrs Craig is going to be mortified when she hears this, especially as she has met Mr Brown on a number of occasions.'

He was right. Any signs of improvement Isabella might have shown were shattered when she heard this new development. She withdrew into herself again, not leaving her studio and refusing to join them for meals.

*

James explained to Celia how Mabel had asked the Craigs to employ her husband. This made Celia feel very awkward. It was she who had brought Mabel into their lives in the first place.

'Please Celia, do not think this way,' James said. 'Do not entertain any ideas that you might even be partly to blame for any of this. It is not your fault.'

'But, oh dear. Mabel seemed such a pleasant character when I interviewed her in England.'

'I am sure she is. Sadly, she has been through hard times. I have been told she never fully recovered from a bout of malaria, and then she fell for Mr Brown's charms. I hear he can be a very pleasant and amusing character when he wants. I would not be surprised if she is feeling as devastated as we are about what has transpired.'

'Do you think that could be the case?'

'Yes, indeed it could very well be.'

'Maybe I should go and see her then? Maybe she is in need of help too, in coming to terms with this ugly turn of events.'

'Yes. That could be a good idea. It may help all of us understand everything better. And especially poor Isabella.'

*

Gonda took Celia to the Brown's house in First Avenue in the Spider. She knocked at the front door three times before it was opened. Mabel stood inside the door looking paler and thinner than she remembered her.

'Ah, Mabel, hello. I was just starting to think you weren't here.'

'Er, no. Good afternoon Miss Braithewaite.' She glanced at Celia and then looked towards Gonda, standing in the street next to the carriage.

'We are all so sad about everything that has happened,' Celia said. 'It is too dreadful.'

Mabel glanced at Gonda again. There was an uneasy silence.

'May I come in?'

Mabel's eyes shifted towards Gonda. After another awkward moment she stepped aside to let Celia in. Celia felt uncomfortable as she was shown to a small front room, and then, before she had a chance to say anything else, Mabel murmured: 'Please excuse me. I will go and make some tea.'

Very odd, Celia thought as she sat down on the sofa and looked about the room. It was sparsely furnished, with one sofa, two hard-backed chairs and a small table in the middle. She took off her hat and gloves and put them on the table, noticing an intricately worked crochet mat on the table. She wondered if Mabel had started crocheting and felt sympathetic towards her, imagining her sitting alone in this drab little room, with nothing to do except crochet. So different to the magnificent drawing room at Sunrising and the lives they lead there. Before this tragedy, of course.

After some time Mabel returned with the tea tray and Celia removed her things from the table and straightened the mat, before

Mabel set the tray down. She poured them each a cup of strong, black tea.

'I hope you don't take sugar or milk because I don't have any.'

'No, no, black is fine,' Celia said. She took a sip and then set her cup back on its saucer, concentrating on not wincing at the smoky taste of the tea. 'I meant to come and see you before, but I just haven't got round to it, what with everything that has happened. I am sorry.'

'My Percy did nothing, Miss Braithewaite. He is being falsely accused.'

'I hope this is the case.'

Mabel looked agitated. 'It is. That is why the people in this town are so angry that he has been arrested.'

'It is distressing for the whole community, and even more so for everyone at Sunrising, as you can imagine.'

'Yes, but it was blacks who did it. Everyone knows that. They have the assegai to prove it.' Mabel's eyes filled with tears, and she bit her lip, trying to stop herself from crying. 'Mr Craig was such a nice man. He was always very good to me. This should never have happened to him.'

'Exactly. Mrs Craig is devastated. We are all devastated.'

'Mrs Craig was not good to me, Miss Braithewaite. I know she is your sister and all, but you need to know, she never let me forget that I was her servant. Unlike Mr Craig. He was different. He should not have been killed.'

Celia took another sip of her tea, surprised at how the conversation had turned. 'But you were employed to be her lady's maid, Mabel. How else was she supposed to treat you? Was she perhaps unkind towards you?'

'No, but everything has always been so easy for her.'

'No it has not, Mabel.'

'We both came to Rhodesia for the same reason. To find a better life for ourselves. I didn't want to be a maid all my life, which is what I was going to be if I stayed in England. Here in Rhodesia we Europeans should all be the same; at least that's what Percy and I think, but Mrs Craig didn't treat me like that. She was always so high and mighty towards me.'

'What did she do, to make you feel like this towards her?'

'Nothing exactly. It's just that she always has everything her own way. But Mr Craig; now he was good to me. He treated me like an equal. He gave Percy his job, so that we could get on in this country. He even helped us with a loan to finish building this house. He should not be dead now.'

'No he should not.' Celia said, deciding she had gleaned as much as she needed. To her, Mabel had lost all sense of perspective. She seemed so bitter and twisted and mixed up. It was almost as if she had lost her mind.

She put her cup and saucer back on the tray and stood up.

'I must go, Mabel,' she said. 'I am very sorry everything has turned out like this.'

'My husband is not guilty, Miss Braithewaite. It is very unfair that he is in the jail now, but he will be released. New evidence will come forward to clear him.'

'I hope this is the case.' She left Mabel's house, feeling less anxious about her. Mabel may need help, but not from anyone at Sunrising.

Chapter 19

THE preliminary hearing began the next day at the police station in Fife Street. There had never been a case like this in Bulawayo, and everyone wanted to witness as much of it as they could. At first the police allowed the public into the hearing room, but it was soon packed, with more people trying to squeeze in. They had to change their ruling and order everyone out, except the witnesses, family and close friends. There were moans and shouts as people left, or tried to stay and argue their right to be there. James and Edward arrived during the ensuing chaos. Ignoring this, they made for the empty seats at the far side of the room. They found themselves staring at the rigid backs of Mabel and two other women.

The room became quiet as the two accused were brought in through a side door, surrounded by police constables. Percy gave his wife a weak smile before sitting down. Finally the judge entered through the same door, and everyone stood as he strode to the front and sat down heavily in his chair. A policeman ordered the gathering to sit down. The judge peered around the room over his glasses, before opening the file in front of him.

The atmosphere was tense with expectation.

'In this preliminary hearing I will decide if there is enough evidence against the two accused,' he looked at his file again, 'Mr Percy Brown and Mr Frederick Payne, to stand trial for the murder of Mr Anthony Craig. Will the accused please stand?'

The floorboards creaked as the two stood up.

'How do you plead?' the judge asked.

'Not guilty,' said Percy Brown.

'Not guilty,' said Frederick Payne.

The judge paused for emphasis, staring at the two men over his glasses. 'Then let us begin. Please call your first witness, Mr Prosecutor.'

'Thank you My Lord,' the prosecutor said, standing up, his chair legs scraping on the wooden floor. 'I call Mr Barry Williams.' Mr Williams's footsteps echoed around the quiet room as he made his way to the witness box. He swore on the bible placed before him and sat down.

'What is your occupation Mr Williams?' asked the prosecutor.

'I am a miner Sir. I work at the Big Rock Mine.'

'And what were you doing in the early hours of the morning of 5th October, 1905?'

'I was riding back to Bulawayo on the road from Big Rock Mine, Sir.'

'At night?'

'Yes Sir. The moon was bright at that time.'

'Were you alone?'

'No Sir, I was with Mr John Barber, who also works at the mine.'

'And what did you notice?'

'A horse, Sir, grazing in the bush, approximately twenty yards from the road. We were surprised, because it had a saddle on it, so we stopped to take a closer look. That's when we discovered the body, Sir.'

'Did you know who the dead man was?'

'Yes Sir, I recognised Mr Craig.'

'Did you touch the body?'

'No, Sir."

'What did you do next?'

'Mr Barber stayed with the body, Sir, while I rode to Umvutcha to alert Sir Charles Fletcher, as that was the closest help. Sir Charles and I went back to the crime scene, Sir. After he saw what had happened, he and I rode into town, leaving Mr Barber there again. I went to the police station to make a report and Sir Charles went to tell Mrs Craig, Sir.'

'Thank you. It must have been a shocking experience. Now going back to the night before; were Mr Payne and Mr Brown at the Big Rock Mine then?'

'Mr Brown left at lunchtime to go home, Sir. He said he was not feeling well. Mr Payne also went off in the afternoon. He wanted to go shooting. He arrived back at the mine before dinner, with an impala ram. A dead impala ram, that is.'

'Thank you for clarifying that. I have no further questions.'

The defense lawyer pushed his chair back and stood up. He questioned how sick Mr Brown was on that particular day.

'He was coughing, Sir. He seemed poorly to me.'

'I see. Just coughing, you say.'

'Yes Sir.'

'And Mr Payne, does he go out shooting often?'

'Yes Sir. He shoots for our rations at the mine.'

'Thank you, that is all.'

Mr John Barber was called next and he corroborated Mr Williams's story. After this, the mine manager was called to the witness box.

'Good morning, Mr Henderson,' the prosecutor said. 'Can you recall, was Mr Craig at the mine the day before he was murdered?'

'He was.'

'What was he doing there?'

'Checking on things, and collecting the gold ingots we had for him.'

'Did he do this often?'

'What?'

'Come out to the mine to collect the gold?'

'Yes.'

'Would the mine workers know he was collecting gold to take back to town?'

'Well, we never shouted it from the roof tops, but I'm sure many have worked it out.'

'And how many ingots did you hand over to Mr Craig that time?'

'Four.'

'Thank you Mr Henderson. Now, turning to the defendants. Is Mr Brown often sick?'

'No, this was the first time since he came to work at the mine.'

'And did you think he was sick enough to warrant taking time off?'

'No, but he was insistent.'

'And has Mr Payne always shot game to supply meat for the mine?'

'No. He only started doing this a month or so ago.'

'To your knowledge, would either Mr Payne or Mr Brown have known that Mr Craig was going to spend the night at his farm on the way home?'

'Mr Brown would have known. One of his jobs was to pack Mr Craig's saddlebags. He would have packed food for him to eat at the farm.'

'No further questions.'

The defense lawyer stood up. Again there was the sound of his chair scraping on the wooden floor.

'Mr Henderson, before Mr Payne started shooting meat for the mine, where did you get your meat from?'

'Other workers at the mine go shooting, or otherwise we buy meat from people in the area; farmers, passers-by.'

'So Mr Payne was doing you a favour, taking over this duty?'

'I didn't see it like this. We never had a problem with our meat supply before he started making a habit of going shooting most afternoons. The way I saw it, he was using it as an excuse to get out of work.'

'But at least no one else had to worry about it.'

'I suppose not.'

'And Mr Brown, you say he had never been sick before?'

'Not that I know of.'

'But he may have been sick and you didn't know?'

'He may have been. I don't make a habit of playing nurse for my workers. All I know is he has never asked for sick leave before, and I didn't think he was sick this time.'

'Thank you. No further questions.'

'We will adjourn for lunch,' the judge said. Everyone rose, and he scurried from the room through a side door.

The crowd was still gathered outside the police station, calling for information from everyone who came out of the room. The two women who had been sitting with Mabel were immediately surrounded, as they started talking about what had transpired. James and Edward refused to say anything, pushing their way, instead, through the throng as they made their way to the Club in Main Street. It was a relief to get away from the police station, but the lunch break was soon over, and they had to get back for the afternoon session.

The first witness to be called after the lunch break was Constable Carruthers, one of the policemen who escorted Sir Charles Fletcher and

Mr Williams back to the crime scene in the early hours of the fateful morning. He described what he saw when he first got there; the body lying in a thicket, as if it had been dragged there, with a deep wound on the head.

'Did he not, perhaps, hit his head on a branch of a tree as he was riding through the thicket?' the prosecutor asked.

'No, we found a heavy log nearby with specks of blood and hair on it. We could tell that it was not a branch that had broken from a tree because it had been cut.'

'What else did you find Constable Carruthers?'

'Not much. There was a storm that night, and the rain washed away a lot of evidence we may otherwise have found. Foot prints or hoof prints for instance. We were lucky there was still some blood on the log. Probably because it had been tossed under a bush.'

'And did you find anything else at the scene?'

'An assegai, near the body of the deceased.'

'Did this assegai have blood on it?'

'No.'

'Does it have any distinguishing marks?'

'It has a pattern on it, but nothing abnormal.'

'Did you take fingerprints from the assegai?'

'No, we could not as it is made of wood. We tried to find some on the metal spear part of it, but there were none.'

'Can you explain the presence of this weapon?'

'No. It appears to have no relevance to the crime.'

'Do you have any idea what time the crime may have taken place?'

'No, but the body was cold and stiff by the time we got there, which means he must have been dead for at least eight hours.'

'And what time did you get there?'

'It was 3.45am.'

'What did you do after inspecting the crime scene?'

'We waited for the cart to arrive, to take the body back to Bulawayo. Then we took the horse to the police station, to examine it.'

'And did you find anything?'

'The saddlebag had clothes and a flask in it. We took fingerprints from the flask.'

'And whose fingerprints did you find on this flask?'

'The deceased's fingerprints, and those of Mr Brown. There were more fingerprints from Mr Brown than the deceased, which led us to believe that he handled the flask last.'

The prosecutor paused, to allow this information to sink in. 'How so?'

'Well, Mr Brown's fingerprints were over Mr Craig's.'

'Was there anything in the flask?'

'No, but it smelt of whisky.'

'One last question. Did you find any gold ingots at the scene of the crime?'

'No.'

'Thank you, no further questions.'

The prosecutor threw himself into his chair and took a sip of his water. The defense lawyer scribbled in his notes and then stood up.

'Constable Carruthers,' he said. 'You state the fingerprints indicate Mr Brown handled the flask last?'

'Yes'

'By looking at fingerprints, is it possible for you establish, with any degree of accuracy, when an item was last handled?'

'No.'

'So, Mr Brown's fingerprints may have been left when he was packing the flask into the saddle bag at the mine? Do you not agree?'

'Yes, except this would mean three things. 1. He packed an empty flask into the saddlebag, 2. Mr Craig did not touch it again, and 3.

No fingerprints rubbed off in the twenty-four odd hours after he left the mine.'

'But none of these suppositions are unreasonable, are they?'

'Not unreasonable, no.'

'How long have the police in this country been using fingerprints in their investigations?'

'This is the first time.'

'Ah, so you are not experts in this field?'

'We have practiced on ourselves at the police station.'

'Mm, but that still does not make you fingerprint experts, does it?' He turned the page of his file without looking up, reading his notes and scribbling in the margin. 'But moving on. Constable Carruthers, you say you cannot explain the assegai at the crime scene. Do you not suppose the perpetrator of the crime may have been a native?'

'We have not ruled this out, but it seems unlikely he would have left his weapon behind as evidence.'

'But not beyond the realms of possibility?'

'No.'

As there were no further questions for this witness, the judge said they would adjourn until ten o'clock the next morning.

The crowd was still hovering outside the police station, desperate to get the latest developments. Again, James and Edward had to push their way through the throng to get to their carriage.

'I am surprised at the level of interest in this case,' Edward said, as he climbed into the Spider.

'Sergeant Smythe did warn me about this. He thinks they will all be hoping the judge rules in favour of Payne and Brown.' James said.

'The hearing could go either way at this stage. The evidence is circumstantial, and the defense has been good at contradicting it.'

'Yes, but the prosecution still has to bring on their main witness; Fred Payne's girlfriend. We'll see what the judge makes of her.'

As it turned out, not a great deal. She was the first witness to be called the next day. She rose from her seat and wafted across the room to the witness box, smiling at anyone who caught her eye, as if she was the leading actress in a play. She was wearing a gown of peacock blue, with a peacock feather in her hat. She placed her hand on the bible and purred, 'My name is Melody Madison and I promise to tell nothing but the truth,' before sitting down in the witness box. As she did this, the peacock feather floated into her face. She blew it away, but it drifted back, so she took the pins out of her hat and turned it to a jauntier angle, with the feather falling over her ear. The courtroom was captivated by her antics, until the prosecutor broke the mood by jumping up and clearing his throat.

'Miss Madison, please can you tell us where you work.'

'At Haddon and Sly, Your Honour, as a sales lady in the newly established woman's department, Your Honour.'

'Not Your Honour.'

'I beg your pardon?'

'Please don't call me Your Honour.'

'Oh, sorry Your Worship.'

'Not Your Worship either.'

'Sorry?'

'Don't call him anything,' the judge interrupted. 'Just answer his questions.'

'Yes. Your Lordship.'

'It's "My Lord".'

'Yes, Your Lord.'

The judge stared at Miss Madison. 'Please continue, Mr Prosecutor,' he said.

'Miss Madison, what is your relationship with Mr Brown?' the prosecutor asked.

'I do not have a relationship with him, Your, um, your…' she fidgeted. 'He is married.'

'But are you friends?'

'We are not close friends. I have only met him a few times.'

'And Mr Payne? What is your relationship with him?'

'We were courting for a while, until September, that is.'

'But you have remained friends?'

'Yes, he takes me for tea when he is in town. To the Grand Hotel.'

'And did he take you there recently?'

'Last time he was in town, yes.'

'And what did he tell you about Mr Craig?'

'That he worked for him.'

'And what else?'

'Nothing that I can recall, except what a shame it was that he had been killed, and all.'

'And?'

'That's about it.'

'But you told Constable,' the prosecutor checked his notes. 'You told Constable Craven something else.'

Miss Madison lifted her hand to her head and shifted her hat again.

'Miss Madison, please tell the court what else you told Constable Craven.'

'Um, I can't think of anything else.'

'Surely you can.'

'No.'

'You told Constable Craven that Mr Payne told you he was involved in the murder. He wrote this in his notes which I have in front of me.'

'Well exactly, because the murdered man was his boss.'

The prosecutor took a paper from his file, and read through it. He spent some minutes looking for the part he wanted.

'Here,' he said, giving it to Miss Madison. 'You made a statement here that Mr Payne confessed to you that he was involved in actually killing Mr Craig, and that Mr Brown was his accomplice.'

'His what?'

'That he was involved too.'

'Oh he was, because he worked for Mr Craig also. That's what I meant.'

'But that's not what is written in this statement.'

'Oh really? The constable obviously misunderstood what I was saying.'

'Then why did you not put him right before you signed the statement?'

Melody Madison fumbled in her sleeve for her handkerchief. 'I'm sorry, your, um your, I'm, I don't know what to say.' She whimpered, dabbing the corners of her eyes with the handkerchief. 'I didn't realise he had misunderstood me. I thought he knew Fred and Percy worked for Mr Craig. I didn't know I had to explain anything more to him. Honestly, I did not.'

'So what is your testimony now?'

'I don't know anything, except Fred and Percy worked for Mr Craig. That's all I know.' She dabbed her eyes again with her handkerchief, then used it to blow her nose.

The prosecutor stared at Miss Madison for a long time, before flicking through his notes again.

'I have no further questions for this witness, My Lord.' He sat down.

'Miss Madison,' the defense lawyer said, leaping to his feet. 'Can you read?'

'A little, Your... um...'

'So did you read Constable Craven's report?'

'No, but he read it to me, I think.'

'Do you understand the seriousness of what has happened? That a man has lost his life?'

'Oh yes. It is very sad, very sad indeed. Especially with the baby and all.'

'So why did you get confused?'

'It was not me who got confused. Constable Craven misunderstood me, when I was telling him about Fred working for Mr Craig. I didn't realise he'd written the wrong thing in his report.'

'Thank you, no further questions.'

Miss Madison put her hand to her hat, as she stepped from the witness box and tottered back to where she had been sitting.

'Do you have any more witnesses to call?' the judge asked.

'My lord,' the prosecutor said. 'I would have called Constable Craven, to clarify the discrepancy in the previous witness's testimony, but as the court knows, the constable died last week when he fell off his horse and broke his neck. Therefore, I have no further witnesses.'

There were murmurs around the room, as they digested this.

However, the defense lawyer had more witnesses to call. Mr Robinson and Mr Sarsons gave testimony of Percy's good character, and two more testified for Fred Payne. Finally he called Mrs Peggy Pingstone to the witness box.

'What is your relationship with the defendant, Mr Brown?'

'He is my neighbour.'

'And were you home on the afternoon of 4th October 1905?'

'Yes. I was there with my children.'

'And your husband?'

'No, he was away.'

'And did you notice anything that afternoon?'

'Yes, that Mr Brown had come home?'

'Did you see him?'

'No, but I saw his horse and I wondered why he had come back during the week. The horse was grazing in the paddock behind the house.'

This wrapped up proceedings. The judge said they would gather the next morning at ten o'clock, when he would announce his decision.

'I have never, ever, in my whole life come across anyone as stupid as Miss Melody Madison,' James said, when they were travelling home in the Spider. 'What a total farce that woman has made of the case.'

'Such a tragedy Constable Craven had his accident and died before he could verify what she said, and did not say,' Edward said.

'Well yes, that's how it is, when you live in the wilds, like we do.'

The judge delivered his verdict the next day. There was not enough substantial evidence to try Mr Percy Brown or Mr Frederick Payne for the murder of Mr Anthony Craig. They were released from custody, and both headed straight for the Exchange Bar to celebrate.

James went to find Isabella in her studio, as soon as he got back to Sunrising. He did not go into details about what an idiot Miss Madison had seemed to be, only that there had not been enough evidence against Mr Brown and Mr Payne.

'Oh my, I am so relieved to hear this. It is bad enough that Anthony was murdered, but to think it could have been someone we knew who did it. I hated the idea of this. I am sure the police will eventually find out what happened.'

Chapter 20

IT was James's turn to feel depressed now. The preliminary hearing left him despondent and unmotivated as the reality of his loss sank in. Every morning he would drag himself to the MEC offices in Bulawayo, or out to the mines, trying to make sense of the operation. But he knew he was only going through the motions. Life seemed pointless and meaningless to him now.

He would try to rationalise his depression by thinking about Isabella, and how she must be feeling. For him, losing his partner and friend was terrible, but for her, it had to be shattering. And yet, since the preliminary hearing, she seemed to have made an improvement. She was no longer closing herself in her studio and losing herself in her work. Now, she was joining the rest of the household again for their meals and other gatherings.

She seemed to be coping better in every way, except when it came to her son, Oliver. She still showed only the remotest interest in him, and Celia was left with the task of being his primary carer. No one said anything about this, preferring instead to pretend that Isabella's behaviour was normal, and hoping she would gradually become more attached to her son.

Celia went to find Isabella in her studio, taking little Oliver with her. She propped him up in an armchair, shifting the cushions around him so he wouldn't roll off. Archie jumped up from his mat and ran across the room to sniff him.

'Ah, no,' Celia said. 'Shoo!'

'It's all right, Celia, he's just being friendly. Don't worry.'

Celia walked to the window and looked out. The day was warm and humid, but she could see dark rain clouds in the north. 'I think it may rain again tonight,' she said.

'That would be nice. I always love a storm. Especially when I'm snug in my bed and can hear the rain pounding on the tin roof, and then in the morning the sky is clear and blue again.'

'It's good to hear you sounding content, Isabella.'

'It's thanks to all of you being here, keeping the house busy and vibrant.'

'Yes, Edward's boys are noisy.'

'I'm not talking about Henry and Johnny, although I don't mind hearing their squeals and yells when they are playing different games to occupy themselves. No, what I'm talking about is all of you, in general. Just being here and getting on with your lives. I do not know what I would have done without you.'

'We are glad to be here. There is nothing like the support of one's family.' Celia paused as she drew the curtain back a little more. 'Talking of 'getting on with our lives', I've been thinking about Christmas, and whether we should invite Muriel and Philip and their new baby to spend it with us. You haven't even met little Barnaby yet.'

Isabella looked up from her painting. 'Why Celia, that is an excellent idea, I would so love to have them around. Yes, please, do ask them.'

Before Celia came up with this suggestion, Isabella had been trying to push all thoughts of Christmas out of her mind. Last Christmas she had been mourning the loss of her baby, William, and now she was mourning the loss of her husband. She still could not accept she had lost the two most important people in her life, one so soon after the other. But somehow, she knew, the idea of Muriel and

Philip being with them would help her face the 'festive season' with a little less trepidation.

A few days later she resolved to go into the bush and find something that could be used as a Christmas tree.

'Can we come with you, Aunt Isabella?' Henry yelled, when he saw her heading across the vlei with Archie.

'Yes, of course.'

Johnny jumped up from the sofa on the veranda, where he had been lying, and sprinted after them. 'Where are we going?' he called.

'I want to find a tree we can put Christmas decorations on.'

Both boys looked about. 'I don't see any Christmas trees.' Henry said. 'We get them sent from Cape Town, when we are at home.'

'There aren't any here, and Cape Town is too far away to have one sent from there. No, what we need is to find something in the bush that we can use as a Christmas tree. Let each of us start looking, and once we have all found something we can decide which one is best. Remember to watch for snakes when you are running through the grass.'

It took a while to find something they could all agree on. Johnny was keen on a green feathery bush, but Isabella managed to convince him that in a day or two it would wilt and look sad. Henry pointed to a branch on a tree which he thought was the right shape, but it was full of leaves, and they all agreed the leaves would soon die and make a nasty mess on the floor. Finally, they found a dead tree lying in the path near the stream.

'That's the one, that's the one,' Johnny yelled, running up to it and jumping on the end, breaking a piece off.

'Now look what you've done,' Henry shouted. 'Get off, stupid.'

'Now, now boys. No harm done, but yes, keep off it, Johnny. We don't want any more breaking off,' Isabella said. 'In fact, why don't you two stand it upright, so I can take a better look?'

They struggled to lift it, wobbling as they heaved it upwards.

'Yes, I believe this will do. It's got lots of branches and twigs for us to hang our baubles and decorations from. What do you think boys?'

Neither of them could see it properly, standing next to it as they were, but Henry said, 'I think it will be very nice, Aunt Isabella.'

'Excellent, thank you. Now, do you think you can carry it to the house, without breaking off any more branches or twigs?'

They struggled as they made their way back, shouting reprimands at each other as first one, then the other, dropped their end of the tree and managed to lose more bits. But finally they had it on the veranda.

'Stand it in the corner, and go and ask Somani to fill a bucket with sand. When he has done this put the bucket near the piano and push our tree into the sand. Can you do this boys, while I go and find the decorations?'

'Yes, Aunt Isabella,' Henry answered.

Isabella went to the library to look for the Christmas decorations in a cupboard there, and found James sitting at her desk, writing a letter.

'Ah, Isabella,' he said, putting down his pen. 'You are just the person I wanted to see.'

'Oh yes?'

'I am writing to my solicitor, making sure there are no problems with transferring Anthony's shares in the MEC and the farm into your name.'

Isabella said nothing.

He sensed her reluctance to discuss anything to do with Anthony. 'I'm sorry to bring it up, but we do need to make some changes.'

'Yes, I know.'

'There is another sensitive subject I would like to discuss with you. Can I do this now? There is a matter I want to clarify with you as soon as possible.'

Isabella glanced at the door. The boys would be a while, she concluded.

'Yes James, of course.'

'Have you any idea what you may do in the future? Where you want to live, what you want to do?'

Isabella hesitated. 'Well, at first I thought I'd go back to England and live with my father again. But the more I think about this, the more I do not want to. I came out to Africa to get away from the dreary English light, and since I've been spending so much time painting in the last few weeks, I realise, more and more, how much I want to stay here and paint this light.'

'Well, I'm happy to hear this,' James said, taking his pipe from the ashtray and puffing on it. 'You know, many would say that Rhodesia is not a place for a woman, er, on her own.'

'Yes, I know, and of course it's a worry for me.'

'I have been giving your situation a great deal of thought, and now that you have told me that you want to stay, there is something I am going to do.' He puffed on his pipe again. 'I am going to transfer Sunrising into your name. At least you and Oliver will then always have a roof over your heads.'

'What? But, James. You cannot.'

'It is what I want to do.'

'But, this is your house.'

'True. It was I who had it built. However, it is you who made it into a home.'

'But still.'

'I would feel much less worried about you if the house belonged to you.'

Isabella fumbled for a chair and sat down. She put her hand to her head, and bit her lip, trying to stop herself from crying.

James resisted the temptation to get up and comfort her.

'But, what about you?' Isabella asked. 'Will you still live here?'

'I am thinking of moving to The Club in the New Year. It will be so much easier to get to the office from there.'

'Oh no, please don't. You have your wing here. It will always be your wing.'

'That's kind. Maybe I can come back for weekends.'

'But this is your home,' she repeated.

'No, it is yours.'

'You cannot call The Club your home?'

'True. I'm thinking that I may build a new home for myself on the farm. I will have to wait for the rainy season to be over, and the rivers to go down again, but do you not think that sounds like a grand idea?'

Isabella felt too overwhelmed to have an opinion about anything right then.

'It's alright,' James said. 'We do not need to set anything in stone. I just want you to know what I am thinking.'

They could hear arguing in the hall. 'Well thank you James. As always, you are too kind, but I had better go and separate those boys before their argument gets any worse. We are trying to decorate a Christmas tree in the drawing room.' She opened the cupboard and found the box of decorations. 'Thank you again,' she said, briefly touching his shoulder as she left the room.

*

The Weirs arrived at teatime on Christmas Eve. They found Isabella sitting on the veranda sketching Archie, who was sleeping in a chair opposite her. He jumped up and ran to meet them as soon as he saw them.

'Ah, now look what you've done. You have disturbed my model,' Isabella laughed, putting her sketchpad down. She stood up to greet her friends.

193

'How wonderful to see you both again.'

Muriel threw Isabella a glance. She had not seen her since the day after Anthony's death, and she could see that the pain she had been through had taken its toll. She had lost weight, and despite smiling, there was an aura of sadness about her. Muriel gave her an extra tight hug.

'But, where is Barnaby?' Isabella asked, looking over her shoulder.

'Nanny has taken him straight to their room to freshen up.'

'Nanny?'

'Oh yes, Nanny Whittle. We employed her last week. She's wonderful. We need to find a nanny for Oliver too. It makes life so much easier.'

Gonda appeared at the door. 'Good afternoon Mr and Mrs Weir,' he said, honouring them with one of his splendid bows. 'We have brought your tea.' Hlabano put the tea tray on the table next to the door. 'Can I pour for you Madam?' Gonda asked Isabella.

'No, don't worry. I will do it. Has everyone been shown their rooms?'

'Yes, Madam. Moses has done this.'

'And very comfortable they are too,' Philip said, eyeing the Christmas cake on the tea tray. 'This looks delicious. Our journey from town seemed to take forever. Muriel packed some food, but, by Jove, I'm feeling peckish now. Where are the others?'

Isabella cut a slice of cake and put it on a plate.

'Please, have some now,' she said, handing it to him. 'Everyone went for a walk before tea, except James, who is still at the office. He is there for horrendously long hours, trying to make sense of everything.'

'Yes, he will need to find a manager as soon as he can. It cannot be easy for him, and especially with the MEC doing so well now.'

Isabella fell silent. She hated the idea of anyone taking over Anthony's position at the MEC.

Muriel noticed her discomfort. 'Now come, my dear. Let's have our tea so that we can go and admire each other's babies. I cannot wait to show you my gorgeous boy and introduce you to the delightful Miss Whittle.'

*

'Celia, you look lovely,' James said, as Celia walked into the drawing room where everyone had gathered before dinner that night. Isabella heard this, as she was crossing the hall on her way to the drawing room too. She stopped and looked at herself in the hall mirror. She doubted he would say the same to her and mean it, she thought to herself. She had lost far too much weight, and all her sleepless nights had taken their toll.

They usually had their drinks before dinner on the veranda, but there had been a vicious storm earlier, making it damp and cool outside. The drawing room was a much more comfortable option. Isabella took a deep breath, and entered the room just as Celia was accepting a glass of champagne from James. How right he is, she thought. Life in Rhodesia is agreeing with her. All the fresh air and rides had done her a world of good.

'Champagne, Isabella?' James asked when he saw her.

'Yes please, thank you.' She accepted a glass from him and sat on the sofa next to Muriel. 'How wonderful it is to have all of you here,' she said.

'We are delighted too,' Muriel said.

Edward walked to the fireplace and clinked his glass with his finger before putting it on the mantelpiece. 'Family and friends, I would like to make an announcement,' he said. 'Please, may I have your attention? Alice and I have made some exciting decisions these last few days.' He picked up his champagne glass again. 'I have been offered a job as a surveyor here in Bulawayo and have agreed to accept this position. Is this not splendid news? Please, let us drink a toast to what we are sure will be a long and satisfying time back in Bulawayo.'

'Oh, how wonderful,' Celia said, jumping up and kissing her brother.

'So what are your plans? When do you start?' Philip asked.

'I start the job in the New Year. Alice will travel back to Victoria West at some stage in the next few months to pack up our house, but I will stay here.'

'And the boys?'

'We are looking for a governess, until they are older.'

'Aha,' Muriel interrupted. 'Speak to me later. I believe I know just the right person for you.'

'So James, may we trespass on your hospitality for a few months longer?' Edward asked.

'Ask Isabella, this is her home.'

Isabella blushed and looked at her hands.

'I have announcement to make too,' James said. 'Sunrising has been transferred into Isabella's name. We signed all the necessary paper work last week. At first she resisted my offer, but eventually she understood that it is what I want for her and Oliver. Isabella told me how much she loves living here in Rhodesia. It makes sense, therefore, for Sunrising to belong to her, don't you think? I know it would make Anthony very happy.'

'Goodness gracious, absolutely,' said Muriel.

'But that is so generous of you,' Edward said.

'And such a weight off our shoulders,' Alice murmured. 'We were starting to worry about what Isabella would do.'

'Well I am glad it's all settled then,' Isabella said. 'I am grateful to you James.' The dinner gong sounded in the dining room. 'Ah, ha. Let us go in for dinner, I am determined to make the most of having you all here for this Christmas season.'

Chapter 21

'You cannot live in that uncivilized country as a single woman,' Isabella's father had written in his last letter. His words had unsettled her, until Edward's announcement that he and his family would be living in Bulawayo again. Isabella hated upsetting her father, or going against his wishes, but surely he would have no complaint now that her brother and sister-in-law would be living here too? Not that the Braithewaites intended living at Sunrising. They were already considering where they should build, or buy, a house. The Weirs told them how much they enjoyed living in the Avenues, near the town centre. But the Heymans said they preferred the Suburbs, over the stream and near the golf course where Mr Heyman played a round every weekend. Then Edward bumped into Colonel Napier at The Club who waxed lyrical about living in the Hillside area, with rocky kopjies and undulating vleis.

'What is a kopjie?' Celia asked.

'A small hill, or maybe it is better described as a pile of large rocks, balancing one on another,' Edward said.

'Mmm, sounds like it could be a haven for snakes,' Celia said, having encountered a cobra on her walk through the bush the day before. She still shuddered at the thought of it.

'My fear exactly,' Alice said. 'I know you cannot get away from snakes in Africa, but I still prefer to be in open areas where there is less likelihood of coming across them.'

'Yes, my dear,' Edward said. 'But they almost always try to make themselves scarce. Snakes avoid humans as much as they can. Always remember this.'

'I know, but that's why I don't like the idea of living amongst piles of rocks. They may just try to hide themselves amongst the rocks, and become angry if they are disturbed.'

'Well at least we don't have to make a decision for a few months yet,' Edward said.

Alice had asked Isabella to accompany her to Victoria West "sometime in March", to pack up the Braithewaite's house. They were unable to set an exact date because James had requested they go only after making another expedition to the farm with him. He had plans to erect and unveil a gravestone for Anthony. He also wanted their help in choosing a site for his new home. But he could not be specific about when they would do this because they had to wait for the rains to subside and the rivers to go down. At the moment it was raining every day, and the rivers were full and flooding. They would not be able to travel to the farm when there was so much water about, because the Umguza River was impossible to cross.

'How exciting and unpredictable life is in Rhodesia, that we have to make our plans around flooding rivers,' Celia said.

'Frustrating, more like it,' Edward said. 'I'm looking forward to having my own home in Bulawayo, filled with my own possessions. The sooner the rivers stop flooding, the sooner this will happen. I look forward to the day when we start building bridges in this country.'

'I understand,' Isabella said, 'but we have to go along with James and his plans. I am longing to go out to the farm again. The last time was so difficult, but now it will be better. I want to see how young Toby Tate is getting on. I believe he is a very bright little boy.' She sighed. 'Going back to James. I so wish he had not felt the need to go and live at the Club. Sunrising will always be his house, as far as I am concerned, even though he insists it's now mine.'

'Well, he left Gonda here, so he must still consider it his home, to some extent,' Edward said. 'And of course he will be back most weekends.'

'True.'

'But Isabella,' Celia said. 'While we are waiting for the rivers to go down, why don't we start working on our bird project? Remember, I mentioned it a while back?'

'Yes.'

'You paint whichever birds you like, and I'll find out as much as I can about them and write down all their details. While you, Alice, and Oliver are in Victoria West, I can put our work together. Then, when I go back to England, I can have it set out properly and books printed. I spoke to James about it, and he said he would pay to have this done. Would it not be wonderful for our family and friends to have a book like this?'

Isabella could not think about books. Something else Celia had just said was worrying her. 'You aren't planning on going back to England anytime soon, are you?'

'I cannot stay here forever. I have to save poor Papa from Aunt Elizabeth at some stage.'

'Oh no, I hate the idea of your going back. I am sure Aunt Elizabeth is doing a fine job looking after Papa.'

'But I promised Aunt Elizabeth I would eventually return. However, I would love to do our bird book first. As you know, I have always been fascinated with the bird life here.

'All right. I will start by painting the crested cranes we see in the vlei every day, and I will do my paintings on paper so they are easy for you to transport. They don't have to be big paintings, do they?'

'No, not at all. If you want to start with a crested crane, I will study their behaviour and make notes. I will speak to others about them.'

Isabella left her family, having their sundowners on the veranda, and went to her studio. The thought of Celia leaving upset her more than she wanted them to know. It was at times like these she knew how vulnerable she still was. In reality, she felt as confused as ever and still had no sense of real purpose to her life.

*

Muriel telephoned. 'Isabella, darling. I believe I have just the right person for you to employ as Oliver's nanny.'

'Oh my. That would be so convenient. Celia and I have started working on our bird project, so we need someone to look after him more. He's a good little fellow, and sleeps a lot, but sometimes it's hard to concentrate when he is around.'

'You need to learn to separate work time from baby time, Isabella. But come for tea tomorrow morning, here at the house, and I can introduce you to Miss Estelle Harrison. Bring Oliver with you.'

When Isabella walked into Muriel's drawing room the next day, holding a sleepy Oliver in her arms, Miss Harrison rose like a heron from her chair.

I have been painting too many birds, Isabella thought to herself, as she looked at Miss Harrison and the painting of the grey heron she had done sprung to mind. Maybe it's the grey dress, with a touch of cream at the throat, she thought. But no, Miss Harrison had the appearance of a heron. Tall and thin with a long neck, accentuated by her grey hair pulled back in a bun and small round glasses perched on her long, narrow nose.

'How do you do,' Isabella said, holding out her free hand as Oliver pushed his flushed face against her breast. Muriel was pleased to see that Isabella was carrying him, and not Celia. She had given her a stern talking to over Christmas when she saw how little attention she was giving her baby. It seemed to have paid off. She was finally making more time for Oliver.

'Why don't you lie him on the mat next to Barnaby?' Muriel said. 'Let's see how long they can stay quiet.'

Celia had been tying Queenie's rein to the hitching post. She joined them just as Muriel was handing Isabella and Miss Harrison a cup of tea. 'Ah, Celia, can I give you a cup?'

'Yes please.'

'And may I introduce Miss Harrison.'

'I am known as Harry,' Miss Harrison said.

'Aha, well that's easy enough.'

'What have you been doing in Rhodesia?' Isabella asked.

'I came to this part of the world in an ox wagon with the Clarks,' she said.

'Oh my goodness.'

'Yes, and when my services with them were no longer required I was offered a post with the Greaves family. I've been living on their farm in Nyamandhlovu ever since. But now they are going to go to the convent school in Bulawayo. Mrs Greaves hoped I would find enough to do around their newly built farm house to keep myself occupied, as they are very isolated where they live and she enjoys having me there. She thought I could keep myself busy with household chores, but quite frankly, they already have enough staff, and I have found myself getting very bored with no children to look after anymore, so I handed in my notice.' She fumbled in her pocket, before removing a letter, which she handed to Isabella. 'Here is my reference from Mrs Greaves.'

Isabella unfolded the paper and read it. 'I do not know Mrs Greaves well, but she seems to have been happy with the way you looked after her children' she said, handing it back.'

'Such delightful children,' Harry said. 'I will miss them a great deal. I was their governess. I taught them to read and write, as well as their

numbers. They are bright children and learnt everything I taught them.
,

'They are very young to be going off to boarding school,' Isabella murmured, glancing at the reference again and then handing it back to Miss Harrison. 'Well I am sure you will find my Oliver delightful too. He is a very easy baby. When would you be able to start with us?'

'As soon as you would like, Mrs Craig. The Greaves are in town at the moment, staying at the Palace Hotel until the rivers go down and they can return to their farm. I brought most of my possessions with me, when we left the farm, so I am ready to leave them whenever it is convenient for you. Mrs Weir took the liberty of telling Mrs Greaves about your predicament, so they will understand if I do not stay with them any longer.'

*

Harry carried baby Oliver up to Isabella's studio. Isabella had asked her to bring him to her every afternoon when he woke from his afternoon sleep. Harry knew about the tragic events in Isabella's life and how fragile she was. She could see she had to make an effort to stop working and spend time with her son.

They went through the same routine every afternoon. Isabella would take Oliver from her and kiss him on the head then walk with him to her easel.

'And what do you think of this bird, Olly?' she would ask.

Oliver would gurgle and kick and she would then take him to the window where they would stand and look at the view together. But then Oliver would start wriggling and writhing in her arms. That's when she would lay him on the mat with her dog. Oliver would roll around and reach out for Archie, who would wag his tail and try to lick him.

Harry felt sad for Mrs Craig. What a traumatic few years she had had, no wonder she was still struggling. On the face of it, Mrs Craig seemed to have so much. She was charming, she was talented, and she had a beautiful son, yet Harry could see that the tragedies in her life had left deep scars.

When she had been staying at the Palace Hotel with the Greaves, she had heard people talking about the alleged murder and the farcical preliminary hearing. But if they never found out who did it, how could Mrs Craig ever have closure on the whole ordeal?

Isabella interrupted her train of thought. 'If you were to be one of these birds I've painted, Harry, which one would it be?'

Harry looked about. There were little paintings of birds everywhere; on surfaces, pinned to the wooden rafters, lying on the floor.

'I think I would like to be this one,' she said, pointing to a small painting pinned to the doorframe.

'A Lilac Breasted Roller. How interesting.'

'I am attracted to the vibrant colours. The blue, the green, as well as the lilac breast.'

'Yes. It is striking. A good choice. Unfortunately I am still having great difficulty trying to make up my mind which bird I want to be.'

"How about this one?" Harry said, pointing to a painting of a yellow bird.

'A Golden Oriole? Do you think so?'

'Yes. It is you.'

'Well then I shall be a Golden Oriole. I do so love their melodious call.

Chapter 22

THE rains subsided in the middle of February and by the end of the month James estimated it was dry enough to plan their trek to the farm. He felt under pressure to do this as soon as possible. Alice Braithewaite was desperate to get back to Victoria West so that she could pack up their house there and bring all their belongings back to Bulawayo.

Once he had made his decision he went out to Sunrising at the first opportunity to organise the expedition.

'Although the rivers have stopped flooding, there will still be a lot of water about, as well as mud and thick bush. We will take the ox cart rather than the mules as the oxen are stronger and hardier,' he said.

Celia looked worried. Ox carts, mule carts, mud, thick bush, it was still all so foreign to her, despite having gone to the farm for Anthony's funeral. However, it had been October then, at the end of the dry season when the bush was dry and sparse.

'I think I will ride this time,' Isabella said. 'On Gunner. I have had breeches made so I will not even have to use my side saddle.'

'Are you sure you can manage?' Celia said. 'It's such a long way. Of course James and Edward can endure such a long journey on horseback, but you?'

'I can, and I will enjoy it.'

Isabella did, and as they made their laborious journey she concluded it was much easier on a horse than in the cart. The roads and tracks were overgrown with thick, long grass, but Gunner could push his way through it while the cart had to keep stopping to clear the way. When they crossed the rivers she gave Gunner his head so he was free to pick his way through the shallow water, unlike the oxen who had a much harder time, yoked together as they were. When one stepped into a hole and stumbled, they were all pulled over, and the cart lurched. The poor beasts struggled to pull the loaded cart, showing their displeasure with loud lows and bellows.

They reached Anthony's huts late in the afternoon. The grass had grown wild around them too. Isabella remembered when she'd tried to walk in long grass in a skirt the first time she had visited the farm. She did not want the others to have to go through the same uncomfortable experience.

'Stay where you are, until they have cut some of the grass,' she called to Celia, Alice and Harry, who were sitting on the cart.

'Oh gosh, I'm desperate to stretch my legs,' Alice said.

'Wait a while. It won't take long for Somani to slash the grass around here. You don't want to have grass seeds sticking to your underclothes. It happened to me once and it took forever to get them out.'

Gonda tried to make a fire, but could only find damp wood, so the air was soon filled with pungent smoke.

'Oh no, we cannot have that,' James said. 'I thought we may struggle to find dry wood after all the rain we've had, so I threw in some dry logs from Sunrising.' He dug in the back of the cart, and tossed them to Gonda. 'Mananga and Hlabanga, please help Mr Braithewaite offload the camping gear from the cart.

'I feel so useless, sitting in this cart while the men rush around setting up camp,' Celia said.

'It won't be for much longer,' Isabella said. She was feeling stiff and sore after her long ride, but she had no intention of telling anyone this. Wearing riding breeches and long boots as she was, at least she was able to walk about the campsite without fear of grass seeds sticking to unwanted areas. She opened the door of one hut, wondering what creatures may have chosen to make it their home. Nothing too serious, she discovered with relief. Just some spider webs in the rafters. The same with the second hut. She and Celia would sleep in one hut, while Harry and Oliver would take the other. The Braithewaites would have their own tent, and James would have another. The workers would make up their own campsite a short distance away in the bush, as they always did. The ringing sound of a hammer beating on metal pegs could already be heard, as tents were being erected.

With dry wood on the fire, it was soon crackling away, this time with little smoke. Gonda found the canvas chairs and set them out, and the women and children were able to get off the cart and sit around the fire.

'Are you alright?' Isabella asked Harry, taking Oliver from her and setting him on her lap.

'I am used to these rough conditions. When I first came to these parts with the Clarks we lived in tents. And then, when I moved to the farm in Nyamandhlovu with the Greaves family, we lived in pole and *dagga* huts, very similar to these. It was only last year that they were able to build a brick house. So don't worry, these conditions do not scare me.'

'Good, because they scare me,' Celia said.

Isabella reached over and squeezed her hand.

'This trip will be much nicer than the last time you were here, and you will love it in the end. James brought his tin bath. We will set it up in my hut tomorrow morning and get Gonda to boil some buckets of water from the river. I am sure we will all appreciate a scrub by then. I am afraid we will have to make do with wash bowls tonight.'

Archie jumped up from where he had been lying at Isabella's feet and ran across the campsite, barking. Toby Tate had appeared on his chestnut pony. He jumped off and tied the rein to a tree, before walking across the campsite to where they were sitting around the fire. He took off his hat, twiddling it in his hands.

'Toby, how pleased I am to see you,' Isabella exclaimed.

He looked embarrassed. 'Good afternoon Mrs Craig. I saw the smoke and came to see what was happening.'

'And so you should. Well done. We have come to stay here for three nights. Sir James had a stone carved for my husband's grave. We are going to set it up there tomorrow. After that we will spend our time riding about the place. Sir James wants to build a big house for himself out here, made from bricks, so we are going to look for the best spot. Maybe you can help us with this?'

Toby looked self-conscious as he glanced at everyone around the fire.

'This is my sister, who you will remember from last time we were here,' Isabella continued, 'and this is my brother and his wife and children, Henry and Johnny. They must be nearly your age.'

'Do you want me to bring more horses for them?'

'Grand idea,' Edward said. 'How many do you have to spare?'

'Three Sir.'

'Excellent. The boys can each ride one, and you ladies can fight over the other.'

'Count me out,' Harry said. 'I've never enjoyed riding horses.'

'Me too,' Alice said.

'Good. Well that leaves Celia, who has become a competent horsewoman since she's been in Rhodesia. Can you bring them here tomorrow morning?'

'Yes Sir,' Toby said.

He arrived back at the campsite the next morning just as everyone was starting to rise, except for Henry and Johnny who had been wide awake since before dawn. They were pleased to see him. There was just a moment of awkwardness before he suggested taking them to the river to show them his favourite fishing spots. They came back soon after looking for fishing rods.

'Ah ha, good thing I thought to bring some,' James said, standing next to the rekindled fire, drinking his morning cup of tea. 'You will find them in the back of the cart. Don't go far away. Remember, there are wild animals everywhere.'

'How charming it is, that children can mingle so easily, despite coming from such different backgrounds and cultures,' Harry said as she watched them rush off to the river again.

'Toby may be of mixed race, but he is bright, and has the good fortune of having a benefactor in Isabella. She has been supplying him with books and pencils these last eight months or so,' James said.

'And what is his parentage?'

'His father is the Englishman who lived on this property from the eighties until we bought it. Thomas Tate. His mother is a native, and when the father went back to England last year, Isabella stepped in and insisted they continue living here, making sure they have what they need.'

'With Anthony's help, and now yours,' Isabella said.

'True.'

'And is the father coming back?' Harry asked.

'He said he would,' Isabella said, 'but I have not heard from him in months, so I am no longer sure what is happening.'

'And if he does not return, what then?'

There was silence, while everyone pondered this.

'The mother's family?' Harry asked.

'No, they don't want them.'

There was silence again until Harry broke it.

'These situations are always so difficult and confusing,' she said.

*

On their last afternoon, James suggested to Isabella they go and visit Toby's mother, Lokuthula, before they left. They had seen a great deal of the boy during their visit. He, Henry and Johnny had been inseparable over the last few days, and thanks to him, Henry and Johnny now knew all the special and interesting places in the vicinity. And thanks to him too, James had found an interesting and attractive site for his proposed new house. It was along one of the tributaries going into the Umguza River and elevated, so it had views all around. James most liked the western vista, overlooking a now dry oxbow lake, with an enormous acacia galpini in the middle of the crescent.

Celia asked if she could go with them to see Lokuthula. She had a special regard for her after their shared experience of helping deliver Oliver. James suggested all three boys accompany them too. They took their time riding to the Tate's huts, going along the riverbanks in the hopes of spotting some wild animals. They were not disappointed, coming across a herd of impala, as well as two giraffe and some zebra in the distance.

When they arrived at the huts Toby and the other boys took the horses and tied them to some trees. Lokuthula came out of one of the huts, looking as shy as ever, her toddler hanging onto her leg.

'*Sebebuyile ukuzokubona Mama*,' Toby said.

'Yebo'

He ran into the hut, but came back holding a cloth bag in his hands. 'We have made some things for you,' he said, scratching in the bag. He brought out an exercise book and handed it to Isabella.

'I wrote you a story in this book, Mrs Craig, and I drew some pictures to show how the story goes.'

Isabella paged through the book. The pictures were rough, but bright and interesting looking. 'How clever of you to do this,' she said, passing the book to Celia. 'Thank you Toby. I will enjoy reading your story when I get home.

'It is about a young boy, who gets lost, but the birds guide him home.'

'Sounds like a good story line, and so clever of you to do the pictures.'

'They are with the pencils you gave me. I will write another story for you next time.' He dug in the bag again and brought out a crochet mat. 'Mama, she made this for you, Mrs Craig. It is like the last one she did for you.'

Isabella took the mat and held it to the light so she could see the intricate stitch work better. 'Oh my, this is beautiful. You are talented, Lokuthula.'

'Can you see that it is like the first one?'

She cast her mind back but could not remember another one. 'Sorry, I'm not sure which one you are talking about?'

'The one I gave Mr Craig, for you, on his last visit here, before, before he, he died,' he stammered.

Isabella was silent. The last thing she wanted was to think about that time. It had been difficult enough erecting Anthony's gravestone yesterday. She was about to change the subject when Celia grabbed the mat from Isabella and stared at it.

'Celia? What on earth? What's the matter? You look very strange.'

'I have seen a mat like this one before,' she said, looking flushed with excitement. 'Are you sure the other one was just like this Lokuthula?'

'Yes. I used a pattern from the book Mr Tate gave me, and he also bought me the cotton, before he went to England.'

'And when do you remember giving it to Mr Craig?'

'The night, no the day, when he was here last. He came to drop off the books and things for us. That is when I gave it to him.'

'And I gave him an assegai then too,' Toby piped up. 'I made it for him. I have made others too. Would you like one Sir?' he asked James.

Isabella was still confused, but James was starting to piece things together. 'Yes, please. Have you got one for me now?'

'Yes.' He disappeared into the hut again.

'What is going on?' Isabella asked Celia. 'Why are you looking so, well, so agitated? '

'When I went to see Mabel before the preliminary hearing, I sat in her front room. She had a mat like this one on her table,' Celia said.

Isabella paused. 'What a coincidence.'

'You think so?'

'Maybe she has the same crochet book as Lokuthula?'

'Another amazing coincidence?'

'But surely? No, surely not? But how?'

Toby came back with the assegai and gave it to James. James looked at it, turning it over and over in his hands. 'Was the other one exactly like this one?'

'Almost, Sir. I always put my initial on them when I have finish making them. T T, standing for Toby Tate. The other one had it too.'

'My God, we have stumbled on some important evidence,' James murmured.

Isabella was agitated, Celia excited, the boys had no idea what was going on, and Toby and his mother were equally confused. But James was now more determined than ever to solve the mystery surrounding Anthony's death. He had always had his suspicions that Percy Brown was involved, and these clues made him even more convinced. He now needed to find a way to have him convicted. He knew he could not go to the police with the mat and assegai and expect them to arrest Percy Brown. The man had public opinion on his side, and he would soon find enough excuses to worm his way out of any accusations like that. But there had to be a way he could be caught out. It would take time, but James would not rest until the mystery was solved once and for all.

Chapter 23

THE Grand Hotel was the place where the women-folk of Bulawayo liked to meet on Thursday mornings for tea. Quite how this custom came about, no one knew, but the manager, Mr Scott-Roger was making the most of his good fortune. A piano had been wheeled into a corner of the dining room, and Miss Cynthia Jones would play her way through a delightful repertoire of tunes she had taught herself. Mr Scott-Roger also made sure there were freshly baked scones and decadent chocolate cakes for his lady guests. He knew how much they enjoyed something delicious to have with their tea.

Like many others, Mabel Brown and Peggy Pingstone had made a habit of meeting for tea there on Thursday mornings. They usually sat at a table on their own; although they would spend a great deal of time greeting everyone they knew.

Mabel Brown had become something of a local celebrity since her husband had been wrongly implicated in the unfortunate alleged murder of Anthony Craig. No one ever mentioned this unpleasant episode to her, but they were pleased to see how well she and her husband were now doing. He had been offered a new job at the Near Enough Gold Mine, and, judging from how prosperous they now appeared, he must be receiving a better salary there than when he worked at the Big Rock Mine.

Mabel was wearing her new gloves and hat, and feeling good about herself, that is until her morning was shattered by the appearance of Isabella Craig and Celia Braithewaite at the dining room door. They never came for tea here anymore; this was one of the reasons Mabel liked it so much. She had to stop herself from gasping out loud when she saw them. Isabella, in turn, spotted her as she was walking into the room. She went white, and a strange look crossed her face, but Celia touched her elbow and whispered something, as she guided her sister to the only empty table on the far side. As such, they had to pass Mabel and Peggy, and Mabel saw Celia mouth the words, 'act normal,' as they approached them. Bitch, she thought, but she managed to arrange her face into a tight smile. The sisters stopped as they were passing her table. It seemed as if the room hushed for a moment, and all eyes were on them.

'Mabel, how are you?' Celia asked.

'Never better thank you.'

Isabella's smile looked more like a grimace.

'Very good to hear this,' Celia said to Mabel. She glanced at Peggy Pingstone, whom she did not know, but no one offered an introduction. There was a long and pregnant pause. 'Well, good to see you again. We won't keep you from your tea any longer.' They continued to their table.

'Those women are so stuck up,' Mabel hissed, once they were out of earshot and everything seemed normal again.

'But Mrs Craig has had a terrible time, you can't deny that. Look how thin and sad she looks,' Peggy said.

'Don't you worry; she'll be just fine. I heard Sir James gave her his house. Can you imagine that; just being given a house? While the rest of us have to work like slaves to acquire ours. Some people have all the luck in the world. She always gets what she wants.'

'I think you are being a bit harsh now. I'm sure she didn't want to lose her husband, especially with a new baby and all.'

Mabel regained her composure. She realised she might be sounding too vindictive. And she had so much more to be grateful for herself now that Percy was getting so well paid and they were expecting a baby of their own.

'You are right, Peggy, and Mr Craig was such a nice man. It will always sadden me that he died so young.'

*

Isabella could not wait to get away from Bulawayo. Bumping into Mabel at the Grand Hotel like that had been the final straw. She had hardly been able to walk to her table; her legs had been shaking so much. There was no doubt in her mind now that Percy Brown was involved in Anthony's murder. How else could Mabel have the crochet mat Lokuthula gave Anthony the day before he was murdered, if Percy had not taken it from him after he had been killed? Of course she had no way of knowing if Mabel was implicated in the murder, but seeing her sitting there, in all her finery, looking so smug and self-satisfied, was almost too much to bear.

James had warned Isabella and Celia not to say anything to anyone about their discovery. He had to find a way to get more evidence. He told them that if the Browns became aware of their suspicions, they might try to hide other clues, but if they thought they had got away with their crime, they could become complacent, and would then be more likely to drop their guard.

*

The train tickets were bought and their departure was imminent. Alice, Isabella, Oliver and Harry were going on the journey. It would take them three days by train to get to Victoria West in the Karoo Desert of South Africa. Alice thought it may take them up to a month to pack up their home, but she was looking forward to showing Isabella that part of the Northern Cape, with its Dutch and Afrikaans influences. Celia would remain at Sunrising to look after Edward and the boys while they were away. Isabella's only sadness about leaving was that she couldn't take Archie, but Celia assured her that he would be well looked after.

Finally they were on the train and chugging out of Bulawayo. They were in a four-sleeper First Class compartment. The top two bunks folded up during the day, leaving two benches facing each other for them to sit on.

'Well, this is comfortable enough,' Isabella said, 'and we can go to the dining carriage whenever we feel like a change. When I first came to Bulawayo over eight years ago, it was one of the first rail journeys since the opening of the railway line. It took us five days to get from Cape Town to Bulawayo and we did not have a dining car then. Every time the train stopped there were vendors, running up and down the tracks outside, selling eggs. Hard-boiled eggs to be exact, and little else. I ate so many eggs on that journey, I have never wanted to eat another hard-boiled egg since.'

Alice snorted. 'You think that was bad. Edward and I first travelled here in one of Mr Zeederberg's mule drawn coaches. Whenever the coach stopped we had to sneak into the bushes to relieve ourselves, far enough away from everyone so that we could not be seen. But I remember I always used to be scared that a wild animal would choose to attack me at that moment.'

'Oh my,' Isabella laughed. 'The thought of you bounding through the bush with your drawers wrapped around your ankles.

'Stop it; it was a nightmare.'

'Yes, I can well imagine. I do not know how you travelled in that coach for so long, Alice. I would have gone mad.'

'It was frightfully uncomfortable. What I remember most about the journey was a middle-aged woman sitting next to me. Every few minutes she would take out her handkerchief and wipe her brow and say, 'Oh it's just so hot!' When I think of that journey, it was she who drove me crazy. When I look back on it now, I do not know how I managed.'

'I am always grateful for modern comforts,' Isabella said. 'At least we can relax and enjoy the sights on this journey.'

'True,' Harry said. 'I will not even start telling you of the discomforts I had to endure on my initial journey here in the Clark's ox wagons.' She adjusted the pillows around the sleeping Oliver.

'While we are talking about being able to appreciate our journey this time, I came up with a wonderful idea,' Isabella said.

'And what is this?' Alice raised a suspicious eyebrow.

'Well, it was Toby who gave me the idea when we were out at the farm. I showed you the story book he made for me, with the story illustrated.'

'Yes.'

Isabella leant down to dig in the bag next to her feet. She brought out three sketchpads. She then scratched in the bag again and found three pencils. 'I took the liberty of buying these for us,' she said, handing one to Alice and another to Harry.

'But what for?' Alice asked.

'So that we can do little sketches of the things that attract us on our journey. We can draw pictures to illustrate our trip, so to speak. Is this not the most wonderful idea, and then we will have them for always to remember what we saw?'

'You can count me out,' Harry said, handing the sketchpad and pencil straight back.

'But Harry, I have even brought some water colour paints, to liven up our pictures.'

'That's all very well for you, but I have never had an artistic bone in my body, and at the age of forty something, I am not going to start developing one now. I will enjoy watching you do yours, but I will not even start attempting to do any of my own.' She pushed her thin buttocks deeper into the seat, winking at Alice as she did this.

Alice laughed.

'Isabella, you are the limit. You mean well, but we just don't have your talent. I will give it a try, while we are sitting in this train with little else to do, but don't expect too much.'

'Good, well I may just begin by sketching my son lying where he is.'

'And I may just go off to the dining car for a cup of tea, while the mite is still asleep,' Harry said. 'Would you care to join me, Mrs Braithewaite?'

'Indeed, I would. Anything to get out of doing my first sketch.'

*

Brilliant blue skies, distant horizons, sparse vegetation, churches with tall steeples and houses with Dutch gables. Isabella found a lot to inspire her in Victoria West. She painted as much as she could when she was not wrapping up glasses and crockery, taking down curtains and paintings, going through cupboards, and discussing with Alice what furniture she should take to Bulawayo and what should be left behind.

Just when the end was near and they were thinking about booking their train tickets back to Bulawayo, Isabella received a letter from James. She sat and stared at his small, neat handwriting for a long time, before reading what he had to say. She had missed him a great deal more than she expected while she had been away. Celia had written to her on numerous occasions, but never mentioned him, which left her wondering how he was getting along.

My dear Isabella, he wrote.

I trust you are well and enjoying your break from life in Bulawayo. You will be relieved to hear that your sister is taking good care of your dog.

I continue to be very busy learning how to run the MEC, with many people still visiting with the intention of investing in our projects. It is in connection with one of these visitors that I am writing to you now.

Sir Henry Parksville visited from the Cape. He is second in command to the Chief Justice there, and he mentioned they were looking to commission an artist to do a painting of the newly completed courts of law in Cape Town. You came to mind when he told me this. Sir Henry is back in Cape Town now, and I would like to suggest that you travel there and meet him, to discuss the painting. I took the liberty of telling him about you and hinted that you might be interested in this project. I showed him some of your work when we dined at Sunrising, and he was most impressed with it.

My house in Cape Town will be at your disposal, should you take up this suggestion. My butler, Mr de Villiers, lives there, and I have already informed him that you may be arriving soon.

I hope to have a positive response from you.

Yours affectionately,

James.

Isabella stared at his letter, stunned. She had never painted anything for anyone other than family and friends, how could he expect her to do something like this? She read the letter again. Surely he knew she was not good enough?

Alice spied her sitting at the window, deep in thought. 'Is there a problem?'

Isabella gave her the letter.

'How exciting. Oh Isabella, you would do such a good job of it, I am sure.'

'I don't think I would at all.'

'But you would. Look at the wonderful painting you did of the Victoria West church. You even said how pleased you were with it.'

'I know, but I was talking from a personal point of view. I would not think so if someone was paying me good money for it.'

'Rubbish dear. It is good by anyone's standard. I think this is a splendid idea. It will give you an excuse to spend a bit of time in Cape Town, which will do you the world of good.'

'But what about you?'

'We are nearly finished here. I will catch the train back to Bulawayo, while you, Harry and Oliver go on to the Cape.'

'But that would mean you would travel on your own.'

'I have done it before. I will be fine. Now please, no more arguing. Write back to James straight away and tell him how excited you are about his suggestion, and ask him how soon you should get to Cape Town.'

Chapter 24

THE first thing Isabella noticed when she walked into James's house in Constantia, Cape Town, was a portrait over the mantelpiece of a striking looking woman. She walked up to it and tried to read who the artist was.

'Miss Georgina Harrington,' the butler, Mr de Villiers, said.

'The artist, or the subject?'

'The subject Madam. I cannot recall the artist.' Isabella could not read the signature in the bottom right hand corner either.

'And should I know who Miss Georgina Harrington is?' she asked, sliding her hand along the bottom of the gilt frame.

'Sir James's fiancée, Madam.'

Isabella's hand stopped in its tracks. 'Who?'

'I should say, his late fiancée. She died in 1901. Buried at the Claremont Cemetery. Lovely lady. We are still very sad about her passing.'

'I am sure,' Isabella managed to answer.

This information whirled around in Isabella's head for days, as she found herself sitting in the drawing room and staring at the portrait of Miss Georgina Harrington. It made her aware that, although she thought she knew Sir James Brooke, there was in fact a great deal she did not know about him. He had told her his mother, brother and sister, all lived in England. He had also explained that his passion for Africa had been ignited when Courteney Selous, an alumnus of Rugby School, the same public school he had attended, came to give the boys a talk about his African exploits. But other than these details, Isabella accepted she knew little else. And while she sat there, thinking about how little she knew, she realised how much more she wanted to know.

As she continued to ponder these thoughts, the future course of her life became crystal clear. She and James must marry. Of course, it was the most obvious thing to do. She thought about how connected they were in so many ways already. Their shares in the MEC and the farm; how convenient it would be if they could combine these, which they would if they were husband and wife. And then there was Sunrising. She still felt bad that he had given it to her, but, if they were married, this would no longer be an issue.

Isabella had never considered James in a romantic way before; not until she saw the portrait of his late fiancée, that is. Miss Harrington was a beautiful looking woman, and James must have won her heart. Until then, Isabella had always thought of him as rather old, a more refined and elegant version of Mr Forsyth. But now she saw him differently. He may be a good deal older than her, in his mid-forties now, but he was charming, sophisticated, amusing, and most of all, the most kind and supportive friend she had ever known. Furthermore, they would be united in their grief for Anthony, as well as their understanding of what it was like to lose someone you loved.

Oh yes, Isabella said to herself, it makes perfect sense for us to marry. Not soon, mind. No, it would have to be after a few years, after what was regarded as an appropriate period of mourning.

She became more settled once she decided on this. She now looked forward to enjoying her time in Cape Town, secure in the knowledge that she knew what her future held.

221

Sir Henry Parksville did indeed commission her to do a painting of the courthouse, and she spent her first weeks in Cape Town working on it. She had just finished this project when she received another letter from James. When Harry gave it to her, she scurried to the drawing room to be alone, like a dog that had been given a delicious bone. She wanted to enjoy it and savour it, without being disturbed. But this was not to be, as she soon found out.

My dear Isabella, James wrote.

I need to tell you about what has transpired in Bulawayo, before you hear it from anyone else. Be warned, you will find what I say disturbing.

After our last visit to the farm, I hired someone to keep a close eye on Brown and Payne. As you know, they had found new jobs at the Near Enough Mine, and my investigator managed to secure a job there too. His suspicions were soon aroused when he discovered that Brown and Payne had been given the task of smelting the extracted gold. This would be a job for tried and trusted workers, well known to the management. Not newcomers. The investigator's suspicions were further aroused when the mine owner, a Mr John Breedon, started making it known that he had found a new and much larger vein of gold than any other they had discovered there before. From what my investigator could deduce, this was not the case at the mine. Yet, true to what Breedon was saying, their gold production did increase. My investigator managed to weasel his way into the smelting shed and found out what was happening. He discovered Payne and Brown melting an ingot. They then mixed the gold from this ingot with gold extracted from Near Enough Mine.

When the investigator reported his findings to me, I went to see Sergeant Smythe again. I took the mat Tate's woman had given you, and explained everything to him about the mat and the assegai. The first thing he did, after hearing my story, was to go to the Brown's house in First Avenue, on the pretext of investigating another case. Unfortunately, only Mabel was there. He saw the mat Celia had seen in their sitting room but did not allude to it as he did not want to make her suspicious. However, I believe she must have been, because, after leaving their house, he picked up a police detail from the police station and went straight out to the Near Enough Mine to question Brown, Payne and Breedon, only to find they were not there.

It is my belief Mabel sent word to them to disappear as soon as Sergeant Smythe left her house.

However, while the police were at the Near Enough Mine they questioned other workers, who could not verify the sudden increase in gold production at the mine. As far as they were concerned, they were finding the same quantity of gold as they always had. Which was not much, by all accounts. No one could explain the sudden increase in production reported by Breedon.

On their return to town, the Police went straight back to the Brown's house in First Avenue in the hopes of finding one or more of the suspects there. But, alas, this was not the case.

They then went to the places Payne and Breedon frequented, or stayed at, when they were in Bulawayo. But no one could be found.

Percy and Mabel Brown, Fred Payne and John Breedon disappeared off the face of the earth within hours of Sergeant Smythe's first visit to Mabel.

While all these searches were going on, the Brown's neighbour, Mrs Peggy Pingstone, brought her son to the police station. The son reported that he had seen Mabel Brown digging in the paddock behind their house after Sergeant Smythe left her. On hearing this, the police sent cables to police stations all over the country, as well as neighbouring territories, to be on the lookout for the suspects.

The police followed up this report with another visit to the Brown's house and found the freshly dug hole the Pingstone boy had reported. But more than this, after a thorough excavation, which took a few days, they found an ingot with MEC stamped on it. In other words, one of our ingots Isabella.

My theory, which Sergeant Smythe shares, is that Mabel deduced the police were onto them when Sergeant Smythe went to see her and sent word to the men at the mine warning them. She then went into her paddock and dug up one of the two remaining ingots that she knew were buried there, so they would have money to see them on their way. Why only one? Maybe because she did not have time to dig up the other. It was deeply buried and the earth was hard.

So do I think these people are guilty of Anthony's murder? Percy Brown and Fred Payne, absolutely; and Mabel knew all about it. And then Breedon was brought into the loop as a means of releasing the gold onto the market without raising suspicions. They had probably smelted and sold two of the ingots, pretending it was gold from the Near Enough Mine, and would have done the same with the other two. No wonder they were all looking more prosperous.

Will any of this ever be proved? Probably not, unless the suspects are found, and Sergeant Smythe warned me he doubts this will happen. Africa is a vast and wild continent. It will be easy for them to move and settle elsewhere. They are wily enough characters to reinvent themselves.

One more piece of information I need to share with you. When they went to the Brown's house on the second occasion, looking for Percy and Mabel, they found Mabel's baby. She gave birth to a baby girl a few weeks ago. She left this baby when she fled, and is now in the care of Mrs Peggy Pingstone..

You will need to be strong, Isabella dear, I know you are going to find this news difficult to comprehend or accept. Everyone at Sunrising, myself included, has been quite overcome by it all. We wanted formal closure on Anthony's premature death, and now it looks like we never will.

May I suggest you stay in Cape Town for a few months longer, and wait for the dust to settle here? As you can imagine, Bulawayo has been rattled to its core by these events, with many people still refusing to accept the facts. Some are even accusing me of chasing innocent residents away.

I will let you know when I think you should come home.

Your most faithful friend,

James

Isabella sat on the window seat in James's house in Constantia, staring at his small, neat handwriting.

What refined writing he has, she thought.

But as she was thinking this, the words he had written began to blur, and her hand started to shake. She sat, watching the paper flapping in front of her. She was transfixed by this, until Harry found her ten minutes later. She walked up to Isabella and touched her shoulder.

'What is the matter Mrs Craig?'

Isabella pushed the letter at her, letting out a long, haunting wail.

*

The first cold front of winter swept in from the northwest, bringing high winds and stormy days. When Isabella had passed through Cape Town the three previous times, coming or going to Bulawayo, it had always been summer. Dry, warm and balmy, with long, soft evenings. But not now. For her, it seemed cold, dark and bleak.

Sir Henry Parksville's wife, Jane, came to her rescue. She told Isabella later, that James had written and explained to her what had happened in Bulawayo. Jane knew Isabella would need all the help she could get. She introduced her to Cape Town society, and Isabella found herself intrigued by it. Unlike other parts of Africa, Cape

Town had an "aristocracy". People with backgrounds, families that had been living there for four or five generations. She found herself visiting homes that contained beautifully framed portraits and landscapes, libraries filled with leather-bound first edition books, dining rooms with gleaming silver and fine porcelain. Houses furnished with highly polished antiques. But what she liked the most about the people she met was their warm welcome; so unlike European aristocrats, who treated newcomers with great caution.

Isabella soaked in the beauty of the Cape, and, although there were more cold fronts, they were mixed with temperate days too. She was awed by the meeting of the two oceans at the Cape of Good Hope, and the grandeur of Table Mountain, standing as a backdrop to the town. The Parksvilles took her, Oliver and Harry on numerous trips to the winelands. Isabella was enthralled to watch the vine leaves turn from vivid green to golden yellow. She found a great deal to inspire her painting, and she was further encouraged when Jane Parksville arranged a small exhibition at her beautiful Dutch-gabled home in Rondebosch. She still could not believe that anyone would want to pay for her work, yet there appeared to be many people in the Cape with money they were happy to spend on her paintings.

One day, Jane arrived at James's house brimful with excitement. She had come up with another idea.

'Do you know Sir Percy FitzPatrick?' she asked, as they were settling down with their tea.

'No.'

'Well neither do I, but a friend of mine does. Sir Percy lives in Johannesburg now, but ten years or so ago he lived in the Eastern Transvaal, working in the gold fields there. He had a Staffordshire bull terrier called Jock, and he wrote a book about this dog.'

'How interesting,' Isabella said, wondering what she would write about, if she had to write a whole book about Archie.

'Well yes. I believe it is a children's book, and it is now going to be published by Longmans in London.' She took a sip of her tea. 'Anyway, the reason I'm telling you this is because they are looking for someone to illustrate the book, and you came to mind.'

'No!'

'Why not? You are a talented artist, and you are fond of Staffordshire bull terrier, from what I've gathered by the way you talk about your dog, what's his name again?'

'Archie.'

'So you know the way a dog like that behaves, its mannerisms, its quirks. Isabella, you'd be perfect at illustrating a book like that.'

'I am sure I would not.'

'Why don't you just give it a go? You could do some paintings of your Archie, and submit them to the publishers, and you just never know. It can't do you any harm to try.'

Isabella hesitated.

'You are right, and it would be fun. The only thing is, I am not sure if I should be going home yet. I have not heard from James again, and my last letter from Celia suggested that, that, you know, that the other matter is still causing a lot of ill feeling.'

'Oh Isabella, I am so sorry to hear this. After everything you and your family have gone through. This is not fair. A project like I am proposing would help take your mind off any negative ill feeling.'

But a week later she did get another letter from James. She opened it with trepidation, wondering if it contained more agitating news.

My dear Isabella,

I hear from Parksville that you have made a great impression on the art scene in Cape Town. Well done.

I am writing to warn you that I am selling my house there and believe the transactions will be completed by the end of August.

I made the decision to sell the Cape Town house because I find it is almost impossible to leave Bulawayo for extended lengths of time the way I used to. I have yet to find anyone to whom I can entrust the running of the MEC to my satisfaction, and, as such, I am very tied to it.

Furthermore, the house on the farm is coming along well. I look forward to showing it to you. I am sure you will be delighted with the final outcome of this project. However it will need furnishing, and this brings me to the second point of this letter.

Can I trespass on your time there and ask you to please pack up my furniture and possessions so that they can be sent to Bulawayo? De Villiers will help you with the task, if you are willing, but I respect your judgment and believe a woman's touch is so much more efficient in these matters. If you are able, you need to decide what should be sent here, and what can be sold there.

The dust has settled in Bulawayo, as far as the other issues are concerned.

I am your humble servant,

James.

Isabella looked up from the letter, her eyes darting around the room, viewing it in a different way. What needed to be packed up, what needed to be discarded? It would take a lot of work, but she knew she would enjoy it.

How interesting, she thought. So he was planning on settling more permanently in Bulawayo. Of course she would help him. She felt it was her natural position to do so, whenever she could. It also meant that her sojourn in Cape Town would be forced to come to an end, which was for the best. She missed Bulawayo now, her beautiful home, her family, her friends, and her dog Archie.

She went to find Harry to tell her the latest developments. She knew she would be pleased about this too. They had been away from home for long enough now.

Chapter 25

THE train shuddered into Bulawayo station and Isabella looked out of the window to see who had come to pick them up. She saw Celia, and Archie with her. 'How sweet,' Isabella murmured. Celia was surely not thinking this. Archie was straining and pulling on his leash, and she was struggling to keep control. Isabella laughed as she watched her yank at him and reprimand him, but he took no notice and continued pulling.

'We'd better get off this train and save Celia from my dog,' she said to Harry.

However, Celia's face lit up when she saw them stepping out of their carriage. She started walking towards them, but, when Archie noticed Isabella, he leapt forward, dragging Celia behind him, running to meet them, leaping up in dizzy excitement. Harry clutched Oliver to her chest, disapproving of such boisterous behaviour.

'Ah, you naughty boy. Down,' Isabella said, stroking his head and rubbing his ears, before pushing him down. He leapt at Harry, overcome with delight at seeing his old friends, but she lifted her booted foot and shoved him away. He jumped up at Isabella again, unperturbed.

'Maybe it was a mistake bringing him,' Celia said.

'Don't worry, he will soon calm down,' Isabella said, taking the leash and giving her sister a warm hug. 'It is so lovely to see you again, Celia darling.'

'You too,' Celia said, squeezing Isabella. She then turned towards Harry and took the startled looking Oliver into her arms. But he was only interested in Archie, who he pointed at and said, 'da.'

They all laughed. 'Oh my, how grown up he is, and almost talking now, I see.' She gave him a firm kiss on his brow, before settling him on her hip. 'How I have missed this beautiful boy.'

'We have missed you too.'

'Well thankfully we're all together again now. I came with Gonda. He is over there, near the luggage carriage, looking for your trunks. We are using the mule cart. I hope you don't mind.'

It took a while to track down all their possessions and load them onto the cart.

'Would you like to stop at The Grand for a cup of tea, before we continue to Sunrising?' Celia asked, as they were heading down Main Street.

'I think I would prefer to get home,' Isabella said. She turned to see what Harry wanted to do, and could not help smiling at the sight of her. She was perched on a bag and, wearing a straw bonnet, she looked like a crowned crane.

'I can wait till we get back, thank you,' Harry said.

'Are you all right there, amongst all the luggage?'

'I have had many a worse journey than this, when I used to travel to Nyamandhlovu with the Greaves family. I will survive.' She gave Archie a threatening look. 'As long as this dog does not try and knock me over again.'

Isabella, Celia and Gonda were squashed on the front seat, with Gonda holding the reins and Oliver sitting on Celia's lap.

'It has been very tense here,' Celia said.

'I heard.'

'James was adamant you should not be here when this was all going on.'

'Thank goodness, it would have opened all the old wounds again.'

'Exactly. It was horrible. Nasty rumours were circulating. Some people were going around saying James had made up the evidence. They were saying he had bribed the investigator, as well as the police'

'How awful. But why would anyone think he'd want to incriminate those people? Surely they know we always hoped they were not involved, especially as we were responsible for Mabel being here in the first place. I still cannot bear to think they were involved, oh my, it's too awful.' She shuddered.

Celia squeezed Isabella's hand. 'Exactly.'

'So how did James deal with it?'

'Well you know James. He rose above it and ignored all the rumour-mongering.'

'But it must have hurt him.'

'It did, but it is all behind us now. Let us not talk about it anymore.'

Isabella glanced at her sister. 'How good you are looking, Celia dear, despite everything. I would say you are positively glowing.'

'Well thank you. Despite having gone through a hard time, life in Bulawayo agrees with me.'

'It looks like it.'

'I love the openness, the weather, the birds, the animals. Every morning I take Gunner for a ride around the property, and every evening I take Archie for a walk along the stream. I am active, and feeling fit.'

Isabella wanted to ask her what plans she had made for going back to England, but resolved now was not the time to broach such a depressing subject.

'And the bird book? How is it going?'

'I have finished working on it. I will show you when we get home. It is going to be wonderful once it's printed.'

Everyone was waiting in front of the house to greet them when they came up the drive. Everyone, that is, except James. Edward, Alice, Henry and Johnny stood on one side of the steps leading up to the veranda, all the staff on the other side. Everyone looking formal and serious. Isabella was reminded of the first time James came back to Sunrising after they had moved in. She remembered they had done the same for him then. How charming, but unnecessary, she thought.

'We have invited James for dinner tonight,' Alice said, once they were settled on the veranda and having their tea. 'I hope you are not going to be too tired.'

'Not at all,' Isabella said, struggling to hide her excitement. 'In fact, I am delighted he is coming. I look forward to giving him the latest news on his friends, the Parksvilles. Such a delightful couple, they are.'

She then went on to tell them about Jane Parksville's idea about her trying to do the illustrations for Sir Percy FitzPatrick's book about his Staffordshire bull terrier, Jock.

*

Isabella took her time changing for dinner that evening. She wanted to make an impression. She had not seen James for over five months and she wanted him to see her in a different light. She no longer wanted him to regard her as the grieving widow of his long lost friend and partner. She now wanted to be seen as a successful artist and an independent woman.

Soon after tea, she had excused herself and gone to her rooms. Celia, as thoughtful as ever, had arranged for the tin bath to be filled with hot water and put in there for her and Isabella climbed into it. She felt dirty after her long train journey. There was nothing like a long soak to wash away the grit and grime from the

233

train journey, and she spent a long time doing just this. When she finished she unpacked her trunk and put her clothes away.

Gone are the days I would have a maid doing this for me, she thought, as she found space for her possessions. After what had happened with Mabel, she vowed she would never have a 'lady's maid' again. Always watching her; always expecting more than she could give; always feeling jealous. Isabella looked about her bedroom with fresh eyes and was pleased and comforted by everything she saw. She had a strong sensation of being back where she belonged. It was wonderful to be home again. To appreciate all the beautiful furniture she and Anthony had chosen when they first moved in; to recall, without too much pain, what it had been like for them then; to look with fresh eyes at each one of her paintings on the walls; to have Archie lying in his basket next to her dressing table, licking his foot.

She selected one of the new dresses she had bought in Cape Town. Not too smart, as tonight's dinner was just a family affair, but it was elegant and showed off her figure. She was pleased she had filled out while she had been away and no longer had that gaunt, haunted look she had had before she left.

After she finished changing for dinner, she went to check on Harry and Oliver in the nursery. She spent some time with them, and was therefore the last person to get to the veranda for their pre-dinner drinks. As she walked across the drawing room towards the French door opening onto the veranda, she could hear the chatter of everyone there; James's deep toned murmurs as he offered drinks, a giggle from Celia, a comment from Alice.

She saw James the minute she stepped through the door, standing at the drinks table talking to Edward. He had not changed in the five months she had been away. Tall and elegant, immaculately turned out as always. His face lit up as soon as he saw her.

'Isabella, my dear, welcome back,' he said, walking to her and gripping her hands as he kissed her on both cheeks. 'It seems I am the last person here to welcome you home and offer my congratulations for the successful trip you had.'

'Thank you James. I heard you riding up the drive when you arrived earlier but did not want to disturb you. It's so lovely to see you now.'

'Likewise.' He squeezed her hands again before letting them go. 'What can I offer you to drink? We are all having champagne, to toast your homecoming. Can I pour you a glass too?'

'Oh yes, please.'

Celia and Alice were sitting on the sofa and smiled at Isabella as she settled herself in the chair opposite them. She looked up at James as he handed her the glass of champagne, and felt a surge of affection towards him.

'Now, everyone,' he said, 'we are drinking this delicious bottle of champagne for two reasons. The first is to welcome our dear Isabella home, and to congratulate her on her successful time in Cape Town. It appears she took the art world there by storm.'

'Not quite,' Isabella said, embarrassed.

'But you did. Everyone was very impressed with your work, and therefore we must congratulate you.'

'Hear, hear,' Edward said, taking a swig from his glass.

'And now for the second part of my toast,' James said. 'This may surprise all of you, but I too have had some success recently.'

'Oh yes?'

'Most definitely. I have been successful in my quest in getting your dear sister, Celia, to agree to be my wife. She has accepted my proposal.' He walked up to Celia and laid his hand on her shoulder. She felt for his hand and squeezed it, leaving her hand covering his.

Alice and Edward whooped with joy, but Isabella was too stunned to respond. The smile on her face faded, and then came back, slowly and awkwardly, as the words sank in. She was taken aback. Everyone noticed her reaction and laughed, thinking it was the shock and delight at hearing this news. Celia rose from the sofa and went to Isabella's chair.

'Sorry to surprise you like this. We knew how delighted you would be, but we wanted to tell you when we were all together.'

Isabella pulled herself together. 'I understand, but of course I cannot help being surprised. There has been no hint of this in your letters, so yes, it is a great shock. But wonderful, wonderful news Celia.' She smiled, as best she could, and was grateful that James topped up her glass of champagne. She took a large gulp.

'Edward and I had our suspicions,' Alice said, 'as we have been here all this time and we have noticed how close James and Celia have become. But I can imagine that you may not have expected this, as you have been so out of touch with everything here.'

'Exactly,' Isabella said.

'And when is the wedding? Have any arrangements been made?' Edward asked.

'Oh yes. It is so exciting', Celia said. 'We will be married in three weeks. James and I have been making all sorts of plans, and the most exciting one of all is that Papa and Aunt Elizabeth are coming out for the wedding.'

'No!'

'Even as I speak, they are on board the Avondale Castle, sailing towards Cape Town.'

'I can hardly believe this,' Edward said. 'Who would think our father would ever leave the comfort of his home, to make a journey like that, and accompanied by his spinster sister.'

'I know, it is amazing. But James wrote to them, and told them that Sunrising is a very comfortable house. He assured them they would not be attacked by anyone or anything wild.'

'Let us hope he is right,' Edward said, laughing.

'True. But what made them finally decide to come, was when James's brother, Jack, offered to accompany them here. They should all get to Bulawayo in two weeks. We knew we had to hurry up and get it done before summer sets in. The weather should be mild enough, and there will be the minimum of mosquitoes and bugs now, before the rainy season starts.'

Dinner went on as planned, of course, and Isabella made every effort to behave normally. But she struggled. No one had dropped even the smallest hint that there was anything going on between Celia and James. She knew she should be delighted. And she was. Yes, she was. It meant her sister would not be going back to England. How lucky was she that she would have both her brother and sister living so near to her?

It's just that she had planned everything so differently, and her plans had not included Celia as James's wife. Not that she didn't love Celia. She did, and she could see that Celia was thrilled with this turn of events. Finally, after two glasses of champagne and the same amount of wine, she was able to behave in a relaxed manner.

*

The following morning Isabella made her way to her studio before breakfast. She needed to collect her thoughts, and what better place to do this than in the room she felt most comfortable.

She unlocked the door and pushed it open, breathing in the familiar smell of oil paint and turpentine. Archie rushed past her and darted around the room, sniffing in each corner, hopping into his basket and then jumping out. He looked up at her, to make sure she wasn't going anywhere, then climbed into the arm chair and lay down, swallowing and sighing as he settled his face onto his front paws.

Everything was as Isabella had left it. She had never let anyone clean her studio, and she could see that her wishes had been respected, even while she was away. There was a fine layer of dust on all the surfaces. She did not mind this; at least she would be able to pick up from where she had left off, all those months ago. Although, of course, she would now be moving onto what she had come to think of as 'her bull terrier project'. Quite different from what she had been doing before she left. Sketches of birds were still pinned to the sides of her easel, to the window frame, to the beams. They aren't too bad, she thought, as she examined them. These were the leftovers, as Celia has taken the best ones for her book.

She started to unpin the bird sketches, but stopped when she heard the steps creak. Even before he appeared at the door she knew who it was. James. Her heart beat more quickly, and she could feel a blush rising from her neck to her face. She started fanning herself with the sketch she was holding.

'Isabella, good morning. I knew I would find you here,' James said. She could smell his shaving soap, from where she was standing at the other side of the room.

'Good morning James.'

'Can I come in? Am I disturbing you?'

'No, no. I was just taking a look around. You know how it is when you've been away for a long time.'

'I do indeed.' He walked over to the window and looked out. 'Shall I open this? You are looking hot.'

'Yes please, it is rather warm in here, despite being so early. It is lovely to be back though. I have missed home very much.'

'And we have missed you. But you are looking so well. I think the long break did you good.'

'It did.'

'I am sorry I insisted you stay in Cape Town for longer than you may have wished.'

'Well, yes.'

'But things were awkward here for a while, after the Browns disappeared.'

'I still find it hard to understand why.'

'I think the main problem was that most people in Bulawayo could not tolerate the idea of a white man being killed by other white men.'

'And you think this is what happened?'

'I do, we all do; your whole family and I, that is. The rest of Bulawayo prefer to put it down to an unexplained death. They did not want me trying to prove that it could be otherwise. Our circle of friends understood my motives, and supported me, but many people here were angry. That is why I did not want you returning earlier. I did not want you getting caught up in any of the hostility.'

'I am so sorry it was like this.'

'Yes. But, most of all, I will always regret that we did not reach a final conclusion, so that you could have proper closure.'

Isabella felt the need to sit down. She shifted Archie over, from where he was sleeping in the middle of the arm chair, and squeezed in next to him. She felt comforted by his warm body against her leg.

'Do you think it was intentional, or an accident?'

'We think it was an accident; their main motive being to steal the gold. But, if proved guilty, they would still have been in serious trouble, maybe even executed, and that it why they fled. They will have changed their names, their stories, their backgrounds.'

'But leaving their baby?'

'A newborn baby would have made things more difficult for them. It would also have made them more conspicuous. The Pingtones have taken the baby in and will bring her up as their own.'

'So sad.'

'They will give her a good home, but the idea of a tiny baby being abandoned by her parents did not go down well with the general public either, and I was to blame. They blamed me for chasing the parents away.'

'Oh my, how awful.'

There was a long pause. Isabella stroked Archie's head, while James stared out of the window.

'Your sister was a tower of strength during all this,' he said, still staring outside.

'I am sure she was. Celia is the most loyal and caring person I know.' She rubbed Archie's ear, and bent to kiss him on his forehead, not daring to look up at him.

'Isabella, I, I um, I.' James shifted, turning around.

She glanced at him now, and caught an expression on his face she had never seen before. She looked down at Archie's head.

'Maybe I rushed into things. Maybe I should have waited. Maybe I, um.' He adjusted the window catch. 'Is it too late, Isabella?'

A francolin called outside the window, making Isabella jump. She could feel her heart pounding again. She could not speak.

'Is it, Isabella?'

'Yes,' she finally said. 'Celia will make a most wonderful wife, and must never be hurt. As for closure on Anthony's premature death. It is almost a year now, and I am getting used to living without him.'

He turned to look out of the window again, staring at something in the distance, saying nothing.

'I will always regret things did not turn out differently,' he murmured so softly, she could hardly hear him.

She did not reply. Then Archie started licking his foot and the tension eased.

'We will always be here for you.'

'Of course.'

'Well I suppose I had better go for breakfast then. Will you come too?

'Not now. There is a lot I want to sort out in this studio. Please will you ask Gonda to arrange for the trunk of art materials, I brought back from Cape Town, to be carried up here?'

'I will indeed.'

She did not trust herself to get up from the armchair until he had left the room.

*

Isabella overcame her disappointment by immersing herself in her painting again. She was grateful that she had her bull terrier project. As she worked on her paintings, she spent hours convincing herself that James and Celia's marriage was by far the best possible outcome. She persuaded herself that she was not in love with James. No, it was more the idea of being married to him that she had found so attractive; the tidiness of having him as her husband. That is what she had been in love with, she concluded. Granted, she was very, very fond of him and he had been incredibly good to her over the last year, but would this fondness have ever turned into real love? No, she told herself. He deserved much more, and from the way Celia was behaving, it looked as if she was willing and able to give it. Oh yes, he deserved more than she, Isabella Craig, could give. She, who had lost her beloved husband, and was now simply looking for companionship and a tidy way of sorting out her affairs.

Every now and then though, a thought would niggle at her, deep down, that she was not being honest with herself, but she would push this away. She focused instead on what she should do with her life. Could she stay here as a single woman? She had asked herself this question constantly a year ago, and now she was asking it again.

*

Isabella and Celia stood at the bottom of the garden, looking out on the vlei and watching the sun set. One minute it was there, and then it was gone. The stillness and peacefulness was profound.

Isabella broke the silence. 'How wonderful is this? Let's hope we have as good a sunset tomorrow evening, when we are all gathered here to witness your marriage.'

Celia glanced at the sky. The rainy season begins at the end of October, but this did not rule out the odd early shower. 'Yes, it would just be my luck if we had an almighty storm tomorrow.'

'Then we will move the ceremony to the drawing room. It will still be a lovely setting there. It is big enough to accommodate everyone.'

It had been Isabella's idea to have the wedding at Sunrising. To have the ceremony at the bottom of the garden, and then dinner on the veranda. Sunrising would be big enough to accommodate the family, plus Mr Forsyth (whom James had asked to be his best man) as well as the Weirs and Chapmans. Other guests were staying with the Fletchers at Umvutcha for the night. It promised to be a most joyous occasion.

'You are happy about all of this aren't you?' Celia asked.

'But of course, was it not my idea?' She was pleased that she had come up with it. She found that the more involved she was with the arrangements, the more excited she became at the thought of her sister marrying James. She would never, ever tell anyone that she had had designs in that area herself. Never.

'I am not talking about the actual wedding. I am talking about James and me,' Celia said. 'You seemed a bit strange when you first heard the news.'

Isabella blushed. 'Oh Celia, I could not be more delighted, now. It was just a bit of a surprise at first, as you had not given me the slightest hint of it. That is all. Everything has turned out as it should have.'

'I felt a little awkward, because I know that James is your special friend.'

'He is, of course, and he always will be. That is why I am so pleased he is going to be my brother-in-law. And a more suitable wife he could not find.' She smiled at Celia and took her arm, as they continued watching the ever-changing sky. 'I am very excited for you both, and for me too, knowing that you will always be here if I decide to continue living here after all. But Papa and Aunt Elizabeth are giving me a hard time about this. They expect me to pack my bags and go back to England, as soon as the festivities are over.'

Chapter 26

AUNT Elizabeth took a good-sized gulp of her gin. 'Those frogs,' she said. 'I do not know how you put up with their incessant croaking.' She took another sip of her drink. 'They just do not stop.'

'They will be quiet in a few weeks' time. They only croak like this during their breeding season,' Isabella said.

Aunt Elizabeth pursed her lips. 'Please. I cannot bear the thought of it.'

Isabella smiled.

'I have not wanted to interfere, or make a nuisance of myself, so I have not said anything before now. But, I do think you need to get rid of that fishpond in your garden, Isabella dear. Then you won't have problems, at any time of the year, with their croaking. Let the frogs go and find somewhere else to, um, to breed.'

'I find their croaking comforting. It is not as if they are right outside our bedroom windows.'

'No. But from here, on the veranda, they are very loud. It quite spoilt the wedding dinner for me. Having to make myself heard above frogs. Goodness, whatever next?'

Isabella couldn't help laughing this time. 'Oh Aunt, you are funny.'

'No I am not. And many of the other guests agreed with me, when I asked them what they thought of the croaking.'

I am sure, Isabella thought, they would not dare disagree with you.

'Don't worry Aunt. This time tomorrow we will be on the train, bound for the Victoria Falls. There will be no frogs on the train to disturb us, I am quite sure.'

James and Celia had left for Cape Town on their honeymoon, and it had been agreed that Isabella would take Papa and Aunt Elizabeth to the Victoria Falls, while James's brother went to Salisbury with Mr Forsyth. Isabella had jumped at this opportunity, having never been to the Victoria Falls before, although it had taken a lot to convince Papa and Aunt Elizabeth. Isabella could not wait to see this spectacular waterfall. If it had not been for Thomas Baines' paintings of the Victoria Falls, she may never have come out to Africa. It was these paintings that had ignited her interest in Africa. But, besides this, she also needed to get away. As much as she convinced herself she was pleased James had married her sister, she knew she needed to keep busy.

The railway line to the Victoria Falls, three hundred miles north of Bulawayo, had been completed in 1903. Isabella and her aunt shared a first class compartment while Papa had one to himself. They left Bulawayo at midday and were scheduled to be at the Victoria Falls by mid-afternoon the next day. They had agreed it was best to leave Oliver at Sunrising with Harry, for fear of malaria; although James had assured them that the chances of getting it at this time of the year were remote, especially if they covered themselves up properly.

'Now, my dear,' Aunt Elizabeth said, as soon as she had finished sorting out her suitcase and putting her belongings into the space provided. 'I vote we have a nice long nap; we need it after all the activity we have been having these last few days. And then we will go to the dining car for tea. Does this suit you, for the short term?'

'Yes, Aunt. That sounds good, although I may cut my nap short and do a bit of work on these sketches I've brought. Let me go and tell Papa our plan. Shall I suggest we meet him for tea at four-thirty?'

'Yes, that sounds reasonable,' Aunt Elizabeth said, settling herself into a corner of the bench that would later become her bed for the night.

But, it soon became apparent that sleeping on the train during the day was impossible. It kept stopping, and on each occasion the brakes screeched, the carriages knocked into each other, and the natives ran up and down the tracks yelling for customers.

'Dear God, give me patience,' Aunt Elizabeth sighed, when the train stopped for the third time. 'Why, oh why, can we not just keep moving?'

Isabella leant out of the window to see what was going on. There seemed no reason for their stop, but a vendor came to her window, with some mangos in a basket on his head. She nodded at him, and he took the basket off his head and put it on the ground, ready to pick out the best mangos for her. But, before he had a chance to complete his sale, other vendors saw what he was doing and rushed to Isabella's window, trying to sell fruit to her also.

'No, no, just him,' Isabella said, but no one noticed, or appeared to understand, as they thrust pieces of fruit at her.

Aunt Elizabeth rolled her eyes and puckered her mouth. 'Now look what you have done. Please Isabella, do not encourage those people anymore.'

'I will just buy two from this man,' Isabella said, holding up two fingers and trying to ignore everyone else. As soon as the mangos had been passed through the window, she closed it, as well as the blind, trying to quell the commotion she had caused.

'Goodness gracious, 'Aunt Elizabeth said.

'Let me see,' Isabella said, ignoring her aunt's snorts, 'I am sure I have a palette knife in my paint box. I will use it to skin one of them. I do love mangos, don't you Aunt?'

Aunt Elizabeth grunted, and then gasped, as juice squirted from the fruit as Isabella cut the skin. 'Now look at you,' she said, staring at where it had splattered across Isabella's white skirt.

Isabella could only laugh, as she cut a slice and put it in her mouth. 'It is good though, do try some Aunt.' Aunt Elizabeth relented and had a piece.

*

After tea they returned to their compartment to 'repair for dinner', as Aunt Elizabeth put it, glancing yet again at Isabella's skirt. They were back in the dining car for their evening drink at seven p.m. sharp. The sun had set by the time they took the first sips of their sherry, but the western sky was still glowing from the striking sunset. Since leaving Bulawayo the countryside had been open and flat, giving a sense of spaciousness, and allowing them to see for miles beyond the train. Isabella commented on this.

'Yes, lovely,' her father said, as he looked at the menu, trying to decide what he should have for dinner. 'Mmm, Elizabeth. The beef may be the safest bet. Not sure I would risk the fish, and definitely not the pork. One wonders what their refrigeration facilities are like. Nonexistent, I'd hazard a guess. What about you, Isabella? What do you want?'

'I have not looked at the menu yet, Papa. I will make my decision once the beautiful sky has faded and I cannot see outside anymore.'

Her father glanced out of the window and then continued to scrutinise the menu.

'Apple crumble and custard. That sounds like a safe enough bet, Elizabeth?'

'I wonder what this "Zambezi Mud" is.' Elizabeth puckered her lips in distaste.

'Oh goodness, do not have that my dear. The last thing we need is either of us getting sick, which will happen if we eat anything exotic. Now, let me look at the wine list. Mmm, quite a respectable selection. Hurry up, Isabella; make up your mind what you want to eat, so I can order the wine. Are we going to have red or white?'

And so the evening went on. Aunt Elizabeth and Papa had the vegetable soup with a roll, followed by roast beef and Yorkshire pudding, and then Papa had the apple crumble and custard while Aunt Elizabeth opted for the bread and butter pudding, by way of a change.

'Middling, middling but not too bad, when you consider the conditions,' Aunt Elizabeth said, dabbing her mouth with her starched table napkin and caressing a petal of a flower in the silver vase on the crisp white linen table cloth. 'One shouldn't complain, should one?'

'No Aunt,' Isabella said. 'My pork turned out to be warthog and was delicious, and the Zambezi Mud was a most memorable chocolate pudding. I must try to get Mananga to make it for my next dinner party.' She enjoyed stirring these two up.

'Now, ladies, what shall we order as a nightcap?' her father asked, signalling to the waiter. 'Garcon, garcon. Please bring the wine list again.

'We are not in France Papa. I am sure he does not know he should respond to 'garcon',' Isabella said, smiling at the waiter as he walked down the aisle towards them.

The waiter smiled back, and then he stumbled. He lurched forward, grabbing the nearest table as he tried to steady himself. His tray went flying and hit the floor with a loud clatter. The train was skidding and the whistle was shrieking.

'Oh my, oh my goodness.' Aunt Elizabeth clung to the table, her face ashen.

'What on earth?' Papa gripped his seat in alarm.

The train continued to brake and finally came to a shrieking halt. The passengers in the dining car strained to look out of the windows, trying to see what was going on. The half-moon had risen in a sky filled with stars, but it was still too dark outside and no one could see properly.

'For goodness sake. What, what on earth is going on?' Aunt Elizabeth stammered. She glanced out of the window but only saw darkness.

The man at the table next to theirs had all the answers. 'Elephant on the railway track everyone. Stay calm! By Jove, those blighters can be a nuisance. This happened to me the last time I made this journey also.'

Aunt Elizabeth's ashen face turned pink as she stared out of the window. 'Oh my dear, surely not?'

'Afraid so. Difficult to keep them off the track, there are so many.'

Aunt Elizabeth looked at Papa in horror. 'Now, now,' their fellow diner said. 'Don't worry yourselves. Elephants may be big, but they are no match for this iron lady. We are safe here.'

'This is all too much. Too much indeed,' said Aunt Elizabeth, twisting her now crumpled napkin between her fingers. Isabella could see that she was hating every minute of their trip and longed to be in the comfort of her cottage near King's Lynn.

The train finally moved onwards and the passengers watched in amazement as they passed a herd of elephant, running from the railway track.

'Oh my,' Isabella murmured. 'Oh my, what magnificent animals. I am in total awe of them. This is the first time in my life I have ever seen them.'

'You are right, they are magnificent,' Papa agreed. Even he could not help being impressed.

*

The Victoria Falls Hotel was a small bungalow made of corrugated iron, built close to the station, so the elderly Braithwaites and Isabella could disembark and stumble to the hotel; porters following close behind with their luggage. The travellers were dirty and soiled, after the long night on the steam train, with the engine billowing black smoke and soot. It seemed to have settled everywhere. They longed for their hotel rooms and a chance to bathe and freshen up.

Although the hotel was unimpressive, it overlooked the imposing bridge spanning the Zambezi River, the bridge Rhodes had commissioned in his bid to build a railway line from the Cape to Cairo. Isabella, Aunt Elizabeth and Papa all had commanding views of this bridge from their separate bedrooms. They could see the bridge from the terrace too, where they all met for an evening drink before dinner.

'What a lovely view,' said Aunt Elizabeth, making every effort to rally, now that they were ensconced there. 'I am sure we are going to enjoy our stay here.'

'I hope so, Aunt.' Isabella said. 'To make up for the discomfort of the train journey.'

'No. It was no more uncomfortable than our train journey from Cape Town. Just a little troubling with the elephant on the track. I did feel very sorry for the one that was killed. But I could not complain about anything else. Absolutely nothing else.'

'Good,' Isabella said. 'Tomorrow I will try to find time to do some sketches of the bridge. It is remarkable. How they managed to build it across that deep gorge is a wonder to me. What a feat of engineering it is.'

'Indeed yes, it is, dear. And this hotel, I can see that they are making every effort to make it as comfortable for us as they can. Just such a pity about these mosquitoes. They have been doing their best to sting me ever since we sat down here. Thank goodness I am wearing such thick stockings, even if they are uncomfortable in this heat.'

Papa wiped his brow in agreement. 'Yes, it is rather uncomfortable. And as for those frogs croaking in the fishpond.

Let us hope they give up soon, otherwise we will not get a wink of sleep. But come, girls, another sherry before we go in for dinner?'

*

They met before sunrise the next morning. The hotel manager warned them it would be too hot to go to the waterfall in the middle of the day; he suggested they go at dawn rather, and return for a late breakfast.

There had been a tremendous rainstorm in the night, with thunder and lightning crashing all about them and the rain pounding on the tin roof of the hotel. Isabella had snuggled into her bed and enjoyed the drama, but not so for her father and aunt. They were both looking haggard and tired when they met in the hotel reception at a quarter to six in the morning.

'Hardly had a wink of sleep,' Papa complained as soon as he saw Isabella. He was already wiping sweat from his brow with his handkerchief. 'Those dratted frogs kept up their commotion all night long, and as for the storm, I thought the Boer War had started up again.'

'Oh Papa, African storms are always loud like that. At least it has cooled the temperatures down for us.'

'I am going to complain about those frogs to the manager. I cannot have another night of that dreadful noise. It will drive me insane. Do you agree Elizabeth?' 'Absolutely, George, someone must get rid of them. It was bad enough at your house, Isabella; I did not want to complain and make a nuisance of myself so I only mentioned it once then. But at least they weren't croaking outside my bedroom window, as they are here.'

Isabella was relieved when the manager came through from his office.

'Good morning good people, I trust you had a pleasant night's rest?'

Papa was just opening his mouth when Isabella cut in.

'Lovely, thank you, and we are longing to see the waterfall.'

251

'My man,' Papa was not going to be dissuaded. 'I need to talk to you, when we get back, about your frogs. Indeed I do.'

The manager looked surprised, but only for a minute, before he regained his composure. 'Yes, Mr Braithwaite, of course. But in the meantime, may I escort you to the rickshaws that will take you to the waterfall.'

'Because of your frogs, my nerves are quite frayed,' Papa said.

'A rickshaw ride to the waterfall. How delightful,' Isabella interrupted.

'Indeed it is,' the manager said. 'Now please come with me. Just a short walk and then I will have you comfortably settled. So much more relaxing, making your way to the waterfall like this, than walking there, or taking a cart. The monkeys and baboons won't worry you on this transport.'

Aunt Elizabeth's eyes widened at his talk of monkeys and baboons, and she looked uncomfortable as she stepped into the rickshaw. She pulled her wide-brimmed hat onto her head, and made sure the ribbons were well secured under her chin. 'I am not sure I like the idea of baboons and monkeys. Oh dear, no I do not.'

'Do not fear, good madam. Livingstone and Judah, here, will chase any animals away, if they come too close. They have sticks tucked into their belts. May I suggest that the two ladies travel together and you, Sir, go in the other rickshaw?'

Livingstone and Judah pulled the rickshaws down to the waterfall. Isabella recognised Livingstone as their waiter from the night before. But now he had changed his waiter's outfit for knee-length trousers and a plain shift top, belted at the waist, with the stick tucked into the belt. The dusty track went down an incline, and they had to take care not to lose control of their rickshaws.

Despite the rain, the early morning was not as cool as Isabella had hoped. She was sensitive to her father and aunt's discomfort. There was not a cloud in the sky, as the pink of the dawn faded, and the sun started showing signs of rising. The rain had raised the humidity level and poor Papa had his handkerchief to his face every few moments, it seemed.

The journey was not long, and the baboons and monkeys kept their distance. Before they knew it, they had stopped and Livingstone was helping them disembark. They looked around, confused, because they were expecting to see the waterfall, but all they saw was thick undergrowth. Bushes, palm trees, long grass. They could hear a faint roaring noise, but otherwise, nothing.

'This way please,' said Livingstone, ushering them towards a clearing in the vegetation. 'We must walk down this path.'

It soon became apparent the ladies were not wearing the right shoes, because, as they proceeded, the ground became ever muddier as the mist thickened into a light rain. The roaring of the falling water became ever louder.

And then, suddenly the forest opened and they found themselves staring at a massive curtain of water, falling into a huge fracture in the ground in front of them. It was so deep and had so much mist rising from it they could only see vaguely into it. The sound of the water was thunderous. Clouds of light spray swirled from the gorge, settling around them, wetting them. They were, to a person, awestruck.

Never, in their wildest dreams, had they expected anything so powerful. Isabella could only think how Baines' paintings were nothing in comparison to what they were now witnessing. No painting could do justice to the grandeur and splendour of it. The ever-faster running river as it neared the waterfall, the islands covered in thick vegetation and palm trees on the edge of the gorge, the glistening black rock of the vertical sides, and the creamy white of the water as it fell.

'Blow me down,' Papa eventually said.

They stood for a long time, mesmerized by the cascading water.

Aunt Elizabeth became distracted by the state of her person. The spray had made them soaking wet. Every so often it would get stronger, as a soft breeze blew a cloud towards them, and then it would ease up again. Isabella took off her hat, so the water sprayed into her face, but Aunt Elizabeth kept hers on, and, as it became wetter, the brim became floppier until it was hanging over her eyes.

She had had enough.

The waterfall spreads a mile across and they could have walked this mile, looking at it from many different points, but Aunt Elizabeth, and even Papa, had seen all they needed to see and were now interested in their breakfast, followed by a relaxing day in their rooms. They beckoned to Judah and Livingstone to take them back to the hotel.

They walked into the hotel foyer and were met by the manager.

'Mr Braithewaite. May I introduce you to Dr Stephen Goldsmith?

Dr Goldsmith has been working at the hospital here, and he tells me he may have something to help you with your nerves, and your sleep, in case we cannot stop the frogs croaking tonight.'

Papa gave Dr Goldsmith a long look.

'You look too young to be a doctor. Are you sure you know what you are doing?'

Isabella blushed. 'Papa, please.'

'London trained, Mr Braithewaite.'

'Good, well you can't be too careful when it comes to matters of health. But in that case, would you care to join us for breakfast, and we can discuss your potions?'

Dr Goldsmith paused. He had not expected a breakfast invitation. 'Thank you. I would be delighted to have breakfast with you,' he said, smiling at Isabella and Aunt Elizabeth.

He looks like he could do with a good meal, Isabella thought.

'We will meet you in the dining room in fifteen minutes as we need to change our shoes and clothes. Will this do for you?'

'Of course, Sir. I will sit on the terrace and enjoy the view of the bridge while I wait for you.'

Chapter 27

THE trip to the Victoria Falls convinced Isabella, once and for all, that she did not want to live in England again. Being with her father and aunt made her realise how much she had changed in the seven years she had been in Africa. Being at the Victoria Falls made her understand how much she thrived on living in Africa, how much it inspired her.

'But you cannot live here by yourself. This country is too wild for a woman on her own,' her father insisted.

'I will not be on my own, Papa. I will have Oliver, Archie, Harry, and all the other staff. Celia and James will be back and forth to Sunrising, and likewise Edward and his family. I will have all my friends.'

Her father grunted his disapproval.

'What about the charming Dr Goldsmith?' Aunt Elizabeth said. 'He seemed to enjoy your company when we were at the Victoria Falls, inviting you to go and see the waterfall with him again. Just the two of you: unchaperoned in that rickshaw; being away for most of the day. I was most taken with Dr Goldsmith, but I did not approve of his forward behaviour.'

'Aunt, you cannot marry me off to the first single man you see me with. As I told you before, we were gone for so long because we chose to explore the breadth of the waterfall, and that meant a walk of two miles, there and back. We kept stopping to admire the view, plus we had to push our way through thick vegetation at times. I went with Dr Goldsmith because he offered to take me. If you had offered, I would have gone with you.'

'Oh, no, I could not have done something like that. It is too wet. My shoes and stockings were sodden after the short time I was there, and as for my skirt, I will never get the mud out of it. It is ruined. Quite ruined. No, I could not walk two miles in those conditions.'

'Exactly.'

'But to go alone with a single man. Isabella! You will get a reputation if you carry on doing things like that. I think of you as my own daughter, and that is why I must caution you against this sort of behaviour. I hate to think what the hotel manager made of it all.'

'Aunt Elizabeth, you do make me laugh. I am sure he thought nothing of it. You know he has commissioned me to do a painting of the Victoria Falls Bridge don't you? That is what interested him the most about me. My ability to paint, not that I went to look at the waterfall again with Dr Goldsmith. But besides this, we were not alone. Livingstone was with us.'

Aunt Elizabeth snorted.

'Well, if you are determined to stay in Rhodesia,' Papa said, 'at least consider sending your son to England for his schooling. This would ensure he is brought up a gentleman.'

'I will think about it Papa. It will be a few years from now, as he is only one year old, and the Convent School in Bulawayo will suit him well to start with.'

Papa and Aunt Elizabeth stayed for one more month. Despite their misgivings, they wanted to be a part of the comings and goings of their family's lives. Celia and James returning from honeymoon and moving back into Sunrising while the house on the farm was being completed. Edward, Alice and the boys relocating to the house they had bought in the Suburbs. Isabella spending many hours in her studio, working on her paintings and sketches for the book about a Staffordshire bull terrier. She had been told the book was going to go by the title, 'Jock of the Bushveld'.

They might consider Rhodesia uncivilized, but they could see their family were living interesting lives.

Isabella made sure she entertained regularly. She would have preferred to lock herself in her studio and work uninterrupted, but, at the same time, she wanted her father to see that her life in Rhodesia was not as uncivilized as he kept saying it was. And so she invited the Weirs, the Chapmans, the Fletchers, the Heymans, the Meikles and the Napiers on different occasions. Her staff was kept busier than ever.

Jack Brooke returned from Salisbury, and he and James began taking cartloads of furniture out to the farmhouse, which was almost complete now. James wanted to move in as soon as possible, and he needed to transport the furniture that had come from his Cape Town house to the farm before the rains started in earnest. It had been in storerooms at Sunrising since being brought up from Cape Town. James sold most of his MEC shares to his brother, who was going to take over the running of the company, allowing James time to develop the farm. There was no talk of taking Papa and Aunt Elizabeth out to the farm. Everyone knew the journey and conditions would be too much for them, and would reverse all Isabella's hard work, showing them how civilized their lives in Rhodesia were.

The only thing Isabella could not change to suit her father and aunt was the weather. The October heat set in, and the main topic of conversation turned from croaking frogs to the weather. There was no getting away from the heat. Every morning Gonda and Hlabano would shut the house up, closing all the curtains and windows, trying to maintain the cool night-time temperatures, and then, in the late afternoon, once it had started cooling off, everything would be opened again.

'I do not think this system of yours works,' Aunt Elizabeth said. She had collapsed on the sofa on the veranda to read her book, but she could not do this because she kept using it as a fan, flapping it in front of her face. 'I think it may just make the house stuffy during the day.'

'It was Muriel who suggested we do it. She says everyone here does it at this time of the year, trying to keep their houses cool.'

'Mm. It does not work, if you want to know my opinion. I think I will open the windows in my bedroom when I go there for my afternoon siesta. I will keep the curtains closed and hope there will be a breeze.'

But nothing helped. Everyone felt hot, whatever they tried to do. Isabella dared not take her English guests anywhere. She knew the heat would exhaust them even more if they were active.

Then, a week before they left, she slipped up. She suggested taking them for a picnic to the Matopos Hills, south of Bulawayo.

'The Matopos is a place of huge rock hills, Papa. The views are magnificent. It is stunning. I would very much like you to see it before you leave. There is a railway line out there, and every Sunday a train takes picnic goers for the day. Do you think you can manage it?

Well I suppose we could give it a try. A train journey you say?'

'Just for the day.'

'Well, we are getting quite used to these now. We could not find fault with the train journey back from the Victoria Falls, could we Elizabeth?'

'No. It was very comfortable, and such a relief not encountering any animals on the railway line.'

'Well I doubt there will be any animals on the railway line to the Matopos either. Anthony and I went camping there once, years ago, with the Weirs. We went in our carts and camped for two nights. It was truly delightful. There is a spiritual beauty about the Matopos Hills which we felt especially in the evenings when the sun was going down and an eagle was soaring in the sky above us.'

'Spiritual camping?' Aunt Elizabeth interrupted. 'Whatever next?'

Isabella ignored her. 'I have asked everyone to come with us, as it is your last weekend. Edward, Alice, the children, Celia. Unfortunately James and Jack will still be at the farm. But I am sure you will be impressed with these hills made of rock, Aunt Elizabeth.'

But this was not the case. They had hardly left the train when they were swarmed by small flies, buzzing around their heads, trying to get into their eyes, their ears, their noses.

'Mopani flies,' Edward said. 'Do not flap as it just makes them worse. Try to ignore them.'

But of course they could not. Isabella's lasting memory of her father and aunt's visit was of them sitting in the compartment of the train, the windows and shutters closed, waiting to be taken away. They could not get back to King's Lynn fast enough after that.

*

Isabella sat on the veranda of Sunrising watching a rain storm moving in from the north. Huge black clouds rolled towards her, contrasting with the clear of the sky above the horizon. The sun shone below the storm clouds, casting a golden light. She knew this light would soon be engulfed, but for now it spread across the landscape, catching the trees and bushes, making them glow. She was mesmerized by the scene. She could see rain already falling in the distance, forming streaks of greyish blue from the heavens to the earth. She could smell it too; an earthy, musty smell as it hit the parched ground. Lightning zigzagged across the black clouds, followed by a rumble of thunder. Archie came bounding through the French door from the drawing room, jumping onto the sofa beside her.

A movement caught her eye. Harry, running from the bottom of the garden, pushing the perambulator, rushing to get back to the house before the rain arrived.

James and Celia had left for the farm early that morning. They had worried that Isabella would feel lonely now they were leaving. Nothing could be further from how she felt; animated, liberated, and excited about her life. She had promised she would go out to the farm for Christmas.

She was about to go and check on Harry and Oliver when Gonda came through the French door, carrying the silver tray from the hall.

'Madam,' he said. 'Someone has come with an envelope for you. This is his card.' He held out the tray to her.

Her forehead furrowed as she took the card and envelope. She read the card:

Stephen Goldsmith Medical Physician

She looked at Gonda, arching an eyebrow. 'Is he still here?'

'No Madam. He said he needed to leave, to miss the storm.'

'Oh my, I fear he may not manage this.' They both glanced towards the garden and, as if by way of a reply, lightning flashed across the sky, followed by a crash of thunder. Isabella jumped, clasping her hands to her ears.

There was a moment of silence, and then the first drops fell, pitter-pattering on the tin roof. This turned into a torrent. The rain came down in sheets, thundering on the roof, glazing the garden, creating a damp mist on the veranda where they stood.

'We need to go in,' Isabella said, watching Archie who was already running towards the French door. Gonda followed Isabella, closing the door behind him. It was quieter inside, the storm muffled by the ceiling and the furnishings. He took the tray back to the hall while Isabella sank onto the sofa. Archie jumped up and sat next to her, leaning against her for comfort. She stroked his head, knowing how scared he always was of thunder and lightning.

'It's alright Archie Boy,' she said, stroking his head again. 'You're safe here with me.' As if he understood her, he curled into a ball next to her and went to sleep.

Isabella was still holding the envelope and the card. She put Dr Goldsmith's card on the table next to her and looked at the envelope. It read:

Mrs J Craig

Sunrising

By Hand:

Per kind favour of Dr S Goldsmith

She glanced again at the card. How interesting, she thought, that Dr Goldsmith was now in Bulawayo. She wondered what he was doing here, and for how long he would be staying. They had spent the whole day together looking at the Victoria Falls, but in that time he never mentioned he may be coming to Bulawayo. She hoped he would come back for a proper visit at some stage.

She broke the seal on the envelope. It contained one piece of writing paper and a photograph. She looked at the photograph; a gentleman whom she did not recognize. She looked on the back to see if there was any explanation. There was nothing.

She unfolded the writing paper and glanced at the bottom of the page. It was from a Sir Phillip Bourchier Wrey. She had met him a few times, but how strange that he should be writing to her, she thought.

The letter read:

The Bulawayo Club,

Main Street,

Bulawayo.

19th November, 1906

Mrs Isabella Craig,

Sunrising,

Bulawayo.

Dear Mrs Craig,

With great respect for your work as an artist, the committee and I wish to commission you to paint a portrait of our first chairman, Dr Hans Sauer – chairman 1895.

We would like the portrait to be as close as possible to the likeness in the enclosed photograph of Dr Sauer. The background and size would be to your liking.

We wish to hang the portrait in the members' dining room.

We will be delighted if you agree to do this commission. If so, please let me know your fee so that I can arrange to have this paid to you post haste.

I remain, dear Madam,

Your obedient servant,

Sir Phillip Bourchier Wrey,

Chairman.

She looked at the photograph again, then re-read the letter and, as she did this, a smile spread across her face. They want me to do a portrait for their club, she thought, a club no woman is allowed to visit. How ironical is that? She put the photograph on the mantelpiece, next to the photograph of the Victoria Falls Bridge. Now she had two photographs she needed to study before she started painting what they depicted. And before she started these she had the paintings and sketches of Archie to finish off, in the hopes she may be chosen to illustrate the book entitled, "Jock of the Bushveld". She doubted this would happen, but you never know, she thought.

The rain stopped and the room felt stuffy with the door closed. She opened it and went outside again. Archie followed her and jumped up next to her as she sat down on the sofa. As quickly as the rain had come, it was now gone, leaving everything looking fresh and clean. The sun came out again, reigniting the glowing light that had been there before the storm, only it was more intense now.

Isabella sighed, stroking her dog's head. She felt content. She was living the life she had dreamed of, being recognized as the artist she had always wanted to be. She had been through the worst of times, but she had survived, and she had much to be grateful for and to look forward to.

She stood up. Archie jumped off the sofa and looked at her. 'Let's go to the studio and do some work, Archie Boy. You need to model for me, before we collect Oliver for our walk later.'

THE END

Acknowledgments

This a work of fiction. The characters and events are made up. When historical figures are mentioned, it is in a fictional way.

I have many people to thank for helping with the creation of this book.

First, my great grand parents-in-law, George and Helen Mitchell. George Mitchell came to Africa from Scotland in 1889 to work in banks in South Africa. He was sent to Bulawayo in 1895 to open the first bank there. He went on to become the first Prime Minister of Rhodesia (before this they were called Premiers), for just 3 months, in 1933. Helen Mitchell, nee Browne, first came to Bulawayo in 1899, to help her sister-in-law with the birth of her baby. She met George Mitchell while she was staying in Bulawayo. When she returned to England, George Mitchell followed a few months later, to ask for her hand in marriage. They were married in 1900 and lived in Rhodesia for the rest of their lives. Helen Mitchell wrote diaries every year, which we still have. I was inspired to write this novel after reading her diaries. They made me realise how adventurous most of the people, who left their relatively comfortable lives in England to travel to unknown lands, had to have been. The diaries also made me understand how quickly connected many of these pioneers became to Africa, despite the difficulties.

A number of the episodes that occur in the book come from the Mitchells' experiences. Not the way the story evolves, but many of the details. For instance, they used a Cape cart and a Spider for their transportation, and they had troublesome mules. Also, they moved from Hillside into a comparatively grand house north of Bulawayo when George Mitchell joined Hans Sauer in a mining and exploration company. This house had many of Hans Sauer's possessions, some of which we still have to this day. Helen Mitchell made the comment that they 'took over Dr. Sauer's remains.' They also wined and dined many wealthy businessmen who were looking to invest in mining. The story about the guest arriving for dinner with his dinner suit being carried by his trusty valet, after their carriage wheel fell off en route, actually happened. Like the characters in the book, the Mitchells bought a property which initially was uninhabited and undeveloped, except for a few huts, built by the previous European owner. The Mitchells stayed in these huts for some years, before building their own farm house. And like the characters in the book, they would leave their house near Bulawayo before the crack of dawn, to travel out to the property, and they would breakfast at a spot along the river on the way.

The Mitchells lost their first two children before they were even a year old.

After writing the first drafts, I gave the manuscript to my parents, Christopher and Moira Carver, and to Margaret Montgomery and Anne Randell. A special thank you to my mother who worked especially hard for me.

Heather MacDonald, Lisa Kaufman, Tina Booth, Vanessa Cottam, Sarah Bowman, Audrey Moyo, Tara Maidwell, Ruth Galloway, Lyn Rawlins and, last but certainly not least, Paul Hubbard read later drafts. Each one of them made very useful contributions towards this book.

George Mhkwananzi and Bryan Orford helped with synopsis of the history leading up to the period this story is set.

Duncan Watson designed the interesting cover.

My sincere thanks to all these people for their contribution towards this book.

More about the house on the cover

As a point of interest, the house on the cover is the house George and Helen Mitchell lived in at the turn of the twentieth century. It was called Amajoda and it is situated in what King Lobengula called "White Man's Land" (see explanation about White Man's Land in the prologue), near what is today called State House. It was one of three grand old houses that had been built just north of Bulawayo in the late 1890s. The other two houses are called Sunrising and Umvutcha. The real Sunrising is right next door to State House and has been used as a guest house for many years. Amajoda is about a kilometre away, over a vlei and the Amajoda stream. It has been empty and partially derelict for as long as I have known it. Umvutcha is further away and beautifully restored.

The history of Amajoda goes further than just being a house my great grandparents-in-law lived in. Next to it is another building, and this building is Dawson's store. When Forbes, Willoughby, Jameson and their men arrived in Bulawayo in November 1893 to find the entire area in flames and King Lobengula and his army gone, they discovered two white men sitting on the roof of Dawson's store, playing cards. Later, they raised their Union flag in the tree next to Amajoda. This tree still remains there to this day. And next to this tree is a very tall palm tree. Helen Mitchell planted this from a pip she found in some dates she had brought from her honeymoon in Egypt

'The Sun is Bright' is the second book in the Sunrising Series.

From the magnificent wide-open spaces of Africa where he was brought up to haunting recollections of his confinement in Italy, 'The Sun is Bright' is the story of Oliver Craig returning to his farm in Southern Rhodesia after the Second World War.

Things changed significantly in the six years he was away with the birth of his daughter, Amanda, in 1940 followed by the death of his wife in 1943. Amanda went to live with her grandmother, the now famous artist, Isabella Craig, but Isabella insists she moves back in with her father on his return. Having never known each other before, Oliver and Amanda are uncomfortable with this arrangement and do everything they can to avoid each other.

Southern Rhodesia is a vibrant place in the late 1940s with thousands of immigrants moving there to escape the aftermath of the war in Europe. The British Royal Family tour the country in April 1947 and Isabella Craig is commissioned to do a painting of Rhodes's grave, which she presents to the King and Queen when they visit the Matopos Hills. At this presentation, the Craigs meet a Mr and Mrs Sanderson and their daughter Lily, and, as their lives become entwined over the next few months, they discover they have always been connected in a most unexpected way.

The Sunrising Series

The Sunrising Series depicts the lives of fictional families, the Craigs and the Brookes and their relationship with Africa and the people they mix with there, from the time the first generation arrived as pioneers at the beginning of the twentieth century to the modern era. There is a forty year gap between the books, and each is a standalone story. Real life events and experiences are mixed with fiction to reveal the evolving interpersonal and socio-economic landscape as the country moves from a British colony to an independent African country. The first two books in the series are set in colonial times while the second two, to be published in 2022 and 2023, will focus on life in the country after independence.

About the author

Susan Hubert was born and has lived in Zimbabwe all her life.

She has an English and Psychology degree from the University of Kwazulu Natal in South Africa, with Mathematics as a minor.

She taught Mathematics for 16 years at high schools in Bulawayo, Zimbabwe, before retiring so she could spend more time with her husband, who was working as a professor of Equine Surgery at Louisiana State University and then Colorado State University. It was during this time she started writing.

When she was back home in Zimbabwe she tutored Mathematics and looked after her husband's herd of cattle.

She now lives full time with her husband on a farm just outside Bulawayo, where they are establishing a pecan plantation. She has one son, Jack Allard.

Learn more on Facebook: Susan Hubert – Author

Made in the USA
Las Vegas, NV
23 August 2023

76522348R00166